ALIAS THE SAINT

FOREWORD BY WILLIAM SIMON

THE ADVENTURES OF THE SAINT

EntertheSaint (1930), *TheSaintClosestheCase* (1930), *TheAvengingSaint* (1930), *FeaturingtheSaint* (1931), *AliastheSaint* (1931), *TheSaintMeetsHisMatch* (1931), *TheSaintVersusScotlandYard* (1932), *TheSaint'sGetaway* (1932), *TheSaintandMrTeal* (1933), *TheBrighterBuccaneer* (1933), *TheSaintinLondon* (1934), *TheSaintIntervenes* (1934), *TheSaintGoesOn* (1934), *TheSaintinNewYork* (1935), *SaintOverboard* (1936), *TheSaintinAction* (1937), *TheSaintBidsDiamonds* (1937), *TheSaintPlayswithFire* (1938), *FollowtheSaint* (1938), *TheHappyHighwayman* (1939), *TheSaintinMiami* (1940), *TheSaintGoesWest* (1942), *TheSaintStepsIn* (1943), *TheSaintonGuard* (1944), *TheSaintSeesItThrough* (1946), *CallfortheSaint* (1948), *SaintErrant* (1948), *TheSaintinEurope* (1953), *TheSaintontheSpanishMain* (1955), *TheSaintAroundtheWorld* (1956), *ThankstotheSaint* (1957), *SeñorSaint* (1958), *SainttotheRescue* (1959), *TrusttheSaint* (1962), *TheSaintintheSun* (1963), *VendettafortheSaint* (1964), *TheSaintonTV* (1968), *TheSaintReturns* (1968), *TheSaintandtheFictionMakers* (1968), *TheSaintAbroad* (1969), *TheSaintinPursuit* (1970), *TheSaintandthePeopleImporters* (1971), *CatchtheSaint* (1975), *TheSaintandtheHapsburgNecklace* (1976), *SendfortheSaint* (1977), *TheSaintinTrouble* (1978), *TheSaintandtheTemplarTreasure* (1978), *CountOntheSaint* (1980), *SalvagefortheSaint* (1983)

ALIAS THE SAINT

LESLIE CHARTERIS

SERIES EDITOR: IAN DICKERSON

Text copyright © 2014 Interfund (London) Ltd.
Foreword © 2014 William Simon
Preface © 1964 Leslie Charteris
Introduction © 1945 Leslie Charteris
Publication History and Author Biography © 2014 Ian Dickerson
All rights reserved.

Published by Thomas & Mercer, Seattle

www.apub.com

ISBN-13: 9781477842652
ISBN-10: 1477842659

Cover design by David Drummond, www.salamanderhill.com

Printed in the United States of America.

To Douglas Madeley
In memory of the Great Open
Spaces . . . not forgetting the Pont Genois

—Corsica, June 1930

PUBLISHER'S NOTE

FOREWORD TO THE
NEW EDITION

We will go out and find more and more adventures. We will swagger and swash-buckle and laugh at the half-hearted. We will boast and sing and throw our weight about. We will put the paltry little things to derision, and dare to be angry about the things that are truly evil. And we shall refuse to grow old.

We shall learn that romance lies not in the things we do, but in the way we do them. . . . We shall speak with fire in our eyes and in our voices; and which of us will care whether we are discussing the destiny of nations or the destination of the Ashes? For we shall know that nothing else counts beside the vision.

—Leslie Charteris, from The Saint Versus Scotland Yard *(1932)*

Time was, you could tell the Hero just by looking at him.

He was nice looking, perfectly dressed, and goodness glowed from within like a bright white light. You knew that, within the space of fifty minutes (one episode, less commercials), the Hero would a) save the world or at least the small part of it he was standing in; b) get The Girl (yes, there was always a Girl, and in a time when calling her The Girl would not get you demonized, lynched, or worse); c) catch the Bad Guy and turn him over to the proper authorities, or dispense his own brand of justice; and d) do it all over again the very next week.

We had police officers and private eyes, we had reporters and jazz musicians, we had doctors and secret agents, we even had the Hero of Heroes, Superman . . . who, disguised as a mild-mannered reporter for a great metropolitan newspaper, fought a never-ending battle for . . . well, you know the rest.

Through it all, one hero in particular stood head and shoulders above them all, was the standard to aspire to, the perfect representation of the Man to Grow Up to Be, at least in my childish opinion:

The Saint.

To a seven-year-old boy in Chicago, the Saint was a wonder. Tall, broad shouldered, ridiculously handsome, impeccably mannered, debonair in the classical definition of the word, but boy could he deal with Bad Guys. Exotic locations (so the reality was Elstree Studios back lot, back then who knew?), glamorous women, dastardly villains, cool cars, and always, without exception, on top of any situation he ran into. Justice was served, mystery solved, Bad Guys nailed, all with a healthy dose of wit, style, and charm. Mysteriously wealthy enough to do as he pleased, anywhere he went an adventure was waiting for him, and he went a lot of places where adventures were waiting.

(Two questions linger: Why was he almost always introduced as "the 'infamous' Simon Templar"? He was the Good Guy, why would he be "infamous"? Also, many times when he landed in a foreign city, the police were there waiting to tell him zey vere vatching heem classly . . . but he hadn't done anything yet, just walked off a plane; consider the fun his attorneys could have with that bit of business. . . .)

Before I was born, my mother was a high-school English teacher and school librarian. A love for reading and for books was instilled at a very early age and, thanks to her patience, I could read at about a fifteen-year-old level when I myself was nine, back when such things were measured in that manner.

About a year or so after discovering the television series, my mother introduced my younger brother and myself to the wonders of the library. Books. Lots of books. Lots and lots of books. It was like handing a child who loved to read the keys to the golden gates of Oz.

At that point in time, I was obsessed with Houdini and magic and read everything I could get my hands on. Mom drove us back and forth a lot to the library, but as a former school librarian herself, she didn't mind at all. One time I went to the checkout desk with my books, and made a comment about *The Saint* being on tomorrow night and I couldn't wait.

The librarian peered at me over her glasses, glanced at my mother, and said, "There are books, you know."

"Yes, ma'am," I replied. We were in a library; of course there were books. We were raised to be polite, so I said nothing about stating the obvious to this woman who was so old she obviously was a little off. (In retrospect, she was probably forty-ish; no real excuse, but that is OLD to a nine-year-old. She had to be at least as old as my mother, for heaven's sake!)

"You misunderstand," she said with the patience of a woman who dedicated her life to indulging children. "There are books about that show you were talking about. *The Saint.*"

There were *what*????

She looked at my mother, who smiled, shrugged, and nodded simultaneously in that way mothers do. The librarian came from behind the desk, took my hand, and led me into the fiction area. It took her a moment or two, then she pointed, "Right here, young man."

I looked to where she was pointing.

An entire shelf. Book after book after book, all by a fellow named Leslie Charteris. I reached out and picked one at random, flipping through the pages.

The name "Simon Templar" leapt out at me.

Score!

She walked me back to the checkout desk, and I added the book (as I remember, it was *Alias the Saint*), and home we went. Just to show how instant my obsession became, it ended up being one of those flashlight-under-the-covers nights to finish reading it. The next day, with no shame at all, I asked if we could go back to the library. With that special wisdom mothers possess, mom said no, not until I'd read everything else I'd brought home.

Okay, fair enough. I blitzed through the rest of the books, suddenly finding Houdini and his escapades to be second fiddle, and Saturday morning off we went again. I came home with five books, the maximum allowed per person at one time.

Guess what they all were?

It went like that over the entire summer. I never learned the librarian's name, she was "The Library Lady," but she handed a child the keys to the kingdom with a random comment and a moment's kindness.

Jump forward a few months, and my father was transferred to Nevada. We lived in a nice neighborhood with a huge mall within walking distance. One afternoon, sent for a half-gallon of milk, for the first time I noticed the spinner racks of paperback books in the grocery store. Idly spinning them around, a title jumped out and caught my eye: *The Saint to the Rescue*.

Hey, I knew those books! Immediately, I grabbed the milk I'd been sent to bring back, paid for it, ran the eight or so blocks home, raided my bank, ran back to the store, and bought it.

That was the start of a collecting obsession that didn't end until 1997, when I finally found a copy of *The Saint in Pursuit* for a reasonable price. And that completed the entire series.

The original stories were different from the Saint I knew. I was stunned to learn the first novel was published in 1928. The Saint of the novels and short stories was more of a vigilante, and sometimes a brutal one. He had no qualms about offering a permanent solution to a particular villain, something that shocked me the first time I read it. He had a gang, initially, a core group of like-minded individuals; Monty Hayward, Peter Quentin, the tragic hero Norman Kent. Not to mention Patricia Holm, the perfect girlfriend. Simon could gallivant around the world, dally with other ladies (the name "Avalon Dexter" has always stuck with me), but he always came back to Patricia. All through junior high, high school, and the first years of college, I almost always had a Charteris book in a notebook pocket.

Thanks to bookstores over the years, the entire series sits in a special bookcase. Thanks to a friend in a writers group who was downsizing her home, the Fiction Publishing set sits on top of that bookcase. The "September Seven" published to coincide with *Return of the Saint* are there, too. And now, thanks to the advent of DVDs, the vagaries and whims of syndication programmers no longer hold sway. Someone who knows me better than I know myself made the comment that she can always tell when I am dealing with an ugly professional matter: *The Saint* runs on the home theatre almost 24/7.

I carefully considered the comment, marveled at the intuition, respected the intellect, then arched my left eyebrow in the best Saintly tradition, and suavely replied, "So?"

I grew up believing this: the Good Guy triumphed, no matter the odds. Victims were always rescued, maybe at the very last moment, but they were alive and saved. If your cause was Just, and you were Right, you'd win. Bad Guys always lost. (insert pause . . . imagine shrug . . .

picture sheepish look) I was a kid . . . what did I know? Heroes should be above the crowd; polished but not effete, superior but not snide, capable but not arrogant, strong but not uncaring.

They should be special. No, make that Special.

The Saint is comfort food for the brain. A return to simpler times, easier times, when black was black and white was white, and one had not yet learned the infinite shades of grey there are in the adult world.

Simon Templar—the Saint—saw me through my childhood, adolescence, young adulthood, and now sometimes in middle age. Of all the books bought and discarded over too many years to admit now, the Saint Collection was, and continues to be, carefully preserved. Moved across the country three times, moved another three times in the same city, there sits a bookcase filled with my childhood hero. In my own fiction, I actually found the perfect moment in a short story to use the phrase ". . . as the actress said to the Bishop," and it fit perfectly. It was my personal acknowledgement to both a writer and his character that still have an influence to this day.

I recently received an email from a reader about Sometimes, *There Really Are Monsters Under the Bed*. He pointed out that one of the lead characters at the climax is described as being surrounded by a "halo" of light and, in his opinion, the resolution was "very well done and along the lines of how Leslie Charteris's The Saint—Simon Templar—might have handled the situation."

To say my Writerly Ego blew all out of proportion for a few minutes would be an understatement, to put it mildly.

I am genuinely excited to see the Saint back in print. It's been too long, old friend.

Here's a glass of Peter Dawson raised to bopping the Ungodly on the beezer, and hoping The Halo continues to shine for years to come, along with the sincere wish new generations find you as exciting and wonderful and entertaining as a certain nine-year-old did in mid-1960s Chicago.

Thank you, Mr Charteris. You always promised us to "Watch for the Sign of The Saint. . . . He Will Be Back!"

Now, he is.

—*William Simon*

ALIAS THE SAINT

PREFACE

Bibliographiles, who study the small print on the backs of title pages, will already have observed that this book was first published in 1931, which is a longish time ago by ordinary standards. It is, in fact, one of the very earliest Saint books, and the first story in it was actually published serially even before any of the stories in the first collection of novelettes, *Enter the Saint*.

At that time I had no idea that I would still be writing Saint stories more than 30 years later, or that an entire new generation would be growing up to discover them, who would then be working backwards through the list to trace all his adventures to the beginning. Even if I had, I suppose there is nothing I could have done about it: I wrote them as well as I could at the time, and publishers found them acceptable, and they seemed to please enough readers to pay their way. And I wrote them for the years in which they were written, without any thought of posterity, and certainly without even imagining that anyone would read them so many decades later.

And now that the same publishers insist on bringing out yet another edition, I feel bound to explain again to any recent recruits to the Saint's following, who might jump straight from the very latest Saint book to this one, that they must inevitably find great contrasts not only between the styles of writing but also between the characterizations of the Saint himself. For just as I have myself been going through the process of growing up which only ends at the end of a man's life, I could not have written about a man who went through so many adventures without ever changing or developing at all.

But that is a labor which could be endless, as my slothful instinct finally realized in the nick of time, and ultimately pointless anyhow, if my Immortal Works outlives me by a few centuries, as I expect them to.

Therefore let this book go out as another period piece in the making. I only ask readers not to be beguiled by any accidental modernities into forgetting how venerable the stories actually are, and how embryonic was the technology of the world in which they were laid.

And also, if you would be critically tolerant, how young was the author, and how correspondingly youthful was his hero.

—*Leslie Charteris*

THE STORY OF A DEAD

MAN

INTRODUCTION

Knowing how easily I could get tiresome if I went on repeating (as many of you have heard me do before) that most of my notoriously outlandish plots are based on recorded fact, it should be a refreshing change for all of us at this point to introduce a story in which the situation is reversed, and the history of crime later adapted itself to fit a plot which I provided for it.

This is one of the earliest stories of the Saint; and now that you have spent your quarter and been stuck with it I will frankly admit that it is not the best. However, it is not the worst either; and it will always be interesting to me for the light that it throws on an old proverb that "History repeats itself." Because my own theory is that History, being an entirely involuntary concatenation of events, is by definition incapable of deliberately doing anything. My own more careful generalization would be that history is full of people who have tried to repeat the performances of their predecessors, usually with no greater success.

For instance. This story centers, in part, around the desire of a certain man to become officially dead and yet at the same time to remain alive; and the way in which he proposed to achieve this convenient miracle is carefully revealed. He failed. But nevertheless, not long after this story was published, another gentleman attempted to perform the same feat by an identical method. His attempt to repeat History was fully reported by the newspapers of the time. I am obliged to mention this in case any other enterprising individuals should remain at large who still think he had the makings of a good idea. They hanged him.

—Leslie Charteris

1

When Long Harry came out of Pentonville Prison, he was not expecting to be welcomed by a cohort of friends. At the worst he had reckoned an emissary of the Prisoners' Aid Society would be the most he would have to deal with, and consequently the sight of the plump and ponderous Chief Inspector Teal lounging somnolently against a lamp-post a few yards from the prison gates was an unwelcome surprise.

Pulling his hat down over his eyes, Harry tactfully began to stroll in the opposite direction, but Inspector Teal was not so lightly to be deprived of the pleasure of renewing his acquaintance with an old customer.

He hitched himself off his lamp-post, and came up with Long Harry in a few slothful strides that nevertheless managed to convey him over the intervening ground in a surprisingly short space of time.

His hand fell on Harry's shoulder, and the yegg pulled up and faced about uneasily.

"I want you, Harry," said Mr Teal, whose sense of humour was sometimes lacking in good taste.

Harry shuffled his feet.

"You've got nothing on me, Mr Teal," he said defensively.

"I want you, Harry," repeated Mr Teal sleepily, "to come along to the Corner House and have some breakfast with me, and then we'll have a little talk."

Harry said he had had breakfast, but Mr Teal was not so easily to be put off.

"If you won't eat yourself," he said, "you can watch me and listen," he added, with unconscious humour.

As he spoke he was gently shepherding Harry back past the prison gates to a diminutive car that was drawn up by the kerb.

They passed down Caledonian Road in silence. Mr Teal had the gift of investing his silences with a peculiarly disturbing quality, and Long Harry became more and more unhappy as the miles ticked over on the speedometer in front of him.

"I suppose," said Harry, breaking a period of almost intolerable suspense as they turned round Park Crescent into Portland Place, "I suppose you aren't thinking I had anything to do with that Regent Street job?"

"I've stopped thinking about that," said Mr Teal, "since I became certain."

"That's like you flatties," complained Harry bitterly. "Let a man do his time and not say a word, and then wait for him outside the prison to shop him for another stretch."

Mr Teal said nothing. They whizzed down Regent Street in another spell of silence.

"It isn't even a fair charge," said Harry presently with an injured air. "I've got a beautiful alibi for you."

"You always have," said Mr Teal, without resentment. "I've never known you to disappoint me yet!"

They sat over bacon and eggs in Coventry Street, and Inspector Teal then condescended to relieve some of Harry's apprehensions by explaining the reason for his hospitality.

"I want you," said Mr Teal, in his sleepy way, "to tell me a little story about a man named Connell. I've got an idea he's a particular friend of yours."

The other's face twisted up in a vicious grin.

"Connell," snarled Long Harry, "is a——"

"Yes?" prompted Mr Teal drowsily.

Harry's clenched fist opened slowly. His vicious grin became cunning, then mask-like.

"Connell," said Harry softly, "is a man I've met occasionally. I can't tell you more about him than that, Mr Teal."

The detective sighed.

"Sure you can't?"

Harry shook his head.

"You know I'm always ready to help you when I can, Mr Teal," he said speciously, "but I don't know anything about Connell."

Mr Teal looked sceptical.

"Except," said Harry slowly, "that I've a good idea he was the squealer who shopped me for the Bayswater joke."

"You let me down over Bayswater," said Mr Teal reproachfully. "I never thought you carried a cosh around with you."

"Nor do I," said Harry. "Listen!"

He leant forward across the table.

"You and me, Mr Teal," he said, "have met pretty often—on business, as you might say. Now, you know I'm a respectable burglar. You've never caught me with a cosh, let alone a gun, yet. You've put me away six times, and I don't mind admitting now that I asked for the whole half-dozen, but I swear to you I never went near Bayswater that night."

"You ought to have told that to the court," said Mr Teal.

"Look here," persisted Harry with charming simplicity. "You remember pulling me in, don't you? Well, had I got an alibi? Did I say anything about an alibi? You know I didn't. Now, I ask you, Mr Teal, have you ever known me to be pulled in for a job of work that I really did and me not have an alibi ready?"

Mr Teal's eyes were half closed, and he appeared to be taking no notice. That pose of lazy boredom was his one affectation.

"The whole thing was a frame-up from start to finish," repeated Harry, "and you ought to know it, Mr Teal. I never used a cosh in my life, and I never did a porch job, anyway. And the man might have died, from what the papers said. Then I'd have been hanged. Maybe I was meant to be hanged, but Connell—"

Mr Teal's eyes suddenly opened very wide.

"What are you going to do to Connell?" he asked.

Harry relaxed.

"Well, when I see him," he said, "maybe I'll stand him a drink, and maybe I won't. Who knows?"

"And when I take you again," said Mr Teal, "maybe you'll get a lifer, and maybe you'll hang. Who knows about that, either?"

It was an unsatisfactory interview from all points of view, and Mr Teal, who had dragged himself out of bed at half-past five that morning in order to bring it about, was pardonably annoyed.

He got back to his room at Scotland Yard about half-past nine, and his assistant found him in an unpleasant mood.

"I've been thinking," began the recently promoted Sergeant Barrow, and Mr Teal cut him short with a ferocious glare.

"Why?" demanded Mr Teal unkindly. "I'm sure it hurts you, and you know I've always told you to take care of yourself."

"I've been thinking about the Camberwell Post Office hold-up," insisted the younger man aggrievedly. "Now couldn't that man Horring have been in it?"

"He could," agreed Mr Teal carefully, "if they hadn't hanged him at Wandsworth the week before. Go away and rest. You'll be getting brain fever if you go on thinking like this."

After that, Mr Teal felt better.

"And on your way down," he called after the retreating sergeant as the door closed, "tell Sergeant Jones I want him!"

There is a special department at Scotland Yard whose sole function is to indulge its curiosity, and the facts which it brings to light are strange and various. Some of them are gleaned from the reports of patrolling constables, who are instructed to note down any unusual happenings which they observe on their beats. Others are gleaned by painstaking subterranean investigation.

No plain van draws up outside a house at night and proceeds to discharge its cargo without the fact being reported; no man moves suddenly from a bed-sitting-room in Bermondsey to a service flat in Jermyn Street without arousing the interest of this inquisitive department; no man becomes a regular frequenter of the hotels and restaurants in the West End which are shared as a meeting-ground by London society, foreign millionaires, crooks both home-bred and imported, and that curious fraternity which, without coming into conflict with the law, contrives to live in luxury by its wits and the generosity of its relatives, without this prying department interesting itself in the subject.

Of this department, Sergeant Jones was an esteemed ornament. He spent his life in a maze of card indexes, turning over the disjointed and apparently insignificant reports which came in to him from time to time, sorting the wheat from the chaff, filing away accredited information, and requesting the further investigation of those facts which seemed to him to require it.

Sometimes the threads he followed led nowhere. Sometimes, by devious means, they were linked up with other threads, which in their turn tangled up again with yet more threads. And then, perhaps, a house would be surrounded, a couple of detectives would enter, and in a few moments some very surprised men would be hustled unostentatiously into a waiting taxi and removed to a place where they would have leisure to wonder how the seemingly undetectable had been detected.

"Sit down, Jones," said Mr Teal, settling himself comfortably in the big swivel chair behind his desk and closing his eyes, "and tell me all about Vanney's."

Sergeant Jones sat down. He was a long, lanky man, with sandy hair and a large nose.

"Directors," said Sergeant Jones, "as follows: president and managing director, James Arthur Vanney, 48, of 52 Half Moon Street; secretary, Sebastian Tombs, Esquire, of no fixed address; director, Malcolm Standish, 34, solicitor, of Lincoln's Inn."

"Do we know anything about these men?"

"Not much. Standish we know. He's behind half the criminal cases that are defended at the Old Bailey—a lot more than his name appears in. If any big crook gets landed he sends for Standish at once. We've never had anything on him, but I shouldn't be surprised if he'd made a tidy pile out of some of the cases he's worked on. Vanney built that new house at the bottom of Half Moon Street about nine months ago. Two cars—a Rolls and a Daimler. Four servants. Does himself pretty well on the whole."

"Where was he before he moved into Half Moon Street?"

"He stayed at the Savoy while the house was being built. His address was registered there as Melbourne, Victoria. Someone commissioned the architect and got the building job in hand a couple of months before Vanney arrived . . . That man Tombs is a bloke I'd like to know a lot more about."

"And so should I," said Teal.

He fingered his chin thoughtfully.

"Staff?" he queried.

"Very small. Girl secretary, name of Pamela Marlowe, and two clerks. Pamela Marlowe was Stenning's ward."

Mr Teal nodded faintly to signify that the interview was at an end, and Sergeant Jones rose.

He was leaving the room when a man brought in a small parcel.

"One moment," murmured Mr Teal, and the sergeant stopped by the door.

Teal examined the packet carefully, and then held it to his ear. Then he blinked, and the ghost of a smile crossed his face.

"How surprisingly unoriginal," remarked Mr Teal mildly.

Sergeant Jones came back to the desk, and Mr Teal held out the packet to him. Jones took it doubtfully.

"Walk that round to the Explosives Department," said Teal, "and mind you don't drop it. You can also spend your spare time praying that it doesn't go off before you get there!"

2

Vanney's Ltd., who were vaguely described on the glass panel of their door as "Agents," occupied a suite of offices in a new block of buildings opposite Charing Cross Station.

There were four rooms looking out on to the Strand. A private corridor ran the length of the suite, and each room opened separately on to it, while a system of communicating doors permitted access to any room from any of the other rooms without entering the passage. The first room was a waiting-room, in the second room worked two clerks, and in the third were Tombs and Miss Marlowe. The fourth was the sanctum of James Arthur Vanney himself, a thick-set man of medium height, who actually looked short by reason of his exceptional breadth of shoulder. He was dark and bearded, sparing of speech, and gruff in manner.

Chief Inspector Teal knocked on the door marked "Inquiries" one afternoon, and was told by the clerk who opened it that Mr Vanney was busy.

"I'll wait," said Mr Teal philosophically, and the clerk appeared to be nonplussed.

The door communicating the clerks' room with the secretary's office was open. Through it Mr Teal perceived a familiar back. He flowed irresistibly past the clerk, passed through the communicating door, and tapped Simon Templar's shoulder.

"When did you change your name to Tombs?" asked Mr Teal drowsily.

"Quite recently," said the Saint unabashed. "It seemed a jolly sort of name. Didn't the clerk tell you that Mr Vanney was engaged?"

Teal nodded.

"He did," he admitted, "and I said I'd wait."

"Mr Vanney," persisted the Saint, "will be engaged all the afternoon."

"I've got a lot of time to spare," said Teal calmly, "and when I get bored with waiting, you can come and talk to me."

"Mr Vanney," continued the Saint pointedly, "will not be able to see you until tomorrow morning."

Teal extracted from his pocket a small packet done up in pink paper. From it he took a smaller packet, from which he took a thin wafer of chewing gum. With his jaws moving rhythmically, he cast a sleepy speculative eye round the room.

"I can doss down in a corner," he said. "Or have you a camp bed?"

Simon Templar inspected a row of buttons on his desk, selected one, and pressed it. Mr Teal masticated in silence until a knock on the door answered the bell.

"In," said the Saint briskly.

The door opened, and a man in a plain blue serge suit and a bowler hat stood framed in the aperture.

"George," said the Saint, in the same brisk tone, "show this gentleman the way out."

Mr Teal shifted his gum round so as to give the other side of his face its full share of exercise.

"Suppose," he suggested languidly, "that I just had a word with you in private first?"

The Saint shrugged.

"I can give you two minutes exactly," he said. "You can wait outside the door, George. Miss Marlowe, would you mind?"

Mr Teal lounged into a chair.

"Nice girl that," he remarked.

"Very," agreed the Saint briefly. "And now let's hear the bright, brisk business. What has fetched you to this wilderness, old watermelon?"

Teal stretched his arms lazily.

"I was interested," he said. "A name like Sebastian Tombs seemed too good to be true, and when I saw you—well, I was just more interested than ever."

"That must have been frightfully jolly for you," agreed the Saint carefully. "May one ask why?"

Teal closed his eyes, but his jaws continued to maltreat Spearmint with monotonous regularity.

"Somehow," he said, "whenever I find you off your usual beat, I have an idea there's a catch in it. What's the idea this time?"

"I have reformed," said the Saint speciously. "Overwhelmed with the burden of my sins, and gloomily conscious of many wasted years, I have decided to go out into the great wide world and make good. These are paths of righteousness, Teal, but I can't expect you to believe that."

"Then you won't be disappointed," said Teal languidly. "Now can I see your boss?"

"I'm afraid not," said the Saint. "I've told you he's engaged."

Teal looked across at the opposite communication door. The upper pane was of frosted glass, and across this was painted the word "Private."

"Does he always see his visitors in the dark?" asked Teal gently.

"Always," said the bland Mr "Tombs." "It's one of his many peculiarities."

Mr Teal's eyes were half closed.

"And does he," pursued Mr Teal, in the same tired voice, "always hang his hat and coat up in the clerks' room? I can see your hat and coat hanging up in the corner there, and there were three hats and coats in the room I came through."

"That," said the Saint fluently, "is another of his eccentricities. He says he hates to have his hat and coat hanging up in his own room."

Mr Teal nodded, and then he moved.

It has already been mentioned that, for such a large and slothful man, he could, when he so desired, cover ground with a surprising turn of speed.

He had flung open the communicating door marked "Private" before the Saint could stop him, and the lights clicked up under his thumb as Templar reached his side.

The room was empty.

It was sparsely but comfortably furnished, with a big knee-hole desk set crosswise in the corner by the window, a safe in the opposite corner, and a filing cabinet against one wall.

There were two armchairs upholstered in leather, and a plain wooden armchair behind the desk. Facing the communicating door was a fireplace, and on either side of this was a tall cupboard built into the wall. There was no sign of Vanney.

Teal leaned back against the jamb of the door, looking at the Saint's blank face and chewing unemotionally.

"And," said Mr Teal, without changing the bored tone of his voice, "does Mr Vanney automatically vanish, together with his visitor, when this door is opened?"

Simon put his hands in his pockets and settled himself comfortably in the doorway. He looked quizzically at the detective.

"I've never known him do it before," he replied calmly. "But great men are always slightly erratic in their habits. It will be an interesting little problem for you to take home with you."

Mr Teal removed a speck of dust from his bowler.

"On second thoughts," he said, "I don't think I'll spend the night here. Bye-bye, Saint. See you later, I expect."

"I'm afraid so," said Simon affably.

Mr Teal opened the door to find the porter standing patiently outside.

"You may go, George," said Teal. "I'll find my own way out."

He was sauntering down the corridor when a thought struck him, and he returned. He opened the door a few inches without the formality of knocking, and poked his head in.

Simon Templar was writing at the desk, and the girl was tapping the typewriter in the corner.

"Good-bye, old fruit," said the Saint pleasantly, without looking up.

"When Mr Vanney comes back," drawled the imperturbable Mr Teal, "you might tell him, with my compliments, that if he makes any more childish attempts to kill me, I shall be seriously annoyed."

He closed the door again and resumed his leisurely progress towards the stairs, humming gently to himself.

Mr Teal had never been able to overcome a weakness for playing the magazine detective.

3

Simon Templar put the finishing touches to the letter he was drafting. Then, settling himself back in his chair, he reached out a long arm to the neat row of bell pushes which occupied one corner of his desk. Selecting one with a thoughtful air, he pressed it. The small brass plate beside the knob was engraved with the word "Secretary," and the bell rang in the opposite corner of the same room, over Pamela Marlowe's head. The outsider would have failed to see the point of this arrangement, but the Saint had not been in business long enough to get tired of playing with the mechanical gadgets provided in all up-to-date offices for the amusement of the staff.

Simon lighted a cigarette and gazed reflectively at the ceiling.

"Take a letter," he said. "This is to Stanforth and Watson: 'Dear Sirs, With reference to our telephone conversation this morning. Stop.' Something seems to be eating you."

Pamela Marlowe looked up from her pad in surprise.

"Do you want me to put that down?" she asked.

"No," replied the Saint, taking his eyes off the ceiling. "The remark was addressed to you."

He was regarding her keenly, and after a few seconds' silence she looked away.

"You may tell me all," he remarked gently. "I am a Grand Master of the Order of Father Confessors."

She met his eyes again, and the question with which she took advantage of his invitation did not come as a surprise to him.

"Who was that man who came in just now?"

"That," said the Saint, "was the worthy Chief Inspector Claud Eustace Teal, of the Criminal Investigation Department, New Scotland Yard. He has a prying disposition, and he isn't anything like the fool he looks. I grant you that would be difficult."

The girl hesitated, fidgeting with her pencil. But Simon, unruffling himself, made no attempt to fluster her.

"Mr Tombs," she said at length, "I wasn't trying to hear the conversation that went on after you sent me out of the room, but the partition wall is very thin."

"It's these jerry-building methods," sighed the Saint. "I'll dictate a letter to *The Times* about it in a moment."

The girl's lips tightened a little.

"I couldn't help hearing what Mr Teal said."

Simon said nothing.

He, who should by rights have been the one to show embarrassment, registered nothing of the kind.

"You didn't deny his charges," said the girl.

"Naturally not," said the Saint. "George Washington was an ancestor of mine, and I cannot tell a lie."

Pamela Marlowe had heard of the Saint—she would have been an amazing woman if she had not. The Saint realised exactly what was in her mind, but the thought failed to disturb him. He was mildly amused.

"What's the worry?" he inquired.

"Are you really the Saint?"

"I am. Did you really think I went through life permanently attached by the ear to a name like Sebastian Tombs?"

"Well," said the girl bluntly, "I shall hate doing it, but doesn't it occur to you that it is my duty to say something to Mr Vanney about it? That is, if you can't give me some sort of explanation."

Simon smiled without mockery.

"Of course it is," he agreed cheerfully. "And I should like to say that I appreciate the nobility of your impulse. I shall draw Mr Vanney's attention to it. But as for the other matter, I'm afraid you won't be able to tell him anything that he doesn't know. The thought that I am immovably parked in this office is the bane of his life. Try it on him tomorrow morning, if you don't believe me."

He dictated a number of letters, waited while she typed them, and took them into Mr Vanney's private office. He was back in a few moments with the sheaf duly signed.

"You can go as soon as you have addressed them," he said. "George will take them down to the post."

She ventured to be inquisitive.

"Why do we need a special porter for this office?" she asked.

"One should always," said the Saint impressively, "surround oneself with all the evidences of prosperity that one can afford. It creates a good impression. George will have his nice new uniform with brass buttons tomorrow and I shall expect to see an immediate jump in our turnover."

It was an invariable rule at Vanney's that Mr "Tombs" was the last to leave the office. On that particular evening, however, Pamela Marlowe, with her hat and coat on, appeared to be uncertain whether she should take him at his word.

"I've told you you can go," said the Saint, without looking up from the letter he was perusing.

She made a demur.

"Are you sure Mr Vanney won't want me again?"

"Mr Vanney," said the Saint carefully, "never wants you. You know that perfectly well."

It was true. All instructions to the office staff were given by Mr "Tombs," and he dictated all the letters that were sent out, and opened all that came in. The rest of the staff were never allowed to pass through the door marked "Private."

"I've told you that I shall not want you anymore this evening," said the Saint, "and you may take that as official. Mr Vanney has already left."

She stared.

"He hasn't come through for his hat and coat," she objected.

"He left by his private entrance," Simon answered shortly, "without a hat and coat. He has just joined the Ancient Order of Kangaroos, and one of their rules is that no member is allowed to take his hat and coat home with him on Friday."

There was nothing for her but to leave without further argument, but the incident found its place in her memory beside a number of other extraordinary things which she had noticed during the few months that she had worked under Simon Templar.

Mr "Tombs" was in every way an ideal employer. His manner, without being brusque, was at all times irreproachably impersonal, but she had never been able to understand his mentality. Whenever she ventured to comment on any unusual happening, he was never at a loss for an explanation, but the reasons he gave so glibly would have been an insult to the intelligence of an imbecile.

There had been a time when she had wondered if he fancied himself as a wag and was expecting her to laugh, but he made the most outrageous statements without smiling, and if he showed any emotion at all it was one of concealed delight at her annoyed perplexity.

She found another enigma to interpret when she arrived at the office the following Monday, for the Saint, with his coat off, was supervising the finishing touches which were being put by two workmen to a curious erection which had appeared at the far end of the private corridor.

Simon greeted her in his usual affable manner, and invited her to admire it.

"This is George's new home," he said.

It was, in fact, no more than a partition which turned into a sort of cubicle at the blind end of the passage beyond the door that opened into Vanney's private room. It would have been nothing but an ordinary janitor's box but for an unusual feature in its design. The partition reached all the way to the ceiling, and there were only two small windows—one in the partition itself, and one in the door which the workmen were at that moment engaged in putting in position. Furthermore, each window was obscured by a row of steel bars set close together.

Coming closer, she made another surprising discovery.

"But why is it lined with steel?" she asked in amazement.

"Because," said the Saint, "a half-inch deal board is not much protection against a bullet. We should hate to lose our one and only George."

The girl was silent, but Simon was perfectly at his ease, "Observe, too, the strategic position," he murmured, with the enthusiasm of an artist. "No one can reach George without having to cover the whole length of the suite, either through the offices or down the corridor. Consequently, it'll be his own fault if he doesn't hear them coming. Besides, we've got another little safety device. I'll show you if you wait here a moment."

He went down the corridor and as he got near the door a low, buzzing noise came to her ears. Staring blankly about her, she eventually located its source in a small metal box screwed to the wall inside the cubicle.

Simon passed on to the door, and the buzzing stopped. He turned, and it recommenced; then he came back down the corridor, and it stopped again. "What is it?" she asked. "A burglar alarm?"

"The very latest," said the Saint. "Come and have a look." He led her down the passage, and when they were within a yard of the door the low buzzing made itself heard again. She stopped and gazed around puzzledly, but she could see nothing.

"I have them all over my own home," he explained. "It's the best idea of its kind in the world. It's worked by a ray that shines across the corridor on to a selenium cell. It's invisible, but if you get in its path the buzzer gives tongue. It's impossible to put it out of action until it's too late, because only Sebastian Tombs"—the Saint shuddered involuntarily—"and the electrician who fitted it know exactly where it is."

He was amused at her bewilderment.

"Don't you think it's rather neat?" he asked.

"It seems a lot of trouble to take over a porter."

The Saint smiled.

"George," he said virtuously, "is a member of Vanney's just as much as you or I. Isn't it the duty of the firm to see that he is thoroughly protected against the dangers of his position?"

In her astonishment she forgot the lesson which experience should have taught her.

"But why should George be in any danger?" she said, and Simon Templar's face instantly assumed its grave expression.

"Haven't you read about all these armed robberies?" he demanded severely. "Haven't you ever heard of the Black Hand? And do you mean to say that I never told you that the Union of Porters, Commissionaires, Caretakers, Undertakers, and Glue Refiners have threatened to do

George in for allowing us to put two more than the regulation number of buttons on his uniform?"

She turned away in despair, and went into the office.

The Saint followed her, and resumed his seat. Then he leaned back in his chair, put his feet on the desk, and pressed the bell marked "Secretary."

"Take a letter to *The Times*," he said. "To the Editor of *The Times*. 'Sir, —The scamping of work at present practised by the building trade is a disgrace. Stop. In the house which I have recently taken, the walls are so thin that a nail which I drove into the wall last night, in order to hang a picture, was distinctly felt by the occupant of the next room. Stop. Consequently my wife has been compelled to take her meals off the mantelpiece ever since, with the result that our domestic arrangements have been seriously disorganised. Stop. I am, etcetera, Lieut. Colonel, Retired.' And just remember, Miss Marlowe, that George is one of the most important people in this office, and if anybody happened to shoot at him successfully the firm would probably go into liquidation, and you and I would be looking for new jobs."

4

The memory of Mr Teal's visit had occupied a prominent part of Pamela Marlowe's thoughts ever since the afternoon when the Saint had so shamefully acknowledged the truth of that lethargic detective's accusations. But when Simon arrived one morning and told her that he had arranged for her to carry the tale to Vanney, she felt a paradoxical reluctance to go to her employer with a charge against his manager's honesty, even while she welcomed the opportunity of testing the truth of his statement that Vanney knew the whole story of his misdeeds.

Simon Templar, however, appeared to have no doubts about what the outcome of the interview would be.

"Tell him everything you heard," he encouraged, when the bell rang from Mr Vanney's office to summon her. "He will be interested."

She took the Saint at his word, but it was a profitless conversation.

Vanney listened attentively to her story, but when she had finished she could have sworn that he was smiling behind his beard. His voice, however, was quite serious.

"I appreciate your high sense of duty, Miss Marlowe," he said, "but what . . . er . . . Mr Tombs told you is quite correct. I know everything about him, and in spite of that he has my complete confidence."

He had a stiff manner of speaking, and appeared to think each sentence out carefully before he uttered it. He did not once look directly at her, but kept his eyes fixed on a point in space a foot or so away from her left shoulder.

"I didn't wish to do Mr Tombs any harm," she felt compelled to explain. "But I had to remember that you were the one who was employing me."

"I quite understand," said Vanney.

He continued to gaze past her in silence for some seconds, stroking his beard. Then he said, "Did you know that your late guardian's last request to me was that, if anything happened to him, I should look after you?"

"But you were in Australia."

"I know," said Vanney, rather testily. "He wrote to me."

The girl nodded.

"I see. But I never knew much about him, and I never heard him speak of any of his friends. My father knew him a long time ago— they were boys together, but they hadn't met for over twenty years. Just before father died, he happened to meet Mr Stenning, quite by accident; and since I had no other relatives living, and father and Mr Stenning had been such close friends, before they lost touch with each other, it was fairly natural that he should appoint Mr Stenning my guardian. But I only saw Mr Stenning three times, and that was when I was quite young. He discharged all his duties through his solicitors."

"He often mentioned your name to me when he wrote," said Vanney. "I believe that, behind the scenes, he took a great interest in you."

He began to fidget with a pencil on his desk, and she could not help noticing his hands. They were rough and ill-kept, and not at all the hands that one would have associated with a millionaire—for Vanney was reputed to be no less.

He appeared suddenly to become aware of their defects, for he dropped the pencil and hid his hands in his pockets.

"I had a very rough life in Australia before I made my fortune," he volunteered. "And I fear that, as guardian, I should be of very little use to you. Now, of course, you are old enough not to need looking after. But if you would honour me with your company at dinner one evening, Miss Marlowe, I should appreciate the compliment."

She hesitated.

"If you want me to—"

"You don't seem very keen," he said. She had to pause to think of a reply.

"I hardly go out at all," she said at length, and was conscious of the flimsiness of the excuse as soon as she had uttered it.

But Vanney did not appear to be at all put out. He pulled a book towards him and began to turn the pages.

"Very well, Miss Marlowe," he said, with a return to the gruffness of tone which had softened for a moment. "That will be all then. You may go back to your work."

She returned to the outer room feeling vaguely uncomfortable. She knew that her refusal of Vanney's invitation had not been an example of perfect tact, and the realisation was not a congenial one. There was no logical reason that she could see why she should have been so perverse, and she was annoyed with herself for having given way so readily to an unaccountable feeling of revulsion.

The Saint was drawing on his blotting-pad a portrait of his employer which would, if it had been published in a newspaper, have provided more than sufficient grounds for a libel action.

"You are subdued," he remarked, without taking his eyes off his work. "Therefore I deduce that you have been unwillingly forced to admit that I'm more truthful by nature than you believed."

She smiled, but he was not looking at her.

"I owe you an apology," she said. "You warned me that I was making a fool of myself, but I refused to be convinced."

"Your apology is accepted," said the Saint amiably.

He picked up a two-colour pencil and added a roseate hue to Mr Vanney's nose, while she transcribed a letter.

"But," said the Saint, "if you're thinking that one day I shall be revealed as the brilliant and noble detective who masquerades as a criminal, caring nothing for his own reputation and matrimonial prospects, in order to nab the crook of crooks, it is my duty to warn you that nothing so romantic will happen. I am a bold, bad man, and I love it. And the fact that you have one of the most adorable mouths I have ever seen will never alter that."

He said this without the least change of tone, so that it was fully a minute before she realised the meaning of the words which closed his speech. When the point dawned upon her, she stopped tapping the typewriter and stared at him.

The Saint seemed blissfully unaware that he had in any way departed from his usual style of conversation. While she watched him in amazement, he drew a dissipated-looking wrinkle under Vanney's left eye with the blue end of his pencil, and then laid it down and gazed at the ceiling with an air of furious concentration.

She did not know what to say, and so said nothing. This was not difficult, for he did not appear to be expecting her to make any comment. After a short period of scowling rumination, he picked up his pencil again and continued drawing.

Pamela gazed hopelessly at a blank sheet of paper. The situation was impossible, but the Saint gave no sign that he perceived any incongruity in it.

"You are still subdued, Pamela," he murmured, pushing the blotter aside. "I can't imagine that to hear my views on your mouth would affect you so deeply, so I am left to conclude that Vanney has asked you to meet him in a social sort of way."

"I don't think it's any business of yours, Mr Tombs," she began, and then he looked up at her.

"Since the villain has been unmasked," drawled the Saint, "I think you can forget that name. I only chose it in the hope that one day that it would annoy Claud Eustace, and the longer I live with it the less I like it."

"Very well—Mr Templar."

"Simon," murmured the Saint, "is even more soothing to my ears." The girl frowned.

"Did he or did he not?" asked the Saint, returning to the argument. She flushed resentfully at his insistence.

"What if he did?" countered a stubborn Pamela. Simon fingered his chin.

"I was afraid he would," he said. "The morals of the modern employer are appalling. You might remind me to dictate a letter to *The Times* about it. But I'll just ask Mr Vanney not to annoy you anymore."

To her astonishment, he rose at once from his desk and went into the next office. This time she had no compunction about eavesdropping. But, strain her ears as she might, she could make nothing of the faint, almost inaudible murmur of voices.

In a few minutes the Saint returned, and his normally unwrinkled brow wore a frown that was not one of concentration.

"Mr Vanney is inclined to be obstinate," he said. "I hope I've convinced him of the error of his ways, but if it occurs again you will let me know."

Thereafter he ignored her existence until lunch time, but when she had put on her hat she found him holding her coat for her—a courtesy which he had never offered before.

"Pamela," he said, "will you put me in the same category as Vanney if I ask you to lunch with me?"

Pamela looked at him, met the full brilliance of the Saintly smile, and was lost. "No—I don't think so."

"Then we'll go and beat up the Carlton," said the Saint cheerfully; and it was so.

Sergeant Jones, who was loitering inconspicuously on the corner of the block, saw them come out. He followed them to the Carlton, and two hours later followed them back.

Inspector Teal, to whom the most trivial details were always a matter of the most

tremendously absorbing interest, had posted him there to report on the habits of the clients and staff of Vanney's Ltd.; and Sergeant Jones had begun to feel that he had a personal grievance against Simon Templar, for on the previous five days Mr Jones had sacrificed his own mid-day meal in the hope of getting a chance to observe the Saint at lunch, and had been disappointed.

"He's either been dieting to keep his figure, or he's been on hunger strike," Mr Teal was told that night. "Anyhow, this is the first time he's been out for a bite during the day since I started tailing him."

Inspector Teal blinked once, but inwardly he was chalking up the Saint's mysterious fast among the many other peculiar facts which were catalogued in his mind against the firm of Vanney's.

5

On a certain morning a grocer in South London was found lying, shot through the heart, behind his counter, when the assistant came to open up the shop in the morning, with the till broken open and the previous three days' takings missing. The man in charge of the case, before he allowed anything to be moved, sent for the police photographers. The pictures they took were developed and printed in a few hours; and these, together with the inspector's own copious notes, were sent immediately to that department of Scotland Yard known as the Records Office, where are catalogued in one gigantic card index all the known forms, variations, and trimmings of crime, with cross-references to the men who are known to practise them.

The usual scientific process of elimination then began. The extra heavy sentence which is always received by a criminal who uses firearms in his work means that comparatively few burglars go armed. From the list of these men were eliminated those whose known methods of entering a house did not correspond with the method used in that case. The list was reduced again by removing the names of those who, without a serious divergence from their old habits—a rare phenomenon among habitual criminals—would have solved the problem of the locked till in a way other than that in which it had been solved. The list diminished steadily as the names it contained were in turn tested by other characteristics of the crime in question.

Even with these precise methods, several names are frequently left over for further scrutiny; but in this instance the accumulated evidence pointed with the most convincing certainty to one man.

"You mentioned his name to me only the other day," said the man from the Records Office, "So I thought you would be interested."

"I am," said Mr Teal. "But I'd be still more interested if you could tell me where he is."

It was in a pessimistic spirit that he telephoned an inquiry through to the inspector in charge of F Division, and therefore he was not disappointed when it proved fruitless.

"The last time anything was seen or heard of Connell," F Division informed him

concisely, "was in July, two years ago."

Mr Teal, remembering his breakfast of a fortnight ago, took his hat and coat and went for a walk.

He ran his victim to earth in a public-house near Victoria Station, and took the next place at the bar.

"This is a pleasant surprise, Harry," said Mr Teal untruthfully, for he had drawn a blank at several coverts before he found his fox. "What'll you have?"

"A bottle of champagne with you, Mr Teal," said Long Harry.

"Two bitters, please, Miss," said Mr Teal.

He picked up his tankard and nodded towards a vacant table in a corner.

"Suppose we get out of the crowd, and have a little talk," he suggested, and Long Harry knew of old that when Mr Teal made such a request it was useless to refuse.

He followed the portly detective to the secluded spot he had indicated, and they sat down.

"Now tell me about Connell," said Mr Teal.

Long Harry scowled.

"I told you once, I don't know anything about him."

"But he did a job in Battersea last night," said Mr Teal. "I thought you'd have heard—it's in the lunch editions."

Long Harry shook his head. 'I don't know anything about it, Mr Teal," he said.

"Now, I thought you would," said Teal dreamily. "The lunch editions didn't say Connell did it, but I was expecting you to come along and tell me that. Either Connell did it, or someone who knew his methods inside out arranged it so that everything would point to Connell."

Harry grinned.

"If you're thinking I pulled that job to frame Connell, you're right up the spout. I've got an alibi."

The torpescent Mr Teal felt in his waistcoat pocket for a fresh bar of chewing gum.

"Then," he remarked pensively, "it seems as if you must have done it."

"But this," said Harry, "is a copper-bottomed alibi. I spent last night in Marlborough Street Police Station. I'd been entertaining some friends, and we'd had what you might call a sticky evening. It took three policemen to get me there."

Mr Teal raised a reproving eyebrow.

"Drunk, I suppose," he murmured.

"All three of them," said Harry.

The detective ruminated in silence for some moments, and then he said, "Do you get drunk easily, Harry?"

"I can knock back a tank-full and not show it," Harry bragged.

"Entertaining friends, were you?" said Teal slumberously. "Then you must have come into some easy money. I know how fond you are of work, and you haven't been out of stir long enough to earn that much honestly."

"I got a remittance," said Harry glibly. "An uncle of mine who went out to Australia years ago, suddenly remembered his poor, persecuted nephew in the old country, and sent me a tenner."

Mr Teal went back to Scotland Yard very little wiser than he had been when he left it.

That afternoon an idea struck him. He walked up the Embankment to Charing Cross, and he was standing by a tobacco kiosk when Pamela Marlowe left the offices of Vanney's Ltd., and crossed the road to the Strand Tube Station.

"Excuse me, Miss," said Teal, catching her up at the entrance to the subway.

It was not the first time she had been spoken to by a stranger, and she would have hurried on, but something in the business-like tone of his address stopped her, and she looked round.

She saw a big, red-faced, sleepy-eyed man of considerable girth, wearing a rather noisy tweed suit, with a soft felt hat tilted to the back of his head.

"I am Inspector Teal, of Scotland Yard," said the same, "and you might be able to help me a lot, Miss Marlowe, if you'd just step into that tea den with me and have a chat."

Over a cup of tea, at his request, she repeated the history of her association with Stenning and Vanney, in much the same way as she had told it to Vanney himself. Mr Teal appeared to doze during the recital, but as soon as she had finished he was ready with a question.

"How did you get your job at Vanney's?"

"Mr Vanney wrote to me off his own bat. He knew Mr Stenning, and he says that Mr Stenning had often spoken of me."

"What were you doing before that?"

"Nothing. Father was always pretty well off, and he left me everything he had."

"And something went wrong?"

She nodded.

"Most of the money was in Claravox Gramophones. Father put all his eggs in that basket just before he died. The shares were at about 450, but the promised dividends were colossal." She smiled ruefully. "If you remember, the fraud was shown up two years ago, when Stenning died and the company went smash."

"I remember," said Teal. "Claravox Gramophones was one of Stenning's companies. I guess that man must have held the dud company record for this country."

He drank some tea, and cogitated with his eyes closed; and his next query was a surprising one.

"Does the Saint ever make love to you?"

"No," she replied at once, and wondered how she came to lie so spontaneously. Teal, however, seemed to have been anticipating that answer.

"He wouldn't," he said. "The Saint's a clean crook. But what about Vanney?"

"I've only seen him once, and then he asked me to have dinner with him."

"Is that so?" Teal opened one eye. "Did you go?"

She shook her head.

"It was only the other day. I put him off, and he hasn't mentioned it since."

With that he seemed to have come to the end of his intended interrogation, and she took advantage of his silence to make an inquiry of her own.

"What did you mean when you said that the Saint was a clean crook?" she asked.

"Well," said Mr Teal judiciously, "he's a crook, all right—you'll know that if you've ever read a newspaper. He doesn't make any bones about it. The reason he's at large is because on the few occasions when he's left any evidence behind him that could be used in court, the injured parties have refused to kick. The Saint has a way of knowing too much about them. He went off the rails once, and then squared that up by stopping a war, confound him; and at the moment anyone who said he was not a respectable citizen could be soaked with good and heavy damages for slander. To give the devil his due, most of the men he's trodden on have been pretty undesirable specimens, but that doesn't make him an honest man."

"Why do you think he does it?"

"The Lord knows," said Teal wearily. "All I can tell you is that if I've got any grey hairs, he gave them to me. Of course, he's made plenty of money out of it—the men he has gone after had a good deal of boodle on them, a lot of which seems to drift eventually into the Saint's own bank balance."

She was astonished at this revelation.

"Then why does he work at Vanney's?"

"If you could answer that question, Miss Marlowe," said Teal, "you'd save my mind a lot of hard wear. All I know is that I smell trouble wherever the Saint's hanging around."

The implication did not make itself plain to her at once; but when she had grasped it, she stopped with her cup half-way to her lips, and stared.

"Do you mean Vanney's isn't straight?" she asked.

"I've a good idea," said Teal, "that Vanney's is one of the crookedest shows in the history of commerce. If Vanney's is straight, I'm going to ask the Commissioner to call in all the rulers in Scotland Yard, and supply the clerical department with corkscrews."

He gazed at her in his drowsily placid way while she digested this startling piece of information, and his air of heavy-lidded weariness did not prevent him taking in every detail of her appearance. She was pretty. Mr Teal, who by no stretch of imagination could have been called a connoisseur of feminine beauty, would have been blind if he had not recognised that fact. Nice eyes and mouth. A trim figure and well-chosen clothes that suited her to perfection. Mr Teal thought that there would have been some excuse for the Saint, anyway.

He thought of the Saint. The Saint, with his gay, devil-may-care face, his dancing blue eyes, and reckless smile, would have found no difficulty in waltzing into any woman's heart. True, Teal knew that the Saint was theoretically attached to a certain Patricia Holm; but Teal had never thought the Saint was a man to confuse fidelity with fun. Maybe there would have been some excuse for Pamela Marlowe.

"You seem to be rather interested in Templar," murmured Mr Teal. "Are you in love with him, by any chance?"

"No," she replied promptly. "Whatever made you ask that?"

"It just occurred to me," said the detective vaguely.

After a few minutes' more desultory conversation he left her.

Those were turbulent days for her under their superficial calm, and she was beginning to feel the strain. Consequently, it was a most welcome relief for her when, after dinner, the girl who occupied the next room in the house where she lived came in and suggested a visit to the movies.

They went by bus to Piccadilly, and walked up Regent Street.

As they passed the back entrance of the Piccadilly Hotel, two men in evening dress came out, and one of them hailed a passing taxi. They stepped in and were driven away.

One of the men she had recognised at once, for it was none other than Simon Templar. His companion had been a big, heavy-featured man, with a small military moustache, whose face seemed curiously familiar.

It required some minutes of concentration before she could place him, but when she had done so her involuntary gasp of amazement startled her companion.

It was not surprising that she had not been able to identify him at once, for the last time she had seen him he had been wearing a purple uniform decorated with buttons and braid of gold, and he answered to the name of George.

6

Pamela walked on with her brain in a ferment. She felt strangely disinclined to embark on a lengthy explanation of what had startled her, and the other girl, after some futile attempts to draw her, relapsed into an offended silence.

It seemed that she was destined to become more and more lost each day in the network of mystery of which Vanney's was the centre, and no added complication seemed to lead nearer to a solution.

What was the closely guarded secret of Vanney's, and which part was Simon Templar playing in it? Everything she had seen or heard pointed to the secret being a sinister one; and yet, however suspicious a character Simon Templar might be, he had one of the least sinister personalities that she had ever met. But why did so many irregular things mark the conduct of the office which was under his supervision, and why, to cap it all, had he been dining at the Piccadilly with the porter—George?

Pamela's brain seethed with unanswerable questions for the rest of the evening, and the entertainment, which should have been a means of forgetting the perplexities which had worried her for days, was spoilt for her; but her adventures were not yet finished for that night.

She got home to find a note on the hall table informing her that a man had rung her up twice while she had been out. While she was reading it, the telephone bell rang again.

She went to the instrument with an instinctive certainty that the call was for her, and she was right.

"I am speaking for Mr Tombs," said a masculine voice. "An important deal has been concluded this evening, and since the other party is leaving for the Continent early tomorrow morning, Mr Tombs wishes you to come round at once and make out the necessary papers."

"But—"

"Mr Tombs asks me to say that he is very sorry to trouble you at this hour, but he must ask you to come immediately."

"A closed car is waiting for you at the corner of the street. Please come at once!"

Before she could reply, a click from the receiver told her that the man at the other end of the line had rung off.

Pamela put the telephone down slowly, biting her lip. In one sense there was nothing very extraordinary about the request. The circumstances were plausible, and it was not unusual for important business negotiations to be concluded over dinner, although such a thing had never happened before while she had been at Vanney's. And Chief Inspector Teal had said that Simon Templar was a clean crook. She might easily have left without further deliberation, but she did not.

There were one or two things which she could not understand, and they made her pause. First, the message which awaited her when she got in told her that she had been called at 9:30 and at 10:30. If it was so important that papers should be made out without delay, would they have waited so long for her? Another stenographer should have been obtainable; and, besides, the Saint was perfectly capable of working the typewriter efficiently himself—she had seen him do so more than once. Secondly, when she had last seen him, he had been with George; and whatever the reason for that intimacy, it was not likely that the janitor would be present when business was being discussed. And then, what was the reason for the car? Apparently it had been sent much earlier in the evening, so that its arrival would coincide with the first attempt to get her on the telephone, and yet there was no reason for Simon Templar to have suspected a sudden dearth of taxis in Kensington. Finally, why had he not spoken to her himself?

Making up her mind, she picked up the telephone book and found Templar's number. She called it, and his voice answered her almost immediately.

"Yes?"

"It's Pamela speaking, Mr Templar. Did you ring up just now?"

"Certainly not," said the Saint.

She told him about the message she had received, and he whistled.

"You can take it from me, it was a fake," he said. "I don't know who sent it, but I'll try to find out. You say a car is supposed to be waiting for you at the corner? "

"Yes."

"Is it still there?"

"I'll go and see."

Her room was in the front, on the first floor, and she ran quickly up the stairs. Crossing to the window, she looked down, disturbing the curtains as little as possible. There was a car drawn up by the kerb two doors away—a racy-looking saloon.

"It's still there," she said, returning to the telephone.

"Good," said Simon briskly. "Now, you run along off to bed, Pamela, old dear, and forget it. And if you get any more messages like that, give yourself the benefit of the doubt and don't make a move until you've confirmed them. Incidentally, I don't know how you go to the office in the mornings, but I should stick to the tube or bus if I were you. Funny things have happened to taxis before now. Goodnight, child."

She went upstairs, but she did not undress at once. Instead, she put on a heavy coat, opened the window a little at the bottom, and sat down beside it with a book. She read inattentively, with one eye on the car in the street below.

Ten minutes later, a sports coupé droned round into the street, passed the waiting car, and pulled in to the pavement directly under her window. A man stepped out, and stood for a moment lighting a cigarette, and she recognised the Saint.

He sauntered up to the other car and opened the door.

"Marmaduke," said the Saint clearly, "you're a bad boy. Go right home, and don't do it again."

The driver's reply was inaudible, but she heard Simon speak again, and there was a hard, metallic note in his voice.

"You lie," said the Saint. "You are afraid of me, because you know that if I get annoyed there isn't a graft in the world that'll stop me showing it—unpleasantly. Do what you're told."

There was a muttered colloquy which she couldn't hear, and then Simon closed the door and stepped back.

He watched the saloon out of sight, and then walked back to his own car.

He stood beside it, scanning the windows above him, and Pamela leaned out.

"It's all right, old darling," called the Saint cheerfully. "You won't be disturbed again. Goodnight, for the second time."

He climbed into his car and drove off, and she closed the window.

The next morning he seemed to have forgotten the incident, and when she thanked him for disposing of the mysterious driver, he appeared to have to concentrate intensely before he could place the reference.

"Oh, that!" he said at length. "Do you know you've broken a record?"

She showed her bewilderment, and he smiled.

"If I put you in a book," he said, "you'd be the first heroine in the history of thick-ear fiction who has not cantered blithely into the first trap that was set for her. Tell me how you did it."

She told him, ending up with the information that she had seen him leaving the Piccadilly with George, but he did not seem at all upset by this discovery.

"George and I are great friends," he said airily. "But perhaps you didn't know that I was a practical Socialist?"

"But he was in evening dress?"

Simon raised his eyebrows.

"Why not?" he demanded. "The only difference was that mine was paid for, whereas so far George has only been able to cough up the first instalment on his. The hire-purchase system is really a fine gift to democracy. George will own that suit in three years, and the dicky and cuffs will be his very own in a couple of months. Who are we to discourage George's efforts to better himself?"

Presently he asked, "Have you seen Teal lately?"

"He spoke to me in the street the other day, when I was going home."

"What did you talk about?"

"Nothing in particular," she said. "He told me one or two things about you."

"I call myself something in particular," said the Saint, brightening, "even if you don't. What did he say?"

"Oh, things."

Simon looked at her.

"And do you wish to give notice?" he asked.

"I don't think so."

"Good," said the Saint. "For those kind words I'll be more gentle with Teal when I see him again."

That afternoon there was a caller, and Simon frowned thoughtfully over the cheaply printed card which the clerk brought in. "Mr Harold Garrot," it said.

He went through to the waiting-room, and a sallow lantern-jawed man, with shaggy eyebrows and a blue chin, slowly uncoiled his six-feet-six-inches of lanky length from a chair.

"Sit down, Harry," said the Saint, affably, "and shoot us the dope in your own time. Also, you might whisper the important passages, because the walls in this office are very thin."

Long Harry sat down, and put his hands on his knees.

"Mr Templar," he said, "you know who I'm looking for."

"I don't," said the Saint.

"Connell," explained Harry tersely.

Simon frowned.

"Is there a catch in this?" he demanded. "Am I supposed to say, 'Who is Connell?'— whereupon you say, 'Connellady eat asparagus without dripping the melted butter down her neck?'—or something soft like that? Because, if so, I'll buy it—but let's get it over quick."

Long Harry leaned forward.

"Templar," he said, "you know me, and I know you, and we both know Connell. But did you know that I'd just come out of stir?"

"I read in the papers a couple of years ago that you'd just gone in," said the Saint. "How's the old place looking?"

But Harry was not feeling conversational.

"Connell put me there," he said. "I never did that Bayswater job. Connell shopped me, and I'm looking for Connell."

Simon rose.

"Well," he said briefly, "I'm afraid I can't help you. Nobody's seen Connell for two years. Good afternoon."

He held out his hand, but Long Harry ignored it.

"Next time you see Connell," said Mr Garrot, rising, "you can tell him I'm laying for him."

"Good afternoon," said the Saint again, and opened the door. "Call in any time you're passing, but don't stay long."

He returned to his desk with a greater feeling of enthusiasm for his job than he had felt for several days, for the return of Long Harry seemed to him to presage the beginning of troublous times for the firm of Vanney's Ltd., and, in Simon Templar's opinion, that was all to the good.

7

"Talking of disappearances, Mr Teal," said Sergeant Barrow, "I've been thinking."

Chief Inspector Teal fixed his subordinate with a basilisk eye.

"Not again?" he drawled with heavy sarcasm.

"What's more," said Barrow, "I've been talking to Jones and the Records Office, and I've got on to something that might interest you."

Teal waited.

"About the time that Connell disappeared," said Barrow earnestly. "Red Mulligan also vanished. The last thing we hear of Red, he was supposed to be dying of pleurisy. Red was the man who worked the Finchley bank job. He and Long Harry used to run together, and they shared a room in Deptford. Connell made a trio when it suited him. Well, Connell disappears, and a few days after that we stop hearing anything about Red, I went down to Deptford and made a few inquiries, but all they could tell me was that Harry gave out a story that Red had got better and gone out to Australia. Since when, nobody's seen or heard of him. Now, does a man who's been given up for dead get better as quickly as that, and would he jump right off his bed into a steamer, and shoot off without saying a word to anyone? It's not as if there was anything against him at that time—he had a clean sheet."

Teal nodded.

"That's worth thinking about," he conceded.

But it was not Inspector Teal's practice to make his thought processes public, and he switched off almost immediately on to a new line.

"Go out into the wide world, Barrow," he said, "and find me an Australian."

After some search an Australian was found, and Teal took him out, bought his beer, and invited a geography lesson. Then he bought the Australian more beer, and left him.

He went to Vanney's, and the Saint saw him at once.

"Mr Vanney is engaged," said Simon, "but all my time is yours. What can I do for you today?"

"I'm looking for a man named Connell," said Teal.

"Everybody seems to be doing it," sighed the Saint. "Only yesterday we had a man in looking for him."

"Long Harry?" asked Teal, and Simon nodded.

"It's surprising how popular a man can become, all of a sudden."

"Connell's wanted for the Battersea murder," said Teal.

Clearly the Saint was surprised at this item of news, but his surprise did not make him any more helpful.

"Connell is the mystery man of the twentieth century," he said. "Sorry, Teal, but you've come to the wrong shop. We broke off our partnership with Maskelyne's years ago."

"There's another thing," said Teal. "We've got a man in for a bit of work in Curzon Street, and he's made a confession that might put us on to a man we've been looking for for years. I won't go into details, but I will tell you that I'm temporarily stuck, and you might be able to help me."

"Anything within reason, Claud Eustace," said the Saint.

Teal winced.

"The point is," he said, "that this case links up with one in Australia. The trouble is, we haven't got the name of the man who was robbed, and I'm wondering if Mr Vanney could save me the trouble of cabling out to Australia for it. I believe he spent some years in Melbourne."

"That is so."

"Then he might know the name. He's one of the richest men in Melbourne, and I'm told he's got the swellest house in the place. The man I've got couldn't remember the name, but he thinks it began with an 'S.' He remembers that it's a big, white stone building at the top of Collins Street, about five minutes from Brighton Beach. The family used to dash down to the sea for a dip every morning before breakfast, and it was while they were out on one of these early swimming parties that the jewels were taken."

The Saint looked up doubtfully.

"It's some time since Mr Vanney was in Melbourne," he said.

"He couldn't help knowing the place," said Teal persuasively. "Collins Street is one of the big thoroughfares, and everybody knows Brighton Beach, and this man's home was a show feature of the city."

The Saint shrugged.

"I'll ask him," he said, "but I doubt if he can help you. Shall I write and let you know what he says?"

"I can get a reply telegraphed from Melbourne quicker than that," said Teal. "Couldn't you ask him now?"

"I'll see," said the Saint, and went.

He was back in two minutes.

"Mr Vanney is very sorry, but he can't remember the name of the man. He knows the house, of course, but he thinks that the man's name began with an 'M.'"

"Thanks," said Teal, and heaved his vast bulk out of the chair. "Sorry to have troubled you."

"Sorry to have been troubled," said Simon Templar genially.

Teal stopped by the door.

"By the way," he said, "why have you gone off your feed lately? Are you in love?"

The Saint smiled appreciatively.

"That was clever of you, Teal," he admitted. "I didn't find out till a couple of days ago that you were watching the place. No, I don't have luncheon these days."

"Why?" said Teal.

"Because," said the Saint fluently, "it is Lent. In Lent, I give up luncheon, lumbago, lion-hunting, and liquorice."

"I," said Teal, "give up lorgnettes, leeks, leprosy, lynching, lamentation, lavender, and life preservers."

It was the first time for many months that Mr Teal had held his own with the Saint in a verbal encounter, and that, in the auspicious circumstances, put him in a very good humour.

He returned to Scotland Yard, and sent again for Sergeant Barrow.

"Did you look out all the papers connected with the Stenning case, as I told you?" he asked.

Barrow pointed to a bundle recently placed on Teal's desk, but Teal preferred to cut his work down to a minimum. If he had told the Saint that he gave up labour throughout the year, irrespective of Lent, whenever possible, he would have been very near the truth.

He leaned back, clasped his hands in an attitude of prayer, closed his eyes, and said, "Have you studied the case?"

Sergeant Barrow intimated that he had done so.

"Tell me about it," said Teal.

Stenning's death had caused a considerable sensation at the time. His name was well known in the City, and the derogatory rumours which circulated persistently among the cognoscenti were not printed in the newspapers, which were restrained by the law of libel, and therefore did not reach the majority of the public. It was not until after Stenning's death that all the facts of his nefarious career were made public, and then there was a panic among the small investors.

Stenning was clever. For years he had sailed perilously near the wind, and had found it a profitable procedure. But with the passing of time, the encouraging recollection of past successes, and the temptation to increase his income still further by risking sailing manoeuvres closer and closer to the wind, had led him to form companies of increasing instability. He had ended up by organising and directing a project which, for the first time in his career, was flagrantly fraudulent. The result had been to raise his conjectured profits to the seven-figure mark, although at his death his estate was valued at no more than £10,000.

"No man," said Sergeant Barrow, "ever died at a more convenient time."

Stenning had passed over with all his sins when his last and most ambitious scheme was tottering on the dizzy pinnacle of success. Ultimate discovery was inevitable—though whether Stenning realised that, and was banking on being able to leave the country before a warrant was issued for his arrest, would never be known. Certainly, drunk with confidence, he had ended up by over-reaching himself, but then he had died. As Sergeant Barrow remarked, he couldn't have timed his death for a more suitable moment.

One night he had set out from London in an open car, accompanied only by his chauffeur, to keep a business appointment at Bristol. According to the evidence at the inquest, the chauffeur, Arthur Wylie, had attempted to take a corner too fast on a lonely stretch of road between Basingstoke and Andover. The car had skidded and overturned. The chauffeur was flung clear, but Stenning had been pinned underneath the wreckage, and before the chauffeur could go to his assistance, the car had burst into flames, so that it was impossible to approach it. The car was reduced to a heap of twisted scrap-iron, and of Stenning there remained nothing but a corpse charred beyond recognition, and identified only by a ring, a watch, and a bunch of keys. The chauffeur pleaded inexperience, and it was found that he had only held a driving licence for six months.

A verdict of accidental death was returned, and Stenning was buried in dishonour, for upon his death the full story of all his shady transactions was made public. But of the millions he was reputed to have amassed in the course of his career as a swindler, no trace could be discovered.

"That's the story," said Sergeant Barrow. "But what's it got to do with Connell?"

"Nothing, and at the same time everything," answered Mr Teal enigmatically. "And now, if you will listen carefully, I'll tell you a little joke."

Sergeant Barrow produced a smile.

"The joke," said Mr Teal, "is about a man who says that he lived several years in Australia, and who gives Melbourne as his last address. I asked him if he could identify a house at the top of Collins Street, five minutes from Brighton Beach, and I told him how the people who owned the house used to run down to the sea for a bathe before breakfast."

Sergeant Barrow's forehead puckered.

"I'm very sorry, Mr Teal," he said, "but I don't see it."

"Suppose," said Teal dreamily, "that I told you that I'd got a beautiful house in Kensington Gardens overlooking the Embankment. What would you say then?"

"I should say you were a liar, Mr Teal," said Sergeant Barrow diffidently.

Chief Inspector Teal seemed to smile in his sleep.

"I said nothing so insulting," he murmured. "In fact, I said nothing at all. But since the Australian you found me gave me his word that Brighton Beach was at least ten miles away from the top of Collins Street, Melbourne, I think I was justified in thinking a lot."

8

"Take a letter," said the Saint. "To the Editor of *The Times*. Sir, —
The *impudent presumption* of the modern employer is a menace to the
morals of the community. Stop. The other day, I was applying for the
post of secretary to an American business man who is opening a branch
in London. Stop. Finding my qualifications and references satisfactory,
he then asked me how much I wanted. Stop. 'Four pounds a week,' I
said. Stop.

'With pleasure,' he replied. Stop. 'Certainly not,' I retorted.
Stop. Can nothing be done about this? Stop. I am, etcetera, Harassed
Stenographer. I wonder why they never print my letters?" he added.

"Because," said Pamela Marlowe calmly, "I never send them."

Simon regarded her seriously.

"This is very like insubordination," he said. "However, I suppose
you know best. Let's change the subject. Have you got any more
complaints to make against the firm?"

"I did remember something the other day," she admitted.

"Let's hear it."

"What did Mr Teal mean by talking about Mr Vanney making childish attempts to kill him?" she asked, and Simon put down his pen and leaned back comfortably.

"Owing to the recent boom in detective fiction," he explained elaborately, "the public have come to regard it as essential that their detectives should lead dangerous lives, in imminent peril of crafty assassination. To meet the popular demand, the proprietors of the leading newspapers have been compelled to organize private squads of thugs, who at intervals attempt the life of a well-known detective and thereby provide headlines for the front page. The detectives, of course, being public servants, take all this in good part, but they do insist on a certain standard of efficiency about the murders, and when the attempt is below par they feel annoyed. Naturally, any self-respecting detective would object to being killed in any of the crude, old-fashioned ways."

Pamela Marlowe went back to her table, slammed back the typewriter carriage, rattled in a sheet of paper, and began to pound away with unnecessary violence.

Simon Templar signed the letter with a flourish, blotted it, and flicked it into the tray on his desk. Then he leaned back, lighted a cigarette, and proceeded to smoke meditatively.

"Pamela," he said presently, "you seem to be annoyed."

"I am," she said.

Simon took his feet off the table suddenly and smiled. It has already been mentioned that he had a most engaging smile. He left his chair and came and stood beside her.

"Pamela," he said, holding out his hand, "let's call it a day."

"Very well, Mr Templar," said Pamela, and went on with her work.

Simon looked at the hand she had studiously ignored, sighed, and returned to his desk.

After that he did no more work, and spent his idle moments with his feet on the table, smoking innumerable cigarettes, and staring at the ceiling with a frown indicative of furious cerebration.

He had lunch that day with two friends, and the conversation was not particularly inspiring. It was not until the end of the meal that he chose to liven things up.

Then he pushed away his plate, lighted a cigarette, and blew out a long stream of smoke.

"Boys," he said, "we have fortified ourselves with an excellent lunch. Our friend Connell has demonstrated a hidden talent for chefery which has been a delightful surprise, and the brandy is on the sideboard in case any of you want bracing up another notch. Help yourselves if you think you need it, because I've got a shock for you."

He paused, inhaling comfortably.

Connell accepted the suggestion, but the other man did not move.

"The first point," said the Saint, settling himself, "is that now is the time for all bad men and blue to realise that this party is likely to break up without notice."

The other two said nothing. Clearly, the Saint had only voiced their own thoughts.

"The second point," Simon went on, "is that, after all the trouble we've taken, we should go down to history as a set of prize pikers if we beat it now. The boodle should all be in within a week, and if we can only keep our nerve and hang on, we've got a sporting chance of scooping the kitty. The pool isn't as large as it might have been, but that's not our fault. We're being rushed on the last lap, and we've got to make the best of it."

He blew two smoke rings and watched them float upwards.

"Maybe you haven't realised how short our time's getting," he said. "Teal's on to us—that's a cert. He caught us all nicely on the hop the other day over that Melbourne inquiry. I had to let it go through because if I'd tried to stall him off it'd only have made him hotter and it wouldn't have made any difference in the long run. It was only a matter of turning a suspicion into a certainty. Teal knows that Vanney's a fake, as far as his Australian career is concerned anyway, but that's not a crime in itself. But there are one or two other things."

The Saint stood up. He had taken over the chairmanship of the meeting quite naturally.

"There's been some funny stuff about Connell and Long Harry, and it's new on me. Harry was shopped for busting a house in Bayswater. Anyway, Harry said he was shopped, and he said it in a way that makes me want to believe him. He's just out of Pentonville, and he thinks Connell shopped him, and he's looking for Connell. And Teal told me the other day that Connell was wanted for a job in Battersea. Now, I know Connell didn't do that job. Therefore Connell's been framed, too. Now, what's the point of all this framing business?"

He looked straight at Connell, and Connell growled.

"Harry must have shopped me," he said.

"Get that idea right out of your head, son," advised the Saint. "Teal knew Harry thought you'd shopped him in Bayswater, and the first thing he'd think of would be that Harry might have tried to return the compliment and shop you. Teal must have had something to make him quite certain that Harry didn't do the Battersea job, or else he'd have had Harry inside in a brace of shakes."

Simon canted up his cigarette between his lips, and set his hands deep in his trouser pockets.

"Even that," he remarked, "is no particular affair of mine. I just put it up to you to think over in your spare time. But the last two points are personal. First of all, this business of trying to bump off Teal has got to stop. I don't know how it was arranged, but Teal said it had been tried, and Teal doesn't bluff that way. I should particularly object to Teal being bumped off. If Teal passed on to his harp, I should have nothing left to live for. Get that. If Teal makes any more complaints of that sort, Simon Templar goes out of this partnership at once."

The other two said nothing, but the Saint had not been expecting a reply. He passed on.

"Finally," he said, "any monkeying about with Miss Marlowe will also stop. I've let you off once, James Arthur Vanney; but I don't know if I made it quite plain then, that the next time it happens you will not be let off. That's all."

The bearded man came to his feet slowly.

"Are you running this show by yourself?" he asked.

"At the moment—and in this matter—yes," said the Saint.

James Arthur Vanney turned to the third member of the party.

"And what have you got to say?" he demanded.

"I agree with Templar. It's too dangerous."

The bearded man's fist came down on the table with a crash.

"And I say," he blustered, "that if either of you interfere with my private dealings with that girl, I'll quit the show!"

The third man got to his feet also.

"And if you quit the show," he said quietly, "I might have a little tale to tell Inspector Teal about the mysterious Mr Vanney."

The bearded man looked round, savage-eyed.

"If it comes to telling tales," he said, "I guess I could tell as many as anyone. You wouldn't dare risk it."

Simon flicked his cigarette into the fireplace.

"Nor would you dare risk it, my man," he said smoothly. "Think it over, and while you're thinking just remember that it isn't only old fat Teal you've got to be afraid of. I might get you first."

The Saint's tone was perfectly quiet, but he never took his gaze off the other's face, and the bearded man saw murder in his eyes.

Mr Teal had discovered long ago that he was the plaything of a peculiar destiny. Whenever he was engaged on a big case, when once the preliminary trifling and ferreting about was done, things had a habit with him of moving with well-oiled precision and alarming swiftness. Mr Teal, in his leisure moments, attributed to this fact his ponderous and somnolent disposition—for, he pointed out, nobody less stolidly constituted could have stood the strain.

It was so with the Vanney case.

There came a day when Mr Teal felt that he had disposed of every detail of the preliminary investigation, and there was nothing left for him to do but to sit down and wait for the other side to make a move which would provide him with a way out of this temporary impasse.

He said as much to the Chief Commissioner, Sir Brodie Smethurst, and the Assistant Commissioner, Mr William Kennedy, at a private conference which lasted until the small hours of the morning; and they agreed with him, for the Criminal Investigation Department is jealous of its reputation. Evidence upon which a layman would act without hesitation is sifted and contemplated with a suspicious and cautious eye, for Scotland Yard prefers to bide its time and take no action until the possibility of failure has been brought down to an irreducible minimum. The net is spread, and it is spread so effectively that only a genius could find a way out of it. There have been geniuses in the history of crime, but they are rare, and the police routine is not designed to cope with them.

"I think I've got Vanney's where I want them," said Teal. "If I have, they're safe anyway. I'd rather not risk making a fool of myself and the Department by acting before I've got all the threads in my hands and I can afford to lay a thousand to one on getting my conviction."

"What's their graft at the moment?" asked Kennedy, and Chief Inspector Teal produced several typewritten sheets of paper which he handed over for perusal.

"That's a confidential report from Stanforth and Watson," he said. "Stanforth and Watson are handling a lot of Vanney's business. They've had their doubts about it for some time, and when I started making inquiries they wanted to chuck it up altogether. I asked them to carry on to help us, and promised we'd see everything was all right for them when it came to the show-down. Eventually they agreed. You will find all the particulars here—it's the old bucket-shop game, but done more brilliantly than it's been done for years. Stenning was the last expert we had, and this is in the old tradition. But this time he's come back with some new trimmings on the old game. He's not going after the chicken food—the mug punters with a few pounds to throw away here and there. He's got a graft that's specially made up to attract the big men— the men who are nearly as crooked as he is himself. Wads of money have come in to him from every corner of Europe."

"Is it like the Saint to be mixed up with a game like that?" asked Smethurst, and Teal nodded.

"It's just about his mark. The technique may be Stenning, but the basic idea is pure Saint. The only thing that's puzzling me is why the

Saint should have bothered to go in with Stenning at all, instead of carrying the whole thing through on his own."

The Chief Commissioner looked up from the report.

"It's very reminiscent of Stenning."

Teal nodded.

"It's Stenning to the life," he said.

"He died right on his cue, that man," put in Kennedy.

"He did," said Teal grimly. "It suited some people I could mention—down to the ground. I've got a feeling that if Stenning came to life again it'd mean a lot of trouble for the firm of Vanney."

He left the Commissioner's house at Regent's Park as the clocks were striking three, and drove away in his miniature car towards his own modest lodgings near Victoria.

The grotesqueness of the association of his mammoth bulk with that microscopic automobile had never struck him, but a more practical argument against it was forced upon his notice ten minutes later.

Piccadilly at that hour was almost deserted, and Mr. Teal, in defiance of all speed limits, betrayed his satisfaction with the way the Vanney case was going, by allowing the lightness of his heart to manifest itself in the heaviness of his foot on the accelerator. He was doing nearly thirty-five miles an hour when he came level with the Ritz, but even so, a big limousine purred up level and passed him effortlessly.

The detective had been guilty of allowing his thoughts to wander, and he was brought rudely back to earth by a sudden vision of the big car steering in to the kerb directly across his front wings.

Faced with the alternative of crashing into the side of the car in front, Teal wrenched the steering round to the left, forgetting that he had no more than two feet of road on that side in which to manoeuvre. He realised his mistake as he saw the columns which carry the front of the hotel over the pavement to the edge of the road leaping towards him. He tried to swing the car round again; but it was too late, and in an instant the near front wheel touched the kerb and the steering wheel was wrenched out of his hand. The car piled itself up against the stone wall with a crash.

Shakily, Teal picked himself up out of the road, where the force of the collision had hurled him. By some miracle he was unhurt, though his car was a wreck. The car which had caused the accident was vanishing in the direction of Hyde Park Corner; but the tail light was out, and it was impossible to see the number.

He saw his car removed, with difficulty, to a nearby garage, and went home in a taxi. It was not the first time that an attempt had been made on his life, and he was inclined to take these things philosophically. But on this occasion he was annoyed, for the accident, and the consequent necessary arrangements for the disposal of the ruins, had deprived him of two hours' sleep.

The next morning, however, found him in a good temper—for his escape of the night before seemed to him, by all precedent, to mean that the case was entering on its last hectic stages—and he was almost cordial to the long-suffering Sergeant Barrow.

"I think most of the facts about Vanney's are taped out now," said Teal. "I've made a list of them in chronological order, and the list spells something to me."

He took a small notebook from his waistcoat pocket, marked a place with his thumb, and handed it over.

"Take a look at that."

Sergeant Barrow read the neatly tabulated entry:

1928 July   Connell and Mulligan disappeared.

1928 August   Stenning killed.

1930 April	House commissioned for Vanney
1929 June	Vanney arrived from Melbourne, took possession of house, and opened the firm of Vanney.

"You seem to connect Vanney up with Stenning," remarked Barrow, when he had finished, and Inspector Teal closed his eyes and smiled beatifically.

"I didn't do that," he replied. "Stenning did it himself."

The next development came some hours later.

Teal had returned to his office after dinner, and he was still working at ten o'clock, when a messenger entered.

"There's a question through from C Division," said the man. "Connell's been seen in Soho tonight, and they want to know whether they're to pull him in or tail him, or what."

"Tail him till I arrive," said Teal briskly, "I've got an idea."

He spent twenty minutes in another room, and when he emerged the change in his appearance was amazing. The modern detective does not rely on such crude disguises as false beards. Instead, he pins his faith to the creation of atmosphere. In a certain room at New Scotland Yard is kept a file of photographs of representative men of different trades, and the minutest details of their habits and characteristics are chronicled.

Teal, suiting his disguise to the frame-work on which he had to build, had adopted the character of a shady racecourse hanger-on. He changed his sober blue serge suit for a loud check, hung a massive watch chain across his middle, selected spats, and put them on over a pair of pointed yellowish shoes. On each hand he put a ring, and he fixed a diamond pin in the wrong part of a flashy tie. To his face he did little—a skilful darkening of the eyebrows, a broadening of the face by the insertion in the mouth of rubber pads designed for that purpose, and the attachment of a bristly moustache, was sufficient.

Regretfully he discarded his chewing gum, and put four cigars in a pocket of his

waistcoat. He took a bowler hat of the wrong kind, a pair of lemon-coloured gloves, and a silver-knobbed ebony walking-stick, and inspected the ensemble in a full-length mirror. Certainly he was transformed.

At Marlborough Street Police Station he was told that the last report from the men who were keeping track of Connell had placed him in a public-house in Shaftesbury Avenue. Arriving there, Teal was met by a detective who told him that their man had moved on to a night club.

The other detective was lounging against the side of a taxi-cab outside, talking to the driver. The sign he gave Teal would have been unnoticed by a casual observer, but it was enough. Teal went in. He had no difficulty in this, for in his pocket was a collection of membership cards which would have gained him admittance to any night club in London.

He saw his man as soon as he entered the room and established himself in a corner a few tables away.

Sipping the drink which was brought him, he watched Connell covertly.

Connell was there without any attempt at disguise. Gathered together at his table were three or four men whose appearances were decidedly against them. Two of them Teal recognised. There was the usual leavening of "dancing partners."

The party was a hilarious one, and Connell was leading every outburst of merriment. Every drink was on him—one round had hardly arrived before he was shouting for another— and he paid for them from a huge roll of Bank of England notes.

"Drink up!" he shouted at intervals. "I'm on a good thing, and this is my night out."

Teal watched for an hour, and when the party quieted down into a sodden stupor he judged that it was his turn to take a hand.

Taking a pencil and an envelope from his pocket, he scribbled a note: "If you want to make some more easy money, don't say anything to anybody, but follow me out of here."

"Slip that to the gentleman over there," said Teal to a passing waiter, and pointed out Connell.

Connell read the note, and Teal caught his eye. Then the detective rose and walked towards the exit.

Connell caught him up in the street.

"What's this?" he demanded thickly, brandishing the envelope.

Teal took it from him.

"I want you to do a job for me," he said. "There's a place just up the road where we can talk without being disturbed. It's worth a hundred to you. Are you on?"

Connell swayed, and steadied himself.

"Let's hear," he said, and Teal took his arm and walked him up the road.

In half an hour Connell was back at the club calling for more drinks, but Teal did not return. He went back to Scotland Yard, changed into his ordinary clothes, and went home to bed.

He retailed the encounter to Sergeant Barrow the next morning.

"I asked him if he could drive a car, and he said he could. Then I asked him if he could do tricks with one, and he asked me what I meant. I told him I'd got a down on a man and I wanted him messed up in an accidental sort of way. 'This man's given his chauffeur notice,' I said, 'and I can get you the job, references and all, in any name you like. If you're a fool, you'll land yourself for dangerous driving, but if you're clever, maybe you can get away with it and draw the hundred

81

I'm offering.' He was in a boastful mood, and he said he could make a car eat out of his hand and turn somersaults just when he wanted it to. I arranged to meet him at the same place in two days' time, with the money, and that was that."

"And?" prompted Sergeant Barrow.

"And," said Mr Teal, with languid satisfaction, "I think that tells me all I want to know about the later history of Mulligan, and how Stenning managed to die so successfully."

Altogether it was a successful twenty-four hours for Mr Teal; for a few minutes later the man he had set to tail Connell home arrived with his report, and another mystery was well on its way to solution.

Mr Teal now had a very good idea why the Saint had been going out to lunch so infrequently, and this further progress increased his conviction that things would shortly commence to hum.

10

At twelve o'clock on a certain morning, Simon Templar made a decision.

He came to this decision at the end of twenty-four hours' unbroken deliberation. In the office he had been moody, going about his work with his usual efficiency, but with the air of devoting to it no more attention than was absolutely necessary, while all the spare energy of his mind was simultaneously devoted to this far more important thing of which he said nothing. When he was not working, he sat back in his chair, scowling darkly about him.

Pamela Marlowe diagnosed these symptoms as the proof of a misspent night before; but in this she was wrong, for the night before did not occur until the night after. The Saint had gone back to the luxuriously converted garage in Upper Berkeley Mews where he made his home, and had gone to bed before midnight like a good boy.

The decision was finally made at twelve o'clock, and with the removal of uncertainty and the arrival of a definite plan of campaign he brightened perceptibly. His pencil went flying across the room into a corner, the blotting-paper was screwed up into a ball and hurled into the waste-paper basket with the gesture of a challenger throwing down the gauntlet, and his feet returned to their usual position on top of the desk.

"I've got it," he said triumphantly.

"Badly, I should say," agreed Pamela, but he refused to be suppressed.

"Since lunch-time yesterday," he explained solemnly, "I have been tormented by visions of helpless orphans struggling to make their way in the world, with no mother to spank them and no father to borrow fivers from. I think something ought to be done about it. Don't you?"

"Are you going to start an orphanage?" she asked.

The Saint stroked his chin.

"Not exactly," he replied gravely. "I'm starting a fund for distressed orphans, and the fund will be used to help deserving cases to end their days in the luxury to which the hardships of their early years have entitled them. I am an orphan," he added absently.

Clearly he was bursting with some big scheme, but he was too intent upon it to waste time elaborating any more fantastic explanations.

He plumped down in his chair, and rang the bell marked "Secretary."

"Take a letter," he said. "This is to Rolands and Battersby, 240 Threadneedle Street. 'Dear Sirs, —With reference to your advertisement of a thousand-ton, ocean-going motor-cruiser, in the current issue of *Yachting*, I'll buy the darned thing at the price mentioned. Paragraph. I understand that the said hooker is at present lying in Southampton Water. Stop. You will kindly rake up a crew, shove them on board, and tell them to shoot the old tub along to Gravesend. Stop. This must be done immediately, as I am likely to be leaving on short notice. Stop. Communicate these instructions to Southampton by telephone, and drum it into the fat heads of the big stiffs at the other end of the line that the barnacled barge aforesaid has got to arrive at Gravesend within forty-eight hours of your receipt of this letter. Yours faithfully.' Turn that into respectable business English, and type it on plain paper. Vanney's," he said, "will shortly know me no more. Observe my tears."

"Are you serious?" she asked.

"I was never more serious in my life," answered the Saint.

"You're leaving Vanney's?"

The Saint smiled.

"Certainly there's going to be a break in the partnership," he said. "But whether I shall leave Vanney's or Vanney's will leave me remains to be seen."

Business had been getting brisker every day, and that afternoon established a new record. Simon spent the whole of his time in a whirl of letters, telegrams, and telephone conversations, and he had no leisure in which to give vent to the high spirits which otherwise he would have enjoyed indulging.

He was not sorry to leave the office that night, for work was a thing in which he was accustomed to indulge spasmodically, and with the sole object of reaping sufficient profit from it to render further work unnecessary for a considerable period.

With a number of late nights behind him, and the prospect of tiring days ahead, he had intended to go to bed early that night; but unfortunately for that plan, when he was half undressed, he was smitten with an idea. With the Saint, to conceive an idea and to put it into execution were things so closely consecutive as to be almost simultaneous. He sighed, dressed again, and went out.

The next morning, however, he showed no trace of tiredness as he ran up the stairs to the office.

He was always the first to arrive, as only Vanney and himself and one other man held keys, and the other two were invariably late. He was feeling cheerful that morning as he let himself in, but the gay humming died swiftly on his lips as he endeavoured to extract the key from the lock.

He twisted, pulled, and wrenched, and eventually it came away. Then he looked at the lock, and discovered the reason for the jam. It was a Yale, and it took him no more than ten seconds' expert investigation to see and appreciate how neatly it had been broken.

He went quickly through the offices—waiting-room, clerks' room, and his own room. The communicating doors were all open. He might have left them like that himself, but one door was open which he had never by any chance forgotten to close, and that was the door between his own office and the room marked "Private."

He passed quickly through, and what he saw made him pull up suddenly with his face gone strangely stern.

Facing him on either side of the fireplace, were two tall cupboards, which, as has been mentioned, were kept locked. Presumably they were used for storing the private files of the company. But since nobody except himself and his partners ever entered the room, the question was never a subject for curiosity and comment. Now both the cupboards had been roughly broken open, and the doors sagged wide, showing the interiors.

One was empty. The intruder, whoever he was, had drawn blank with his first guess. The other was also empty; but instead of the wooden back, which one might have expected to see, there was clearly visible the raw brickwork of the wall, and this had been broken away so that there was a large gap through which a man could easily pass. On the other side of this gap was a curtain, which had been drawn aside, and through the hole in the wall could be seen a room.

The Saint stood still for a long time. Then he took out his cigarette-case, and very slowly and calmly selected and lighted a cigarette. With this in his mouth he strolled forward, pushed through the doors of the right-hand cupboard, ducked through the aperture in the wall, and came out into the room beyond. It was furnished as a sitting-room, with a safe in one corner and a writing-desk in another. The safe had been smashed by an expert, and its heavy door stood wide open—a battered and drunken-looking apology for a door. Papers were strewn about the floor. The writing-desk was in a similar state of disrepair; every drawer had been forced, and the contents were scattered over it, around it, and across the carpet.

After what he had already seen, these catastrophes were of minor importance, and even the litter failed to exasperate his tidy instincts. Moving very slowly and deliberately, he examined the rest of the flat, and found that no part of it which might constitute a hiding-place had been overlooked.

The Saint smiled faintly, but it was not because he was amused.

He went back into Vanney's office, pulled the cupboard doors to, and returned to his own room, closing the door marked "Private" carefully behind him.

When Pamela Marlowe arrived he was comfortably blowing smoke-rings, and no one would have known from his expression what a jar he had received.

She sat down, and it was some time before he became aware that she was expecting him to do something. He pulled himself together with an effort.

"Oh yes, the letters," he murmured, and swept the pile before him neatly into a drawer, "I've already opened those, and there's nothing to attend to yet."

He played a tattoo on the desk with a pencil.

"By the way," he said casually, "I'm giving you a week's notice, though the necessity for your services may cease to exist before then."

It was some moments before she could recover from her surprise.

"Why?" she stammered. "Isn't my work satisfactory?"

"Perfectly, sweetheart," he said. "But the firm you work for isn't. Later on in the day I shall be giving myself notice, so you needn't think you are the only victim. You will receive three months' salary in lieu of however much longer notice you thought you were entitled to, and a further three months' salary instead of a reference. The procedure may seem strange to you, but it is dictated by my wishes for your welfare. You could have a reference if you wanted one, but it would be quite useless. The money I spoke of has already been paid into your bank account, and you will receive confirmation of that from them as soon as the cheque has been passed through."

"But surely," said Pamela blankly, "six months' salary isn't necessary in lieu of notice and a reference?"

"The firm of Vanney," answered the Saint, "although eccentric to the point of being crooked, has a reputation for generosity to maintain. I have just started to give it that reputation, and you are the first beneficiary."

She hesitated.

"It's very kind of you," she said at length. "But since the money has already been paid over, you must have known that this was going to happen."

"I did," he replied. "But I wasn't sure exactly when. I discovered this morning that it was going to happen today."

Pamela looked straight at him.

"Simon," she said, "since I'm leaving Vanney's, and this looks like the last eccentricity I shall have to puzzle over, is it any use asking you to give me the real reason for it?"

The Saint stood up. He was quite serious.

"I'm sorry," he said. "I've stopped playing the fool from this moment. So I'll just say that it's impossible to answer your question today. Tomorrow, perhaps . . ."

The last words were spoken almost in a whisper, and he was standing quite still with his head bent slightly forward, as though listening.

"One moment," he said, and went quickly into Vanney's office.

"George," said the Saint quickly, to the porter, "yours not to reason why, yours but to promptly fly. In English, pull out of here right away. You also, my King Beaver," this to Vanney. "Go away and sit down and open your hearts to each other. And wait till I come back—it will be within two hours."

He returned to his own office, taking no notice of Pamela, jerked his hat down from the rack, and went out.

A taxi took him to Upper Berkeley Mews. It was there that Teal found him an hour later. There was a half-filled suitcase on the table, and the Saint, having admitted the detective, returned unconcernedly to the task of trying to close the lid of a trunk that was already crammed to bursting point. A selection of clothes was laid out on the bed, and every chair in the room was similarly loaded.

Teal surveyed the disorder thoughtfully.

"Where are you going, Saint?" he inquired.

"Where am I going, old dear? Well, that isn't decided yet. I may be going abroad, or I may not—it just depends how things turn out."

11

Teal did not seem surprised.

"That's what I came to see you about," he remarked, "I suppose there's no chance of your putting in a bit of King's Evidence?"

"Teal," said the Saint, "surely you know me better than that!"

The detective sighed.

"Unfortunately I do," he said. "But I was told to try it."

He picked up his hat.

"There are some men who say no," he observed, "and you wonder whether they mean yes. You don't say yes or no, but one always knows what you mean. Sorry to have troubled you."

"The last man who said that to me," remarked the Saint reminiscently, "is one of the only two possible starters for the Great Burglary Sweepstakes. Tell me, do you boys ever indulge in what you might call judicially sanctioned crime?"

"Not that I know of."

"I just wondered," said the Saint. "Now I know. It must have been Harry."

Teal put down his hat again. If he had not been so obviously incapable of such contortions, one would have said that he pricked up his ears.

"Harry?" he repeated.

"The same. But if you think you're going to get anything out of me before you've got me in the dock, you may have another guess free. Good morning, Claud—and don't forget to close the door as you go out."

Obediently, Teal went to the door.

"By the way," he said from the threshold, "you were working late at the office last night, Saint."

"I was," said Simon, folding a dinner-jacket. "What about it?"

"I made some inquiries, and I found that the rule in those offices is that everyone must be out of them by eight o'clock."

"True," said the Saint. "But since Mr Vanney owns not only the offices but the whole block of flats as well, and since he made that rule, I think one may say that he and his staff are allowed to break it. Good-bye."

"See you again soon," said Teal, and went.

The two hours which the gentleman known as George and the King Beaver had been told to wait had expired to the minute when Simon Templar returned. He knew that he had been followed from Upper Berkeley Mews back to the office, but he was not bothering about such trifling troubles.

He walked quickly down the corridor and turned into his own room.

It was empty.

With a grim foreboding, the Saint swung round on his heel and flung open the door leading into the clerks' room.

"Anybody seen or heard of Miss Marlowe?" he observed.

They had not.

"You're an idle bunch, and you know it," Simon rapped back. "Don't waste your breath telling me you were so busy working you couldn't hear anything, because I shan't believe it. She couldn't have left the office without you hearing the door close. Have you heard her go out?"

They had not.

"Right," said the Saint violently, and closed the door with a contrasting gentleness.

He went through into Vanney's room, closing the door behind him, passed through the cupboard and the wall beyond, and entered the flat. There was only one man there.

"Stenning," said the Saint, "I want to know where Pamela Marlowe is, and I want to know it quick!"

"Miss Marlowe?" repeated the big man blankly.

"You heard me the first time," snapped the Saint.

"I don't know anything about her."

Simon put his hands in his pockets.

"You're a liar and a dog, Stenning, my man," he said. "But I'll settle that account later. Where's your partner in crime?"

The Saint looked round the room.

"He was here when I left you," he said. "He can't have gone without your knowing—unless you weren't here yourself. Which is it?"

Stenning rose.

"I left him," he said.

"I told you to stay here."

"And I chose to leave. Have you got anything to say?"

"A mouthful," said the Saint, "but that'll wait. Where did you go?"

"I went out to buy a bottle of whisky, if you want to know."

Simon's glance fell on the table.

"I see. Well, we'll come to that in due course. I'm only putting it off because I think that when I've finished my interview with you,

you'll be more disposed to tell me all the things I want to know about Connell."

He flung some papers on the table.

"Take a look at those," he said.

Stenning looked.

"A cheque for twenty thousand pounds, which only needs your signature to make it worth that amount, payable to Miss Pamela Marlowe. That is the sum of twelve thousand pounds which you swindled off her father, plus a sum of interest which, I grant you, is extortionate, but which you will pay all the same. A receipt for that sum, signed by Miss Marlowe. I know it'll pass in a court of law, because I forged the signature myself. You may keep it as a souvenir. Also, there's a cheque for fifty thousand pounds, payable to myself, for which I am afraid I omitted to provide a receipt. I'll address it to you on Dartmoor, if you think you'd like something to remember me by."

Stenning's mouth twisted.

"And how do you think you're going to make me sign?"

"Moral persuasion," said the Saint. "Reinforced, if necessary, by physical. Take your pen and follow the dotted lines."

Stenning laughed.

"You're mad!" he said.

"Absolutely," agreed the Saint, cordially. "Sign, please."

Stenning sneered.

"I refuse."

"Right," said the Saint. "If you maintain your refusal, I shall be compelled to inflict divers unpleasant forms of physical violence on your person. But before I start, I'll tell you something. Anything I can do to you may not make you sign. But if my methods of persuasion fail to convince you, I have one argument up my sleeve. Do what you're told, and I'll fade out of the picture and say nothing. Without my assistance the firm of Vanney will probably be seriously handicapped, but I can't help that. I'll get out, and nothing will be said. But don't sign, and the firm of Vanney will be shown up within an hour. Teal's on to you already, but if he's got to make his own way he can't get going in time to stop your getaway— if you're quick enough. But if I help him, there'll be a nasty cold cell waiting for you, Stenning."

Stenning sat down. He seemed to be enjoying the joke.

"Templar," he said, "that one's too old for me. I know the game as well as you do, and I tell you it won't work. There are two things to stop your squealing. One is that if you squeal you'll be in the same boat with the rest of us. The other is that even if you squeal, that won't make me sign."

"Granted," said the Saint. "There are two answers to that. One is that I planned this little meeting, and everything is plotted out on my time-table to the last minute. Within one hour Teal could have all the evidence he needs, and I can be away and out on the high seas. Can you say the same?"

Stenning made no answer.

"The second," said the Saint, "is that even if putting you away for at least ten years' penal servitude won't make you pay Miss Marlowe back that money, it'll be the least I can do for her by way of compensation. I'll do it cheerfully—don't make any mistake about that, Beautiful."

The other showed his teeth.

"You rat!" he snarled.

"Your name," said the Saint calmly, "is Mug." It is my distressing duty to have to tell you that you've been had. Your leg has been pulled to such an extent that if you wanted to pose for your portrait with one foot in the grave and the other kicking the cobwebs off the roof of the Chrysler Building, it would have to be a damned deep grave." The Saint smiled with a beautifully cherubic magnificence.

Stenning sat quite still.

"You seem," said the Saint, "to have thought that I'd change my habits for your especial benefit. And that was your gravest error. It wasn't so very long ago, when I was travelling round the wilds of South America, that I met Arthur Wylie. A good soul, but talkative when he had absorbed the best pan of a bottle of whisky. That's how I learnt all about your fake death. Wylie told me how Connell and Long Harry raked up Red Mulligan for you—who, most fortunately for your purposes, had just decided to die, and who, still more considerately, had contrived to end up his useless days with much the same build as yourself. I came back with your dossiers all locked up in the trunk marked 'Not Wanted on Voyage'—and then you had to let me in. And I know everything that's happened in this firm since I joined it. Long Harry's sphere of usefulness passed over, but he was dangerous. He didn't know much, but he might have guessed a lot. You framed him for a job in Bayswater, but it wasn't your fault that the man didn't die and so put Harry out of the way for ever. Connell stayed in the partnership, but he was always a danger. Because he's a mug, it took him some time to realise how important he was. But you know as well as I do that he was starting to realise that he held the whip hand; and what's more, he had started to put the screw on, feeling his way. You disposed of that—by fixing him for a job in Battersea. That time, you made no mistake about the murder. After that, I expect you felt safer, because if Connell started to get any more uppish you would have a very good way of putting him back in his place."

Stenning remained motionless in his chair, hunched up. His face had gone pale, and in that set, pallid mask, his eyes glowed with hate. The Saint, lounging against the table, went on speaking in the same calm, level tones.

"You were clever," he admitted. "You even realised that since Harry was out and was known to be looking for Connell, Harry might be pulled in by mistake for the Battersea job. Knowing your man, you sent Harry money, and, as you expected, he got very tight on it, and was arrested, thereby establishing his alibi beyond all dispute. In fact, the whole show was a really brilliant piece of work, but you went off the rails badly when you began to think you were sitting pretty with the Saint playing a hand in the game. Did you really think I'd changed my habits so much, dear heart, as to want to share the profits in any swindle with anyone— particularly with a flop-eared simoleon-toad like you? Now sign!"

"You're a fool!" said Stenning harshly. "Even if you made me sign, I could still stop the cheque."

"You couldn't," said the Saint. "Being a thoughtful sort of bird, I shall take care to put you in a place where you won't have a chance of stopping it until it has been paid."

"And even then," said Stenning, "I could recover the money, because my signature was obtained under duress."

The Saint smiled beatifically.

"You'll have a job proving it," he murmured. "In any case, it won't be necessary, because you're going to sign that cheque voluntarily."

"Am I?"

"You certainly are," said the Saint. "Because if you don't sign it voluntarily, I shall now proceed to beat you up."

Stenning came to his feet again.

"You're going to beat me up, are you?"

"I am," drawled Simon, with a certain enthusiasm. "And it will be no ordinary beating-up. I'm an expert in the beating-up game, and I may mention that the mercy of a knock-out does not figure in my programme until—oh, well beyond the thirtieth round. It will be painful for you, and I'm afraid your face will be rather crudely damaged; but unfortunately I haven't any more subtle instruments of torture than my fists."

Stenning came round the table, and the Saint, who was unarmed but prepared for a display of armoury, divined the next move in the game before Stenning's hand had reached his hip-pocket. The toe of his right shoe caught the big man on the wrist as the automatic came into sight, and the force of the kick was shattering.

The Saint fell to the floor a second after the gun, and his legs flailing round in a scissors motion, knocked Stenning's feet from under him. Stenning went down with a crash, but Simon was up again in an instant with the automatic in his hand. He slipped it into his hip-pocket, and shed his coat as Stenning scrambled up again.

"The show devolves on me now—what?" he murmured. "That wrist of yours won't help you a lot."

The next instant Stenning was upon him.

It was not a pretty fight to watch, nor would any boxing referee have allowed it to continue for more than three seconds. Simon Templar was giving at least three stone away, and he was not prepared to take chances. The encounter lasted nine minutes by the clock, and at the end of that period Stenning went to the floor for the eleventh time and stayed there.

"Up, Jenkins!" encouraged the Saint. "You're not nearly out yet, so it's no good shamming. The only Queensberry rule we haven't broken yet is the one which forbids rolling about on the floor fighting, but if you don't come up again quickly I'll break that rule, too."

Stenning came to a sitting position.

"I'll sign," he gasped.

The Saint took him by the collar, yanked him to his feet, and pushed him into a chair.

"Here's your pen, and here are the cheques," he said briskly. "Get on with it, because I'm in a hurry. And mind you don't drip blood all over them, because the bank might ask questions."

12

Simon examined the signatures, folded the cheques carefully, and put them in his pocket. His hair was tousled and his shirt torn, but he was breathing quite regularly. He felt ready to begin again any time, and in spirits he was completely unruffled.

"While I think of it, there's one thing more. Take your pen, and write as I dictate. 'I, James Arthur Vanney, formerly known as Stenning, hereby confess—'

"I refuse! You damned double-crosser—"

"I don't," said the Saint, "want any more unpleasantness. But if you're going to be obstinate—"

He took a step forward, and Stenning, seeing the look on his face, drew a clean sheet of paper hurriedly towards him.

The Saint dictated, and Stenning wrote, and when the confession was completed and signed, the Saint read it through carefully and stowed it away in his wallet.

"Now for Connell," he remarked. "Where is he, Stenning?"

The limp mess at the table buried its pulped face in its hands.

"You may as well know now—he's with Miss Marlowe."

"And where's that?"

"Downstairs. There are vaults under the building that I never told you about. The only way into them is from this flat. I had a private lift put in—I was going to use the cellars to hide in if the police got on to us and there was no time to make a bolt for it. Connell was putting the screw on—he said he must have the girl, and I helped him take her. They're down there now."

Simon took the automatic from his pocket, and thumbed back the safety catch.

"If anything's happened to her," he said, "you're certainly going to collect a bullet, my pet. Where is this lift?"

Stenning gestured weakly towards the wall.

"Press the panel next to that picture," he said.

Simon did so. The panel slipped back a fraction of an inch at his touch, and he waited. For a few moments it seemed as if nothing was going to happen. There was no sound, but then a piece of panelling swung open with a click, and in front of him was a small lift. He stepped in, and the panelling closed behind him automatically.

In the wall of the lift were two switches. He tried one without result, but when he clicked over the other the lift began to move downwards.

Presently it stopped. In front of him was a gap in the shaft, hardly distinguishable in the darkness. He stepped out and then he was able to see better.

A runnel ran to left and right of him. The paving, walls and ceiling were of stone, and the passage lost itself in darkness at either end. But a little way down to his right there was a space in the wall from which a faint light came. That must have been a branch tunnel, and since light came from it, it seemed as if his search would not have to be a long one. He began to creep towards it, moving as silently as possible over the flags, but he had hardly taken two steps before a low hum from behind him made him swing round. He saw the lift by which he had just descended commencing to move upwards, and for an instant he weighed up in his mind the possibility of reaching it and checking its ascent; but the idea was no sooner formulated than it was discarded. That was Stenning, of course—he should have knocked him out completely, or tied him up—but it was too late to think of that now. For a moment again he thought of retracing his steps and waiting for Stenning to arrive, but before he could figure out the pros and cons of that scheme it was driven out of his head by a scream that shrilled and echoed hollowly down the passage.

He leapt towards the turning from which the light came. Another shorter tunnel

stretched before him, dimly lighted by two flickering gas jets. At the end it appeared to open into a room so brightly lighted that at that point the gas jets must have given place to electricity. He could see a chair and the end of a table—nothing else—but it was the only place from which the scream could have come.

Simon Templar was inside the room in a matter of seconds.

Pamela Marlowe was there, and so was Connell. Connell was holding her in his great arms. Pamela was struggling, but she was a child in Connell's terrific embrace. The Saint never took in more than the bare details of the scene. His hand gripped Connell's collar, and literally bounced the man off his feet.

"Connell, my man," said the Saint pleasantly, "that will be all from you."

Connell's fist came up like lightning; but Simon was even quicker, and the big man went sprawling against the wall from a mule-kick of a punch that carried every ounce of the Saint's weight and strength behind it.

Connell reeled and nearly fell. Then he came catapulting back to reply, like a jack-in-the-box. The Saint side-stepped coolly, and landed an uppercut that started at his knees and travelled skywards with detonating force to impact smashingly on the point of Connell's jaw; and Connell went down like a log.

"The conventional situation at last, Pamela," said the Saint sadly, and he was just in time to catch her with his arm as she staggered.

In those few merry moments he had forgotten everything else, and he was brought back to reality with a jar that sent a stream of cold air whistling down his spine.

The sound was slight—no more than a subdued rattle that told of a lock being turned home. But the Saint heard it and whipped round—a few seconds too late.

What had been an unguarded way out back into the tunnel was now barred by a solid iron gate, and on the other side of the gate was Stenning—Stenning leaning weakly against the wall, with his face smashed to a jelly, and his coat spattered with blood, but Stenning vindictive and triumphant.

"Now will you squeal, Templar?" he croaked.

The Saint made no answer.

The nearest gas jet was directly over Stenning's head. Stenning reached up one hand, and the flame was extinguished. A faint hissing sound could be heard.

"Do you know what I've done, Templar?" asked Stenning shrilly.

The Saint's left arm was round the girl. With his right hand he was fumbling behind him.

But Stenning was taking no notice. Forcing his tortured body to obedience by the exercise of a tremendous effort of will, he was reeling back down the corridor, lurching from side to side like a drunken man, keeping himself erect half the time by resting against the wall, but dragging himself, somehow, to the other end of the corridor and the second gas jet. He reached it.

"Shall I tell you what I've done, Saint?" Stenning's voice came booming hollowly down the tunnel, and as he spoke his hand went up and found the tap he sought.

Simon knew then that the man was mad.

The last gas jet went out, and the hissing sound became louder. The only light in the corridor now was that which came from the electric bulb in the room in which Simon and the girl were imprisoned.

"I have turned on the gas," said Stenning.

And he laughed—a harsh, strident, demoniacal laugh. He was still laughing when the Saint shot him dead.

"The late lamented," murmured the Saint calmly.

After the shot the silence that followed was so unbroken that Simon could hear his own breathing. Stenning would never speak again, and Connell was out for a long time.

Slowly the Saint returned Stenning's automatic to his hip pocket. It was no use now. One glance at the massive lock on the barred gate, which went from the floor to the top of the tunnel arch, told him that any attempt to shoot away the fastening would be wasted. Besides, with the gas continuing to escape, even the flash of a pistol would be enough to blow them all up.

He felt quite unperturbed. A tight corner like that never bothered him in his life, though he knew how thin his chances were.

He had thought that the girl had fainted, but he saw that her eyes were open. Even so, he did not let go of her.

"Sorry about this, old dear," said the Saint quietly.

She nodded.

"I understand," she said.

"They took you when I was away, of course," he said. "Something seems to have gone wrong with this conventional situation. Remind me to write to *The Times* about it when we get out."

He told her of the cheques he had made Stenning sign, and took one of them out of his pocket to show her.

"It may be of some use to your heirs and legatees—if you've made a will," he said cheerfully.

She looked up at him, steady-eyed, and it was not only that he was holding her, but she was holding on to him. At that moment, it seemed the most natural thing to do.

"Is there no hope?" she asked; and the gaiety of the old, reckless, Saintly smile was as swift and natural as ever.

"There's always hope," said the Saint. "Somehow or other I'm the most unsuccessful corpse that ever lived. Listen. I'd planned out everything I was going to do today. I wrote a complete account of everything I knew about Vanney—or Stenning, as he really was—and what I proposed to do about him, and left it at a District Messenger office, addressed to Teal.

They were to send it straight round to him at one o'clock, unless I cancelled the order by telephone. The motor-boat is at Gravesend, as I ordered it, and by one o'clock, if anything unforeseen had gone wrong, I should have been miles away. What we've got to consider is whether we're likely to last long enough to give Teal time to get on the job. The gas will spread; it'll have to fill all the cellars. I don't know how big they are, but it will creep up all the same."

There was a long silence, and then the Saint said, "Since the situation is working out in such a cheerful way, I think we ought to make the best of it."

She saw the mocking mischief in his eyes, and even in that hopeless impasse she found his bantering enchantment irresistible.

"Perhaps you're right," she said.

"In these matters, I am invariably right," said the Saint, and he kissed her.

Presently she seemed to grow heavier in his arms. He was stronger himself, and his mind was still clear, but his eyes felt strangely heavy, and his chest was starting to ache with the labour of trying to extract some life-giving oxygen from that poisoned air. There was a rushing as of many waters in his ears, and it seemed as if a thousand trip-hammers were pounding on his brain.

He wondered if she was already gone, but then she spoke. It was no more than a whisper, but her voice seemed to come from a tremendous distance.

"Good-bye, Saint," she said.

The Saint laughed softly.

"Tell 'em to save a harp for me," he said, and kissed her again.

He was starting to feel very weak, and the room was swaying dizzily before his eyes. He leant against the wall, but he still held her with the last of his strength. It seemed to be getting dark, and he knew that he could not last much longer.

13

"There's a man to see you, sir," said Sergeant Barrow, entering the room. Teal looked at the card, and read the note that accompanied it.

"Send him up," he said.

He started a fresh piece of chewing gum, and waited as though asleep. He remained in that attitude when the visitor was shown in, for his party manners were not his strong point.

"Go right ahead," said Teal, without opening his eyes.

The man sat down.

"The circumstances are rather peculiar," he explained. "At about eleven o'clock this morning a rather bulky letter was deposited at one of our branches, addressed to you, with instructions that it was to be delivered at one o'clock unless the order was cancelled by telephone. It seemed a rather extraordinary proceeding to me at the time, especially as the address on the envelope told me that it was likely to be a message with some bearing on your professional activities. So after thinking it over, and taking the opinion of our head office by telephone, I decided that it was my duty to come round and see you at once."

"Have you the letter with you?" asked Teal.

"Naturally, I brought it along."

Teal stretched out his hand.

"Let's have a look at it," he suggested.

He had to open his eyes to read the address, and then he was suddenly galvanised into life. He sat up with a violence that made his chair, solid as it was, creak protestingly.

"The Saint!" he muttered. "I'd know that writing in a million."

"I hope I did right," ventured the stranger.

"You did one of the best things you're ever likely to do in your life," said Teal, and pressed a bell on his desk.

"Barrow," said Teal, as his subordinate entered, "take this gentleman away, fill him up with whatever he likes to drink, and thank him as profusely as you know how. I'm going to be busy!"

Left alone again, he sat down and ripped open the envelope. He read, and he read quickly, and in five minutes he was leaping down the stone stairs in the direction of that wing of Scotland Yard which constitutes Cannon Row Police Station.

"Every man you've got, armed and at the double!" rapped Teal.

And the sergeant in charge was so astonished at this display of energy and hustle on the part of his normally drowsy superior officer that the order was obeyed in what must have come close to record time.

At about half-past twelve, the keen observer might have noticed a number of burly men in plain clothes unostentatiously taking up positions round the block in which Vanney's stood. Teal circumnavigated the block himself, and made certain that every possible exit was watched. Then he went in alone.

A clerk met him in the waiting-room, but Teal had pushed past him before his business could be questioned. He went through the clerks' room, into Simon Templar's office, took in the emptiness of it at a glance, and went straight across to the door marked "Private." His hand was on the gun in his pocket as he walked in.

"Ah!" said Teal.

One cupboard was still open as the Saint had left it, and Teal could see through into the disorder of the room beyond. He went forward cautiously, and squeezed through the hole in the wall.

There was a man in the room, and Teal had him in an iron grip before the other could be quite sure what was happening.

"I'll take you for a start, Harry," said Teal. "Now tell me what you've done with the rest of the gang, and tell me quick!"

Long Harry straightened up.

"I've been in this place all day," he said. "I bust in. I don't mind telling you that now. I was looking for Connell, or something that would tell me where he was, but I couldn't find him. So I waited. I hid in the bathroom. Templar came in early in the morning, saw the mess, and looked round, but he never saw me. Then Connell arrived, but he wasn't alone, and I didn't dare start anything with witnesses. I heard them talking. Then, presently, after Templar had been in and spoken to them, Connell and the other man went out into the office and grabbed a girl who works in there. They had a blanket over her head, so I couldn't see who it was, but I was watching round the corner of the door and I saw Connell take her down."

"Down where?" snapped Teal.

"I'll tell you in a moment. Connell took her down, but the other man stayed here, and I didn't dare follow. Then Templar came in, and there was a fight. He knocked the other man out, and made him tell where Connell had taken the girl, and he went after her. Presently the other man followed. I waited, hoping Connell would come back alone. Then I heard something like a shot."

"Can't you get to the point?" snarled Teal. "Where did they go?"

"There," and Harry pointed.

Teal stared.

"I can't see anything."

"I'll show you," said Harry.

He went across and pressed a panel, as the Saint had done. Presently a larger piece of the panelling opened, and the lift was revealed.

Teal put his head inside, and stepped back quickly.

"Gas," he muttered. "For the love of mud, don't strike a match!"

He came back into the room and stood over Long Harry, who, taking the situation philosophically, had sat down comfortably in a chair to await removal to his home from home.

"Harry," said Teal, "would you like to improve your chances of getting off with a light sentence?"

"Tell me how, Mr Teal!" replied Harry with alacrity.

"Go down out of here any way you like—there are busies at every door. Send them up after me, and tell them I've gone down in that lift. There's been something funny going on with all that gas about, and if you only heard one shot it means someone's likely to be in trouble. Now jump!"

Long Harry jumped.

Teal went into the bathroom, soaked his handkerchief under the tap, and tied it over his nose and mouth. Then he went back and entered the lift.

The door closed automatically behind him, and he was fortunate enough to find the right switch at his first attempt. The lift started to go down. With every yard of the descent the smell of gas, even through his wet handkerchief, grew worse, and Teal knew that he would not be able to live for long in that atmosphere. But he was a man without fear.

Presently the lift stopped, and he stepped out. He saw a faint light coming from the branch tunnel, and hurried towards it. At the end was a lighted room, and in one corner he could see the Saint sagging against the wall with Pamela Marlowe in his arms. With the fumes already starting to make their presence felt, Teal hurried forward.

He tried the iron gate, but it was immovable.

"Saint!" he roared.

The Saint's eyes half-opened dazedly, but Teal knew that he could see nothing. "Saint," he bellowed again. "Where's the key?"

Simon's chest heaved, and Teal had to strain his ears to catch the reply. It came, with a fearful effort.

"Stenning's pocket—"

Teal went stumbling back down the corridor towards the inert figure that he had nearly tripped over on his first journey. He bent down, and fumbled with the man's pockets. The gas lay more heavily near the ground, and Teal wondered if he could hold out. But he found the bunch of keys, straightened up, and went staggering back down the tunnel. Somehow he found the lock. The gate opened. He was in time to catch the girl as the Saint fell.

By this time his heart was pounding furiously, and his head seemed to weigh a ton. Few men could have remained conscious and active for so long, but Chief Inspector Teal was a giant in strength.

He picked the girl up as if she were a feather, and fireman's-lifted her on to his shoulder. He bent down again, and got an arm round the Saint. Carrying the girl, and dragging the Saint behind him, he began the terrible journey back along the tunnel to the lift. It was like a nightmare. At every step he seemed to grow weaker, and it was only by a superhuman effort of grim determination that he was able to move at all. He never knew how he accomplished the journey with his double load, but after what seemed an eternity of ineffective struggling he found the lift in front of him.

It would only hold two at a time. He dragged the girl in, and pressed the switch. The lift crept upwards.

At the end of a thousand years the bare wall of the lift turned into panelling, and the panelling sprang open in front of him, and Teal fell out of the lift into the arms of two of his men.

"Get her to a doctor," he gasped, and somehow reached the bathroom. He felt sick and weak and giddy, but he soaked his handkerchief again, replaced it, and went back to the lift. They tried to stop him, and then he was savage.

"The Saint's down there," he said, "and I owe him something. Let me go!"

This time the journey was not so difficult, for his short relief in the purer air of the room above had revived him a little, but there was a limit even to his endurance. He remembered dragging the Saint into the lift; he remembered pressing the button that started them on their upward journey; he remembered the beginning of the ascent. Then everything went black.

When he opened his eyes again he was in bed. Looking to right and left, he saw a row of beds in which other men lay motionless. The room was almost in darkness, but in the dim twilight he saw nurses moving about, and a man in a white jacket was bending over the next cot. At the side of his own bed a nurse was sitting reading, but she looked up as soon as he moved.

"I gather that I'm not going to die," drawled Teal. But this time he spoke drowsily because he really felt drowsy.

The nurse smiled.

"You'll be back at work in a couple of days," she said cheerfully.

Teal sighed comfortably, and rolled over. As he did so, the doctor moved away from the next bed, and Teal saw who the patient was.

"How are you, Saint?" said Teal.

"I'm fine," said the Saint. "Sorry, old dear."

"Remind me to arrest you when you're better," said Teal, and went to sleep.

14

Four days later, Mr Teal, a trifle pale, but otherwise his old self, rang the bell of No. 7, Upper Berkeley Mews, and the Saint answered the door himself.

"Why, it's old Claud Eustace," said the Saint. "Come right in!"

Teal came in.

"Say when," murmured Simon.

Teal said when.

"Cheerio!" said the Saint.

"Cheerio!" said Teal.

"By the way," said the Saint, "I believe you saved my life, and all that sort of thing. God bless you, damn your eyes!"

For the first time in his life, Mr Teal looked embarrassed, but he shook the hand which the Saint offered.

"And before I arrest you," said Teal presently, "why haven't you tried to jump for it on that boat you've got lying at Gravesend?"

"It didn't happen to be necessary," said the Saint. "I have a little story signed by the late James Arthur himself to show you. Take a look at it, and get ready to laugh."

Teal sat down and unwrapped a fresh packet of his favourite sweetmeat.

"This is our one consolation for having lost America," he remarked. "Let's see this confession."

The Saint passed over the paper. Teal read it through, and glowered.

"When did you write this?" he inquired.

"I didn't write it. Our one and only James Arthur wrote it. It'll stand any test. Sorry, I'm sure."

"You haven't by any chance got his signed permission to shoot him, have you?" asked the detective sardonically.

"Self-defence, old dear. Self-defence. Want to have it argued out in court?"

Teal sighed.

"And how's Connell?" asked the Saint.

"Enjoying a tropical climate, I should say," replied Teal dispassionately. "They got him up later, when the firemen had arrived with gas masks, but he was one of the deadest men I've ever seen."

The Saint lighted a cigarette.

"He was Vanney, of course," he said. "And at the same time he wasn't. It would have been too risky to let Stenning interview people that he had probably done business with before, although he had grown a moustache and made one or two little alterations to his face. But dressed up in livery, as George—a mere porter—nobody ever noticed him. There was a door opening right out of the private office to the passage, only a yard from his cubicle. When I went through to speak to Vanney, I went farther through, and spoke to George. When Vanney had to interview people I got my instructions from Stenning, and conducted most of the interview myself. Connell simply said 'Yes' and 'No' as I tipped him the wink."

Teal nodded.

"I guessed all that," he said.

"I don't suppose you'd have spotted us so soon if we had been able to keep Connell in order. He looked great in a false beard, but he started getting uppish. He had to have money, and wanted more and more. We tried to keep him indoors in case he got tight and spilled the beans, but he got away the other night."

"I found him,' said Teal. "He told me a lot that I wanted to know. It was clever the way he and Stenning arranged for that chauffeur to drive him and the body of Red Mulligan, recently deceased, into the country at night, upset the car, and have Wylie to swear that it was Stenning who had been killed. In fact, it was all very clever, but it wasn't good enough."

"It was good enough for me," said the Saint cheerfully.

"And what have you got out of it?"

"An untarnished reputation, and a glorious escape from the name of Tombs. You can have no idea how tired I was getting of that name."

There was a silence, during which Teal ruminated in a certain atmosphere of gloom.

He rose ponderously to his feet at last.

"Well," he said, "you seem to have done it again."

"I'm always doing it," said the Saint modestly.

They walked together to the door, but on the threshold Teal stopped and gave birth to the expression of his greatest worry.

"Saint," he said, "when you were locked up down in that cellar with Miss Marlowe"

"Yes?"

"Wasn't it—er—um—Well, you know, I've only seen that sort of thing on the movies, but when I arrived you were—er—"

"Teal," said the Saint, "you're a naughty old man. Go home and read the *News of the World*."

And he closed the door gently, and left the detective blinking at a polished brass knocker of very doubtful respectability.

THE IMPOSSIBLE

CRIME

1

The man in the big loose-cut overcoat walked quickly through the dark mean streets that led to Gaydon's Wharf. Although the night was not very cold, the wide collar of his coat was pulled up high about his ears, and his soft hat was crushed down over his eyes. He kept his hands in his pockets, and one of those hands gripped a squat bulk of unlawful metal. But that was from sheer force of habit—as were the swift keen glances with which he probed every shadowy doorway and every patch of shadow. The ingrained instinct which dictated these circumstances of his passage was far too deep-rooted for him to change, although he knew that here in London, for a short time anyway, he was safe.

He paused for a moment at the corner of an intersecting street, and shot a long watchful gaze down the new road over which he proposed to travel, then he went on with the same rapid stride.

A little way down, he stopped to look at the number of a house, then he pressed gently on the door. It swung back at his touch, and he went in, closing it behind him. The gloomy uncarpeted stairs, miserably lighted by a flickering gas jet at each landing, faced him. He went on up them, and stopped again outside a door on the third floor.

He tapped on it softly, giving a signal, and presently the sound of a well-oiled bolt slipping back answered him. Then the latch clicked. He was looking at a little card that was pinned to the door just above the lock; it receded from him as the door opened, and he stepped quickly forward following it with suddenly savage eyes, and abruptly found the view blocked by the body of a man and an automatic pistol in the man's hand that dug into his chest. He straightened up.

"Quit that, you damned fool!" he snarled.

The man who had opened the door backed away, pocketing his gun. He was a tallish man with a pinched face and closely set dark eyes under thick tangled eyebrows, and his sallow complexion was even paler than the shade at which the visitor remembered it.

"Oh," he said weakly. "It's you, Farnberg."

"Who did you think it was?" demanded Farnberg roughly.

He pushed his way into the office, and the other retreated before him awkwardly. "I don't know, Farnberg. I was scared."

Farnberg unbuttoned his coat and glared at him.

"You don't say!" he sneered. "And what were you scared of, Friste?"

"I—I don't quite know. Sit down, Farnberg—have a cigar. If we're going to talk business—"

"This is business! What were you scared of?"

"I—well, I've been threatened a couple of times, but—"

"But?"

"I didn't think much of it—"

"And so you just jump around sticking irons in my chest—just to help stop you thinking. And what next? Haven't you always told me no one could ever get a line on you?"

Friste shuffled back to the desk.

"I thought it was true," he said nervously. "No one ever has had a line on me. But something's happened—I've had two letters . . . I'm glad you're here, Farnberg."

"Who were these letters from?"

"You wouldn't have heard of the man—"

Farnberg turned and jerked open the door. He pointed to the card that he had been inspecting before he entered.

"Is that him?" he snapped, and Friste went dead white.

Farnberg put out his hand and twitched the card away. It was the size of an ordinary postcard. On it had been sketched an absurd little spidery figure surmounted by a symbolical halo, and underneath was one short line of writing.

With the Compliments of the Season.

"Is that the man?" snapped Farnberg again, and Friste nodded dumbly.

Farnberg shredded up the slip of pasteboard and hurled the scraps across the room.

"That—"

"Did you—did you know about him?"

"Know about him?" Farnberg slammed the door and dropped into a chair. "I'd like to know anyone who knows more about him than I do. I know that he's the slimiest double-crosser that was never taken for a ride. He's the guy that helped the bulls to put me away last time. He—"

Farnberg continued the history at some length.

Then he returned to cross-examination.

"He's got on to you, has he? What were those letters he sent you?"

"Just cards—the same as that other one."

"Didn't you tell the police?"

"The police?" Friste cackled hoarsely. "That's one thing you don't know about the Saint. The police may have been aching to get him for themselves once, but they've never forgotten what was behind his record. I should think there are plenty of juries that would hang you just for getting one of his cards. They'd know there was some good reason for the Saint having noticed you."

Farnberg reached out one powerful hand and took a cigar from the box on the desk. He bit off the end and spat.

"The Saint will have to be bumped," he said, and he said it with a gentleness that was surprising after his introductory outburst. "I've been wanting him for a whole year—it didn't need this to happen for me to make up my mind about that. It was one of the things I came over here to do anyway."

"How long will you be over for?"

"Till I've fixed the Saint and loaded the cargo I came for—however long that takes. It can't be a long time, because I've had the wire that Duncarry's on his way over looking for me. What else has been happening?"

Friste shrugged. His first scare was sliding back from his mind, and he was comparatively calm again. Farnberg's virile, confident presence had something to do with that.

"Everything else has been all right," he said. "The Saint's the only one who knows anything. The Cabaret Ship sailed again last week—the usual passenger list. I've got another boat berthing tonight with about thirty pounds of heroin on board—it'll come through the Customs in the usual way." He glanced at his watch. "I'm waiting for it now—they'll be bringing the case in at any minute."

"Distribution O.K.?"

"There's never been any difficulty about that. I do it all myself—the orders come through by post, and the parcels go out by return."

"And what about my cargo?"

"That's ready for you in the warehouse by Deepsands Wharf—all except the champagne. That'll be through at the beginning of next week. The rest is all in, exactly as you ordered it— there's plenty for you to start lading. What ship are you using, by the way?"

Farnberg grinned.

"Got my own—a dandy floating palace provided by Ardossi. He came over with me. We're both running in with Kellory now. Didn't you ever think to ask how I got over? I could never have made any of the regular boats. We came over on that yacht, like a coupla princes. I got off at Southampton, and Ardossi's seeing her through to Deepsands. She ought to be in by tomorrow evening, so if you have your men ready to start work—"

He was interrupted by a ring on the bell over Friste's chair, and Friste smiled.

"That's the heroin. If you'll excuse me—I suppose you closed the door after you when you came in?"

"Yeh! And if you'd closed it before I came in, and let me ring, you'd have saved yourself a fright. What's the idea, anyway, being so damned hospitable? You just trying to make it easy for the Saint to wring your neck?"

"I didn't want to keep you waiting—" Farnberg pulled up out of his chair.

"I guess I won't wait now," he said. "I'll go down with you and see this case in—just to avoid accidents."

He led the way down the stairs, his hands back in his pockets, and stood aside while Friste turned the spring lock. Outside, the dim shape of a Ford delivery van blocked the streetscape, and just beyond the doorway two men in overalls leaned on a coffin-shaped packing-case.

As the door opened, they picked up the case between them and entered without a word. They toiled up the stairs with it, and Friste and Farnberg followed.

"Does it take two Englishmen now to carry thirty pounds up three stories?" asked Farnberg sardonically, when the men paused on the second landing for a rest.

Friste shook his head.

"That case is full of canned peaches—most of it," he said.

The case was dumped into the office, and Farnberg stayed there with it while Friste supervised the departure of the porters.

He was back in a few minutes.

"Those are the only two men resident in this country who know anything about my business," he said. "They've been with me for five years, and I'd trust them with anything."

The successful negotiation of another item of business-as-usual had completed the revival of his spirits. He rubbed his hands together in blatant self-satisfaction, but Farnberg's eyes did not light up in response. They merely glanced over the packing-case with professional indifference.

"That canned-fruit trick is an old one, but it's good enough if it gets by," he said. He turned away and relighted his cigar.

"Now—what's the bill?" he asked. "I'll square it and get out—I feel like some beauty sleep tonight."

Friste sat down at the desk, unlocked a drawer, and drew out a bulky ledger. He extracted some loose sheets and handed them over.

"There are the accounts. You can check them up yourself."

Farnberg skimmed briefly through the papers.

Then he nodded.

"Looks O.K.," he said. "One thousand nine hundred and thirty pounds—that's about nine thousand bucks."

"About nine thousand, two hundred and sixty-four dollars," said Friste carefully; and Farnberg, with a bulging wallet in his hands, stopped counting to stare at him.

"Are you sure you haven't forgotten the odd thirteen cents?" he inquired.

Friste spread out his hands in a noncommittal gesture.

And then a surprising thing happened.

To Jack Farnberg, it seemed as if a third hand—a lean, brown, ruthlessly capable and yet curiously sensitive hand—materialised out of thin air and made contact with the wad of bills from which he was making his selection. And then, before even his lightning-like brain could adjust itself to that amazing interruption, a total quantity of twenty-two thousand, four hundred and twenty-five dollars vanished completely from his ken.

Jack Farnberg was a practical man. He was only hypnotised for an instant; and, then, with a searing oath, he spun round, his right hand flying accurately towards the butt of his gun.

"Oh, please!" said the Saint—almost apologetically.

2

He stood there, a bare two yards away, the perfect picture of insured innocence. His left hand, upraised in peaceable protest, was worth exactly twenty-two thousand, four hundred and twenty-five dollars cash. His right hand was travelling unhurriedly towards his pocket.

"Stop that!"

Farnberg's voice broke the momentary stillness with a bark of command that would have made a sergeant-major jump three feet into the air. The Saint had never been a sergeant-major. He raised one eyebrow three millimetres.

"Why?" he asked mildly.

"Unless you want me to fill you up with lead right now—"

"Oh, but you can't do that! Ask Reginald." The Saint nodded languidly in the direction of Friste. "This, brother, is not Chicago. People are hanged for murder in this country. It's most distressing. Isn't it, Reginald?"

Friste gulped.

"I—I should wait a minute, Farnberg. You don't know what he's got up his sleeve—"

This was quite true. The Saint had a knife up his sleeve, and Farnberg did not know it. He turned on Friste with his lips twisting up contemptuously.

"You moron—"

"That's right," murmured the Saint affably. "Moron and Mack. Shall we do our stuff? But who wants a worm, anyhow?"

Farnberg's gun levelled accurately at the pit of the Saint's stomach.

"How did you get here?" he rasped, and the Saint actually simpered.

"Don't you think I'm a peach?" he said.

The eyes of the other two ranged behind him, to the packing-case that stood against the wall. The lid was open, and it was beautifully empty.

"Of course, I'm not canned," said the Saint, in his earnestly conversational way. "That's very important. And I'm full of heroism, but absolutely void of heroin. Perhaps she arrives in the next chapter. You haven't by any chance got a sister, have you, Jack?"

Farnberg showed his teeth.

"I have not got a sister," he said, and the Saint shook his head sympathetically.

"I was afraid you hadn't," he remarked. "Naturally, your parents could never have done it again. And now, may I smoke?"

Farnberg tossed over a cigar from the table.

"Make the most of it," he said, with venomous geniality. "I've been waiting a whole year to see you smoke it—your last cigar!"

Simon Templar sighed.

"This is not quite the reunion I was expecting," he said, "but I suppose it will have to do." He lighted the cigar, and drew upon it approvingly, "You have a nice taste in these matters, Reginald. How can I reward you? Perhaps by setting your mind at rest. Shall I assure you that the two varlets who carried me up are still to be trusted? I was peachifying long before they took charge. In fact, I had a very jolly voyage, though the hold was a trifle stuffy. I dropped the peaches and other things over the side before we were out of sight of Rotterdam, and all the rest of the trip was free for philosophy and meditation. I grant you they dropped me with a bit of a bump at this end, but that was my fault. I should have marked myself 'FRAGILE.'"

He propped his elbow on the tail of a bronze Chinese dragon that ornamented the top of a filing cabinet beside him, and surveyed it with some repugnance. The dragon was inextricably entangled with the more distant portions of its own anatomy, and clawed limbs protruded from diverse parts of its person with a charmingly simple lack of system, but its head rose clear and solitary above the mess. That head was the most hideously evil thing the Saint had ever seen—a creation without rhyme or reason, without relation to anything human or animal, a fantastic nightmare in metal, and yet it possessed an uncannily living malevolence.

Simon Templar glanced again at Friste, and indicated the graven horror with a wave of his hand.

"George is not unlike you," he remarked pleasantly.

"Now, see here!" Farnberg's jaw went out, and his forefinger tightened dangerously on the trigger. "What game are you playing?"

"Mah Jong," said the Saint.

"If you think you're—"

"Oh, but I know I am," said the Saint lazily.

And then he straightened up.

"I came here this evening," he said quietly, "to give myself the inestimable pleasure of wringing Reginald's neck. Having a useful pair of hands, and a cake of carbolic soap waiting for me at home, I didn't trouble to bring a gun. I admit, Jack, that I wasn't expecting to meet you—you slightly disorganised my very complicated espionage system by coming overland from Southampton. But the difference you make is really immaterial. I shall simply postpone the bouncing of Reginald to a more convenient opportunity. And meanwhile, I shall be able to amuse myself with the charitable distribution of some of these here berries—I think I'm quite a deserving case myself," he added reflectively. "No—don't interrupt me for a moment."

He had dropped his mask of flippant banter as easily as he had put it on, and something in the quiet gentleness of his voice held the other two silent.

For the Saint had stated the circumstances exactly, and it is quite worth recording that everything he had said was perfectly true. He had not been expecting Jack Farnberg. The Saint was blessed with the priceless gift of always knowing exactly how far he could go; and he had also, at one stage of his career, acquired a certain insight into the mentality of the American gunman in general, and of Jack Farnberg in particular. Furthermore, he had taken his Honours Degree in Bluff and Allied Sciences at the age of nine.

And all these facts, taken together, directed him at that moment towards precisely one and only one course of action. The Saint might look the picture of insured innocence, but he was not insured, and the money would have been no use to his widow anyway because he would leave no widow.

Jack Farnberg was showing a lot of gun, and Friste had also begun to do his share since the backchat began. The Saint retired a slight but tactful distance—almost imperceptibly.

"In a few days, Jack, when you've got the lie of the land a bit better," he said, "we may be able to resume the argument. But for the present you'll just have to take my word for it, supported by Reginald's—that it would be highly dangerous for you to bump me off here and now. I've always been a cautious sort of bird. When I go out on a jaunt of this kind, I always let a friend of mine know where I've gone. And if I didn't come back, she would be reluctantly compelled to tell the police." It occurred, sadly, to the Saint, that he was straying a little from the path of strict veracity on which he had entered the scene, but he felt tremendously tactful at that particular moment. "And so, Jack, I'm afraid I can't die today. Besides, it would spoil the story anyhow. It isn't till Chapter Fourteen at the very earliest that I'm tied up in a chair with bombs lashed to my suspenders and the slow fuse bubbling across the floor. So, all things considered—"

Farnberg took a pace forward.

"Is that what you think? Well, let me tell you—"

"Farnberg!" Friste's bleat cut in shakily. "Wait a minute—if anyone knows where he is—"

The gunman's lips curled.

"Aw, hell! I'll soon find a way of fixing that—"

"I doubt it," said the Saint.

And then he took the chance that he had been manoeuvring for.

As he backed away, with Farnberg following him, it had so happened that Farnberg completely covered him from Friste's potential line of fire. And Farnberg's attention was momentarily distracted.

The Saint's left hand knocked the threatening gun aside. His right hand whipped up into the gunman's unprotected jaw, and Farnberg's head clicked back as if his neck had snapped at the base.

Simon stayed to do no further damage. His left hand had made one jerk at the gun, but Farnberg had held it fast. And the Saint knew that his punch had gone just one inch out of place. If it had been dead accurate, no man living could have retained any further interest for the subsequent proceedings; but even a Simon Templar, seizing one slim split second's instantaneous flicker of a chance, with an automatic pistol in the hand of a practised operator fourteen inches from his solar plexus, cannot expect to make every single stroke with infallible precision. Wherefore the Saint did not pause.

He opened the door and ducked through it, and Friste's shot splintered the glass upper panel as he did so.

The Saint took the first flight of stairs in one flying leap, rebounded from the wall of the lower landing like an India-rubber ball, and went down the second flight by way of the banisters. Above him he heard the roar of Farnberg's bull voice, and the more treble yap of Friste. Their feet clattered on the stairs, and the Saint, slipping with elegant rapidity down a second stretch of banister, heard another shot plonk into the rail just behind him, and changed his style of descent abruptly.

He kept his lead to the ground floor; and then, instead of making for the front door, he spun round in his tracks as his feet felt the last step, and doubled towards the back of the building.

Here was darkness, till a ray shot out from his little pocket flashlight to pierce it. He opened a door, passed through, and closed it behind him; his torch and fingers together searched swiftly for a key in the lock, or bolts anywhere, but there were none.

"Now that," said the Saint, "is a nuisance."

He had decided against the front door without a second's hesitation, for he had no overpowering ambition to sprint down two hundred yards of straight street with one very expert shot and one unknown quantity popping bullets after him. And he knew to one-millionth part of a hair's-breadth how flimsy was the bluff that he had put up to discourage that possibility. It hadn't really been a serious attempt at all—it had been nothing but a minor flourish with the object of gaining time and creating a slight dissension among the battalions of the wicked. Which purpose it had served—and that was all.

He flashed a glance round the barely furnished room. There was a table, a couple of chairs, and precious little else. The Saint heaved those three items of furniture against the door, and made for the window.

This did not appear to have been opened since the day when it was first installed—both upper and lower sashes resisted his efforts. And at that moment Farnberg crashed against the slenderly barricaded door.

A small cupboard stood under the window. The Saint snatched it up in his two hands and hurled it bodily through the glass. It left a wide jagged hole which he had no time to negotiate carefully. He stepped back four paces, took a short run, and launched himself through it horizontally, in a high flat dive.

As he went through, he heard the items of furniture collapse before Farnberg's terrific onslaught.

Then the waters of the river engulfed him with a mighty splash.

He came up for a breath and dived again, this time like a porpoise. He swam a dozen yards under water, and let himself rise again gently. Even so, a shot plopped into the water a moment after his head broke the surface. He dived again, changing his direction, and heard the muffled sounds of further shooting as he went down, but there was no more of it when he came up again.

He paddled silently along in the deep shadows under the walls of the buildings that came right down to the water's edge. Presently a little jetty loomed up ahead of him. He turned alongside it, and a few seconds later he was pulling himself over the stern of the light electric launch that he had parked there the previous evening to await his need.

As he started it up, he heard the engine of a River Police launch chattering officiously over the dark stream, and a spotlight wobbled along the line of warehouses and picked up the face of Reginald Friste framed in the broken window. Simon heard the shouted question, and the word "burglar," among others, in reply; and he was smiling serenely as he let in the clutch and was borne swiftly and soundlessly up the stream.

3

Patricia Holm carried the bowl of bronze chrysanthemums from the sideboard to the window seat to give the blossoms a sunbath. The Saint, who was also taking a sunbath, turned his head.

"It dawns upon me," he said, "that we are stagnating rapidly. For a whole fortnight I have done nothing either desperately wicked or stickily virtuous. Also, I have run out of cigarettes. And the thought of having to walk two hundred yards to the nearest tobacconist's makes me want to burst into tears."

Patricia handed him a case of dainty white cylinders tipped with rose leaves. The Saint took one, lighted it, and shuddered faintly; and his lady regarded him with indignation.

"What's the matter with them?" she demanded.

"Probably, like barley water and spats, they're an acquired taste," said the Saint. "They have one good point—a seductive element of doubt. Is the flavour vanilla, or just mulligatawny with a dash of scented hair-oil?"

Patricia detached the abomination from his fingers and sat on the arm of his chair.

"What are you going to do, lad?"

"Blowed if I know," said the Saint gloomily. "Of course, I could always murder a bishop. I could bring you his scalp, and you could use it to trim your new coat—the one that looks as if we'd found a way of using up last year's eiderdowns. But I have a dreadful feeling that bishops are mostly bald. Can you think of a bishop with a really luxuriant growth?"

"Ass," said Patricia, and she kissed him.

The Saint gazed through the brightly curtained windows at the charmingly sunlit scenery of Upper Berkeley Mews. From the middle distance came the swishing and whoofling sounds of the morning wash and brush-up parade. Invisible taxis honked and spluttered in the adjacent streets, but in the quiet backwater of Upper Berkeley Mews brooded an atmosphere of autumn calm.

And then into the peace and quiet burst the rattle of an intruding taxi. It stopped just beyond the open windows; and the Saint, leaning forward, saw the man who alighted from it, and groaned.

"Gawd!" said the Saint sepulchrally. "Our one and only Teal is paying us a visit. Open the door to him, sweetheart, and brain him with the hat-rack if you get a chance. Maybe he's got some decent cigarettes on him."

Patricia departed; and the Saint put his feet on the window-sill and closed his eyes. He was in that position when Chief Inspector Teal came in.

"Good morning," said Teal, and the Saint opened one eye and focused his visitor.

"It was," he agreed wearily, and closed the eye again. "Have you got a cigarette?"

Teal drew up a chair and sat down.

"I haven't," he said.

"That makes you, if possible, even more unwelcome," said the Saint. "You'll probably be murdered before you leave—we were just looking round for someone to kill. Pat, where are your manners? Pass Claud Eustace the garbage tubes."

Patricia obeyed, and Teal took one look at the offering and declined gracefully.

"Beer, then?" said the Saint.

"If you'll excuse me," said Teal, "fat men didn't ought to drink."

"Teal," said the Saint wearily, "if you were a blanket, you'd be the wettest thing that ever happened. But if you'll allow me—"

He proceeded to the barrel in the corner, filled a tankard, and returned to his chair.

"Now what's the worry?"

"What are you doing these days, Saint?"

"To the most casual observer," said the Saint, "it should be obvious that I'm winding up the parish clock."

"Oh, stop it."

"Sorry," said the Saint, "I can't. I'm employed to wind it up."

"Been getting into any trouble lately, Saint?"

Simon appeared to consider the point carefully.

"Not that I can remember," he said at length. "Of course, I may have bumped somebody off in my sleep. Or do you mean something else? There was a little blonde I met at the Berkeley the other night—"

Teal unwrapped a wafer of Mr Wrigley's unrivalled jaw exerciser, and engulfed it ponderously.

"I was thinking maybe you'd have something helpful to say about that Gaydon's Wharf case," he said.

"Don't," said the Saint pathetically. "I'm not well enough. I don't want any of those Sherlock Holmes stunts, my dear Watson. They're as dead as the dodo. You found a cigarette coupon rolled up and concealed in the murdered man's left ear. If he had collected five hundred of them he would have obtained a pair of fish knives and a sardine opener. From this we deduce that the murdered man was fond of fish. Therefore the man whose bitter hatred he had aroused was the local butcher. Arrest the butcher, and the thing's done. Next case, please."

Teal looked at him.

"Suppose you come along and talk down at my office," he suggested, and the Saint sighed.

"Is this another arrest?" he inquired.

"Not yet," said Teal ominously.

The Saint drank deeply.

"Then we'll hear your trouble now," he said. "I'll come for a walk with you later, if it sounds interesting enough."

Teal nodded slowly, and masticated in silence for some moments. Then again he turned his round, red face towards the Saint.

"Have you been lying low because you knew Duncarry was over here?"

"Nope. That hatchet-faced New York sleuth and I have entombed the tomahawk."

"I wondered," said Teal. "Somehow, we got discussing you."

"And what did you hear?"

"Nothing against you," said Teal, almost regretfully. "He doesn't seem to bear any malice. He asked me to get hold of you and give you a message."

"I'll hear it."

"Duncarry said, 'Break the glad news to that reformed and Saintly guy. Give him a big earful of the joyous tidings that Jack Farnberg has busted his corral and is rampaging around somewhere on this side with his war paint on and feathers in his hair.' But what he meant was—"

"I know the language," murmured the Saint mildly. "Did you think you were the only man in London who went to the movies? But what's that got to do with anything?"

"I just thought you might be interested," said Teal. "Also, that's another matter you might be able to help me over. We're looking for Farnberg—we don't want him over here. And as soon as he's found he's going to be put on the first boat and shipped back to his home town. Duncarry had an idea that you'd be the first person Farnberg would want to see on this side."

"But not to give me his love and kisses," drawled the Saint. "Sure—I understand. And if Jack comes beetling in here, all hung around with howitzers, you want me to collect him and pass him along to the Export Department."

"I'd be obliged if you would," Teal admitted. "But that's nothing to do with the Gaydon's Wharf business. Now, look here, Templar—"

"Shoot."

"I don't mind telling you that's stumped me. It's stumped every single man at the Yard. A man shot dead in a room that no one could possibly have got into, and no trace of a weapon. We aren't miracle men, and it just occurred to me—"

"That I might have one of my brilliant inspirations?"

"That's about the strength of it." Teal regarded the Saint seriously. "If you're at a loose end—"

The Saint stroked his chin, and slowly a light dawned in his eyes.

"It's an idea," he murmured.

Then he stood up.

"Teal, it's the hell of an idea! I shouldn't think you'll have another idea like that in the next thirty years—with a brain like yours."

"You'll see what you can do?"

"I will. For the first time in his life the Saint shall hunt on the side of law and order. The coruscations of his astounding intellect shall dazzle the nitwits of Scotland Yard. You have only to lead me to the body."

He swung round with his quick laugh. The idea had fired his volatile brain as the Saint's ideas always did, with a dazzling, dancing suddenness.

"Sorry, Pat, old dear, but you'll have to wait for your bishop. Duty calls, and these lighter pastimes must wait for their turn.

But if a rural dean will satisfy you until Friday—eyes right for a moment, Claud."

Patricia put up her mouth, and the Saint dealt with it suitably.

"The sailor's farewell to his horse. And so we pass on to the perils of our calling. O.K., Claud Eustace."

He swung himself out of the window.

"Your hat," said Patricia.

The Saint caught his head furniture.

"Thanks," he said, smiling up at her. "Don't expect me back to lunch—I have to tell Teal the stirring story of the cardinal and the pig of the aunt of the gardener."

"I haven't heard that one," said Patricia.

"Neither have I," said the Saint. "But I shall invent it as we go along. I've just woken up after a fortnight's sleep, and my brain is buzzing. So long, old darling!"

He disappeared with a gay wave of his hand; and as Teal emerged more sedately through the door, the long, lean Hirondel purred up with the Saint at the wheel.

"I seem," said the Saint, as he spun the great car into Piccadilly in his cheerfully murderous way, "I seem, Claud, to have heard that there's a fair lady floating somewhere in the background of this spot of bother."

"You've seen the newspapers?" The Saint nodded.

"Eileen Wiltham," he said. "I presume you've inspected her?"

"I have."

"Pimples?"

"No."

"Squint?"

"No."

"Bow legs?"

"No."

"Shall I be allowed to meet her in the course of my profound investigations?" "No."

"Teal, as a prophet you're bum," said the Saint happily, and concentrated on manoeuvring the car through a gap between two omnibuses that would conveniently have accommodated an emaciated visiting card.

4

When they arrived at Scotland Yard, Teal was greeted with a message to say that the Assistant Commissioner desired converse with him, and the Saint strolled on alone to the office in which the detective was accustomed to think his great thoughts, earn a certain amount of his salary, and qualify for the pension which the patient British tax-payer would one day have to provide.

The Saint, with his hands in his pockets, kicked open the door, and then stopped on the threshold; and the lean figure of Detective Duncarry of New York City shot out of an easy chair with outstretched hand.

"Hullo, Saint!"

They gripped. Once upon a time, in some gay days on the other side of the Atlantic, when the Saint had been on the run and Detective Duncarry had been doing the chasing, they had fallen down an elevator shaft together; but the smile with which the American greeted the man to whom he owed his limp that would go with him to the end of his life was innocent of all animosity.

"It's good to see you again, Saint."

"And damned good to see you," murmured Simon. "Hell—this was worth waiting for! I always had an idea I'd like to take a look at you without any artillery blocking the view."

"Have a stogie?"

Simon shook his head. He lighted a cigarette and seated himself on the desk, and for a few moments there was a reminiscent silence.

"Did you get my message?" asked the New Yorker presently.

"I did. And has any more stuff like Jack Farnberg leaked out of your tanks?"

"One or two have faded out," said Duncarry, nodding curtly. "We've been having a bit of a clean-up lately. There was some rough stuff down in Canal one night last month, and four of Farnberg's bunch got between the fresh air and some lead that was floating around. But Farnberg was the guy we wanted, and he was the guy we didn't get. From what trickles through he wants you like a butcher wants sheep— in the form of mutton."

The Saint grinned.

"He's not the only one," he murmured. "But he's got more reason for it than some of the others. Those were the days!"

"Is Teal coming along?"

"Some time. He's having a heart-to-heart chat with the Ass. Comm. at the moment. Let's forget him. He's all balled up with a murder case these days—spends all his waking hours on his hands and knees with a magnifying glass and a bottle of glue, looking for clues."

"He said he was going to talk to you about that."

"He has," said the Saint. "You'd better watch your step, Dun—you see in me an incipient sleuth, full of righteousness and chemical beer. Which reminds me—have you started thinking about lunch?"

"I had started," admitted Duncarry.

"Then let's go and see if we can get some poured out," said the Saint. And Duncarry intimated that the idea was O.K. with him.

Simon scribbled a message and spiked it to the desk with Teal's favourite pen. They walked round to the Victoria, and it was there that Duncarry harked back to a matter of curiosity.

"How did you come to get in trouble with Farnberg, Saint?"

"It just happened—that night in Brooklyn. He bothered me, and I had to tread on him. The trouble was that he was just going down for the third time when the raid started. Farnberg stopped a nasty one right at the beginning, and I was slightly plugged myself. I did a two-mile swim that night with a couple of bullets in me for ballast." He smiled. "There always seems to be some water around to spoil my clothes whenever I meet Jack," he said cryptically.

"Have you heard Jack's end of the story?"

"Not yet."

"His yarn is that it was a frame-up—that you just waded into him and got him mixed and held him till the cops came in. That was the story he told the court, and he went over the Bridge of Sighs still saying it."

"And then?"

"Ardossi worked his get-away. Where they went to nobody knows for certain, but we know they got over to Europe somehow, and I've more than a good idea that they're right here in London. That's the reason why I'm over on this side of the big pond."

"That's just your idea?"

"That's all I know so far—I've only been over a few days."

The Saint was lounging with his back to the bar, and for a moment Duncarry failed to notice his sudden immobility. And then the Saint spoke again—quietly and gently.

"Then from information received," he drawled, "I can tell you that that's more than your own private hunch—it's just plain fact."

He shifted off the bar, straightening up with his most Saintly smile.

"Come right on in, Vittorio," he said clearly, and Duncarry spun round. "What the hell—"

The Saint laughed.

"Too late, old dear," he murmured. "You missed the vision."

He strolled forward and picked up a glossy silk hat, and returned with it to the bar.

"He bolted as soon as I spoke—just let go his lid and skidded for the tall timber. But if it wasn't Vittorio Ardossi himself, I'm at this moment selling fish and chips in the Commercial Road. You were dead right, son—there are some bright days coming."

He gazed thoughtfully at the swing doors through which the flying Italian had made his exit; and then, radiant again, he waved a hand to Teal, who at that moment opened them. Something in Duncarry's lean face indicated trouble, and Teal blinked at the two men speculatively.

"What's been happening?"

"Nothing much—I've just been collecting Duncarry part of his outfit for next year's Ascot."

The Saint waved the silk hat.

He up-ended the head-piece on the bar, and pencilled in the lining an artistic sketch of a little man with a circle for a head and straight lines to designate body and limbs. Above the circle he perpetrated something that might equally well have suggested a halo or a starved and suicidally-minded sausage making a ferocious attack on its own tail; and Teal looked over his shoulder and watched the performance curiously.

"What's the idea?"

"*Pour encourager les autres.*" The Saint extended the hat towards the barman. "Some absent-minded bird in a hurry hung this up on the carpet," he said blandly. "If he calls in to inquire about it, which is unlikely, return it to him with my compliments."

"If you have a quiet time, it isn't your fault," said Duncarry appreciatively, and the Saint grinned.

"We may yet see life," he said.

They moved on to the grill room together, and it was there, over the coffee which closed the meal, that Simon checked up what he knew of the Gaydon's Wharf murder.

"I gather," he said, "that Reginald Friste was not very nice to know. Barringer, through some oversight on the part of a deluded parent, had to tolerate him as a guardian up to the age of twenty-one, and thereafter as an infernal nuisance. Barringer, a clever lad, is an analytical chemist attached to Wiltham's Brewery for the purpose of devising fresh horrors to be inflicted on the public in the sacred name of beer; Friste ran a shipping agency, and probably a number of less reputable organisations as well."

"All right so far," assented Teal.

"Enter," said the Saint, "the beautiful heroine, daughter of Sir Enoch Wiltham. Barringer falls. Friste also meets her, and likewise drops with a sickening thud. Friste is wealthy, and Barringer is not, but heroine nobly refuses to be influenced by bank balance. Icy optic for Friste, glad and merry one for Barringer. Joy and black jealousy. Register some black jealousy, Teal."

"I'd like to register you a black eye," sighed the long-suffering detective.

"The melodrama," continued the Saint, unmoved, "follows rapidly. Friste visits heroine, proposes for the umpteenth time, and is turned down. Friste utters some unseemly language, makes threats of hideous vengeance, and exit. Red fire at back of stage, and muffled drums and popping of beer corks off."

Teal slewed his wad of chewing gum to the westward and nodded again. "Then?"

"Barringer hears of scene, visits Friste, and threatens to beat him up if he comes within ten miles of the girl again. Barringer has incidentally discovered a new method of producing commercial alcohol at one-third the cost of the cheapest present process. Roseate gleams of dollars on the horizon. Hopes of wedding bells and cottage with roses round the door and garage for two-seater. Is that right?"

"It's good enough."

"Then the dreadful scene. Sub-title: *Came the Dawn* . . . Friste's staff, after waiting two hours for their boss, endeavour to enter his private office to obtain urgently needed papers. It is discovered to be locked—an unprecedented occurrence. Telephone call to Friste's house reveals that Friste did not go home the night before, and the staff, loyally dismissing all sinful possibilities from their minds, summon the police. Door bust in, and Friste found dead. Enter Chief Inspector Teal, star performer of the Criminal Investigation Department, the Man of Destiny, with a nose for murders like the nose of a china bloodhound on a mantelpiece. 'Ah- ha! Foul play! Somebody has bumped this guy off.' Overcome with his own brilliance, Teal swallows chewing gum. S.O.S. to nearest Vet. to retrieve said gum. What next?"

"Some sense," Teal suggested reasonably.

"Then suppose you let me inspect the scene of the crime," murmured the Saint. "The great brain shall wallow in its atmosphere, soaking up deductions like a curate absorbing ginger-beer at a parish bun-fight. I was wrong, Teal—this sleuthing business is Big Stuff. Where's my violin? . . . Waiter!"

5

"The man who called this place Gaydon's Wharf," said the Saint, "had a cock-eyed sense of humour."

There was certainly nothing hilarious about the place. The three-storied building had almost certainly started its life as a warehouse, but had later been converted into three floors of dingy offices. Friste's office had been on the second floor, and the Saint appeared to grow slightly perplexed as he climbed the dark, narrow staircase.

"If Friste was a man of all this wealth," he remarked, "why did he want to choose a hole like this for his office?"

"Possibly he thought it would be convenient for the docks," said Teal. "If you'd thought of that question before he was killed, I could have asked him."

The entrance to the office was secured with a padlock and chain, and a constable stood on guard outside. The Saint lingered to light a cigarette while Teal produced a key and removed the obstruction. They passed into a large, bare room principally furnished with three desks supporting three shrouded typewriters. It was divided approximately into two equal areas by a counter which confronted the visitor on entering. On the right there were two doors, one on either side of the counter.

Teal opened the nearest one, and they passed into Friste's private office.

"There are only these two rooms," he explained.

The Saint glanced interestedly around the inner sanctum. Near the centre of the room was a large, flat-topped desk; there was a filing cabinet, two armchairs, and a small table in one corner.

"How does it strike you?" asked Teal.

"Hideously," said the Saint. "That wallpaper—"

Teal scowled.

"Do you intend to try to be helpful, or don't you?"

"I will do my wonderful best," said the Saint modestly.

He drifted round the room in a cloud of cigarette smoke. The single window interested him. Looking out, he found that the wall in which it was set ran sheer down to the river. The face of the building, on that side, at least, would have provided no foothold for anything but an athletic fly.

"How was this window fixed when the police came in?"

"It was open about nine inches at the bottom."

"And Exhibit B?" The Saint pointed to a long pole feebly resembling a boat-hook, which lay on the floor, close by.

"That's exactly as we found it. It was used to open and close the upper sash."

"And the deceased?"

"He was lying in a line between the window and the centre of the room, on his back, about six feet from the window."

"How was he shot?"

"Through the centre of the forehead—from a range of about two inches."

"And the doors?"

"Both locked, as I told you. They're Yale locks, and there was absolutely no trace of them having been tampered with. Of course, if they had been unlocked when the murderer arrived, he could have slipped the catches and made them lock behind him as he went out."

"I see that there's a third door," said the Saint, pointing to the wall opposite the window.

"That's a private entrance from the landing. Friste could go in or out without passing through the reception-room. But if you'll look carefully, you'll see that that door is bolted on the inside, and it was like that when we found it. It's the one door which the murderer couldn't possibly have used."

The Saint paced the room in silence for a few moments. Then he said: "What about the office staff?"

"Their alibis are cast iron," replied the detective. "There were two girl stenographers and a young clerk. On this particular morning the girls arrived together, and the clerk came in about five minutes later. Not one of them was out of sight of somebody for one second, and there's no possibility of suspecting anyone. But there's one thing you haven't read in the newspapers."

"What's that?"

"The porter downstairs saw Friste come in at ten o'clock, yet he never passed through the outer office. Friste was alive and well at ten o'clock. He must have let himself in by his private entrance and bolted the door behind him. And shortly after that he was shot dead, but there were three people waiting for him in the outer room who never heard the shot that killed him."

The Saint frowned.

"There certainly seem to be some difficulties about this case," he murmured, and Teal exploded.

"Difficulties! I tell you, when you've sweated your brain over the case as long as I have, you'll see that it's not only difficult—it's impossible! Nobody could have gone into that office by the private entrance because it was bolted on the inside. No one can have gone in through the outer office, because the staff would have seen him. No one can have got in through the window, because it's humanly impossible to get at that window except by a rope lowered from the roof. And that rope would have to pass right in front of a similar window in the offices above where there were whole staffs working at the time. Besides, if anyone opened or closed that window on the outside, he managed to do it without disturbing one particle of dust—and the outside of the frame's thick with it. If someone sat outside that window somehow, and potted Friste through that nine-inch opening at the bottom, I'd like to know how Friste got his head down to that level, even if he was using the pole to try and open the upper sash. If you tell me that someone tied a revolver to a long pole and pushed it across the river from a building on the other side, and Friste obligingly put his head against the gun, I shall have you arrested."

The Saint sighed.

"It certainly is difficult," he repeated.

He knelt beside the window and examined the inside of the sill.

"There's a tiny mark here," he said. "Looks as if it had had a bang."

Teal and Duncarry came up to inspect the discovery, but the Saint sauntered off and lighted another cigarette. He was stretched out in one of the armchairs, apparently asleep, when Teal rose to his feet again.

"Does it mean anything to you, Templar?"

The Saint roused aggrievedly.

"Not yet," he said. "But I thought it might mean something to you. Anyway, you can call it a Clue, and tell the newspapers about it."

He stretched up out of his chair, yawning, and then he suddenly stiffened.

"Where is the dragon?" he asked, and Teal stared.

"What dragon?"

The Saint gazed at him with a slow smile.

"If you don't know anything about the dragon I'm not going to tell you. But that dragon is a good joke. Remember to ask me about it later." The Saint yawned again. "And now I'm tired of this case. Also, I require some beer."

He faded away abruptly, and the disgruntled detective followed with Duncarry. The Saint decanted them in Whitehall, told them to be good boys and to take care not to get brain fever, and headed the car towards home after extracting Eileen Wiltham's address.

As it happened, this was a precaution that he need not have taken.

"Pat," said the Saint, as Patricia opened the door to him, "I have sad news. I've just been out with a bloke whose literary tastes include parish magazines, and he tells me that our chosen bishop has had his hair cut. Now we shall have to wait until it grows again, or that scalp I promised you will look moth-eaten."

"There's someone here to see you," said Patricia. "I thought it might save you some trouble if I raked her up."

Simon gazed at her with admiration.

"Eileen herself? Pat, you're a genius."

He went through into the sitting-room, and a tall, pale girl, who had been occupying his favourite chair, rose as he entered.

"Pleased to meet you, Eileen," said the Saint briskly. "And you're pleased to meet me. Splendid. Have some beer?"

Eileen Wiltham smiled.

"I'm not sure why Miss Holm should have fetched me—"

"Nor am I, unfortunately," said the Saint. "But if you can tell me anything interesting, or let me know anything I can do—"

He offered his cigarette-case, lighted a cigarette for himself, and seated himself on the table.

"I didn't know you worked with the police," said the girl.

"Nor did I," said Simon cheerfully. "In fact, this is a record."

"I've read about you, of course—"

"Then you know my sticky reputation."

"You were pardoned some time ago—"

"Some of my sins have certainly been forgiven," admitted the Saint largely. "The process of reformation continues but very slowly. Now tell me your worry."

"It's not about myself," said the girl after a pause. "But my fiancé, Charles Barringer—since I'm here, can you tell me why he's being followed about wherever he goes?"

"Teal's faithful hounds." The Saint chuckled. "But I don't see what I can do about that. If I gave them a clip under the ear and ordered them back to barracks, they mightn't consider that the orders came from an authoritative source."

"But do they really believe that he committed that murder?"

The Saint looked at her for a moment before replying. She was undeniably pretty, but the strain and worry of the last few days showed in her face.

"It wouldn't be fair to deny that there are temporary suspicions," he said seriously. "Consider the facts. After Friste had made a nuisance of himself with you, your boy went round to his office and bawled him out. He threatened to murder him if the offence was repeated, and he fired off all his stuff in the hearing of Friste's entire staff. That same evening, before the office closed, Friste went out and had a number of drinks at a neighbouring pub and repeated the whole story of the row to anyone who'd listen. He was rather a heavy drinker, but thoroughly booze-proof, and the landlord of the pub swears that he's never seen the little rat the worse for it. Then Friste went back to his office as the staff were closing up, and the next morning he was shot."

"Yes, but—"

"The porter saw him come in at about ten o'clock, but his staff never saw him. Therefore he went into his private office by the other door. No one came through the outer office, and therefore the only man who could have shot him also entered by the private door. And your fiancé had a key to that door."

"But that door was bolted on the inside," Patricia put in. "So the man couldn't have got out that way."

"I know. And yet he didn't go through the outer office because he would have been seen. He might have dived straight from the window into the river, but I doubt it. The whole show is one of the most frantic mysteries of this bleary age. Teal did the best thing he could think of when he pinched your fiancé. But he had to let him go almost at once."

"Then why are they still shadowing him?" asked the girl helplessly.

"It's the system. It's vaguely possible that he might have killed Friste, though no one can think out how he could have done it. Teal had to let him go for the time being when your revered parent butted in and cemented his alibi."

"But Charles couldn't have done it! He was staying with us that night—"

"I know that, too. And your house is at Cookham, isn't it?"

"Yes."

"Until after midnight he was discussing the development of his invention with your father—then some more drinks and smokes, and so to bed. That was the night of the murder. According to the processes of Teal's apology for a brain, Charles might have crept out later and borrowed your father's car to get to London and do the job. But if he did that, he also did big things in the wash and polish line afterwards, for it was a filthy night, and the car was clean when he drove back to London in it with your father and found Teal sitting on his bed with a welcoming smile and a pair of handcuffs. He might have used a car from a neighbouring garage, but the inquiries that have been made seem to rule that out. He might even have used a push-bike—"

"But at ten o'clock he was having breakfast with us."

The Saint nodded.

"Exactly. The whole thing is quite impossible; but it's also impossible that anyone else could have killed Friste."

Eileen Wiltham raised her eyes wearily.

"I don't see it. If everyone thinks that Charles couldn't possibly have done it —"

"The snag," said the Saint, "is that Teal isn't quite sure about the authenticity of the Reginald Friste whom the door porter saw alive and well at ten o'clock."

"What do you mean?"

The Saint shook his head and shrugged. He tried to explain the methods of Scotland Yard when investigating an apparently impossible crime, but it was a difficult and unwelcome task. When he found that he could give Eileen Wiltham no useful help or information of any kind, he changed the subject and tried to sidetrack her mind from it; and when, later, Patricia reminded him that they were invited to fill the Hannassays' box at the Gaiety, he thought he had an inspiration.

"Take Eileen instead," he said. "Kit and Susan won't mind, and it'll do her good."

But the girl shook her head.

"I'd love to go, but I promised to go to a show with Charles."

"When are you meeting him?"

"At a quarter past eight."

"Then you can go to the preliminary dinner," said the Saint. "They're good and cheery souls, and just now I think that the best thing you can do is to jump at anything that'll stop you from thinking too much. Pat, you might get on to Susan and give them due warning. Make my excuses also—I'm afraid I shouldn't have been able to go, anyway. I think tonight is going to be a busy night."

He over-ruled all protests, and at seven o'clock he drove Patricia and Eileen to the Hannassays' house in Hamilton Place.

And from Hamilton Place he proceeded along to the Victoria. He paused briefly at the door, where he received some interesting information; and then, continuing his researches further, he found Duncarry in the grill room, lingering over a menu. The New Yorker offered the glad hand.

"If you've nothing better to do, Dun," said the Saint, "you might join up with me. I'm alone."

"I'm not feeling any too crowded myself," Duncarry confessed. "You've leaped down like a little ray of sunshine out of a dark sky. London can be a darned lonesome place."

"Got a gun?"

Duncarry did not blink an eyelid at this odd question, but shook his head and plumped for smoked salmon.

"Pack this, then," said the Saint, pushing an automatic pistol under the table.

"What's the idea?"

"Vittorio has collected his hat," said the Saint cheerfully. "When he and Jack Farnberg get together to admire the drawing I left in the lining, there will be vitriol in the air. Unless my prophetic powers are getting as punk as Claud Eustace Teal's, we shall see fun and games before tonight is out. What do you say we burst a bottle?"

6

Duncarry examined the automatic more closely when they got to Upper Berkeley Mews.

"Looks useful," he remarked. "That's a neat little silencer."

"German. Did I hear you say one time that Jack Farnberg and Vittorio Ardossi are wandering around together lovingly hand in hand?"

Duncarry wrinkled his long nose.

"Not as a great and solemn truth—only as an intelligent guess," he answered. "Ardossi was never a big cheese before his uncle made a will. Uncle had a chain of salami foundries from Minneapolis to 'Frisco. He must have been some hash-slinger, believe me. There was a dandy sea-going steam-yacht and a fleet of cars among the oddments."

"Sounds good." The Saint was sliding an ingenious specimen of folding steel shuttering across the windows. "Pardon these precautions, but I have a constitutional objection to spilling blood in my drawing-room, and you never know what some gay bird may be doing on the other side of the castle walls."

Duncarry nodded his approval.

"You certainly know how to look after yourself," he conceded.

"If I didn't, I should be ancient history," said the Saint coolly. "And, by the Lord—"

He broke off as a bell rang softly somewhere outside the room. He flicked a little automatic from his pocket and went out into the hall; and as he did so something was pushed into the letter-box. The Saint looked at it for one second, and then leapt like a cat and snatched a cone-shaped metal fire-extinguisher from its bracket as he saw a speck of fire like an angry red eye glowing between the wires of the box. There was a hiss and a splashing as a jet of liquid from the extinguisher deluged the letter-box and drenched the mat below in foaming lather.

"What's happening?" asked Duncarry's voice.

"Watering the garden," replied the Saint genially, pushing the plug back into the extinguisher. "And now we shall have to swab up the mess. I have an idea, Duncarry, that if that guy was the postman he was doing a bit of overtime. You'd better take cover, son—maybe I haven't soaked all the spitefulness out of this kindly gift."

He opened the letter-box cautiously, and withdrew something hard and heavy with the charred and saturated paper wrapping still clinging to it. Duncarry shifted his cigar and peered over the Saint's shoulder. It was a flat cigarette-box that had once contained fifty gaspers of a popular brand. Copper wire had been wrapped round the box from end to end, and the tails of wire were twisted tightly together. In the centre, a scorched half-inch of cotton fuse protruded from a hole punched in the tin.

"Crude," said the Saint pleasantly, "but effective. I guess it would have made a mess of me if I'd met it in action at close quarters. Without dissecting its internals, Dun, I should diagnose a combination of high explosive and hobnails."

"More like Ardossi's visiting-card than Jack Farnberg's stuff," grunted the New Yorker. "That's in exchange for the scare you gave him."

The Saint laughed and made for the kitchen in search of a mop. He found a swab and pail, and was down on his knees giving a good imitation of an industrious housemaid when he heard a hasty step outside, and the bell rang again.

The Saint pushed the pail into the fairway, leapt to his feet, and opened the door with a jerk.

The visitor, who seemed to be in a desperate hurry, rushed in, staggered over the pail, fell, and scrambled up to discover an automatic pistol levelled at him, and behind the pistol the lean face and red-tipped cigar of Detective Duncarry.

"Put 'em good and high, stranger," drawled the American. "Are you claiming this bird, Saint?"

Simon smiled at the amazed and startled visitor, and shook his head.

"Hullo, Barringer," he said. "I'm sorry you tripped over the iron-mongery, and sorrier still that you've slopped all the juice out of it. However—take him inside and give him some beer while I clean up, Dun."

Barringer was a good-looking, up-standing young fellow of about twenty-six. He seemed worried and nervous, and probably he had reason. To be shadowed and dogged at every twist and turn by the watchful myrmidons of the law is not a stimulating tonic.

"I really can't wait, Mr Templar. I just wanted to know: Is Eileen—is Miss Wiltham here?"

The Saint waved his swab affably to a man who was energetically ornamenting the opposite side of the Mews as a living proof of the vigilance of Scotland Yard, and shut the door.

"I'm afraid she isn't," he said, resuming his job.

"She promised to meet me at quarter-past eight—"

"I know. Didn't she turn up?"

Barringer shook his head.

"I waited till nearly nine, and then took a taxi straight here."

"She has been here," said the Saint. "But she left at seven. That bit of mopping isn't bad work for an amateur, is it? Slide into the consulting-room while I shift the bag of tools, and I'll be right with you. Mr Charles Barringer, Mr Duncarry. Barringer, Dun, is the bloke who's slightly tangled up with the Gaydon's Wharf murder, that brain-racking mystery now filling Teal's head with aches and his heart with tears."

Barringer, however, refused beer and declined cigarettes. The Saint rang up Hamilton Place, and the butler informed him that the whole party, including Miss Wiltham, had left at eight o'clock in Lord Hannassay's car. This provided the sum total of the information which the Saint could give. And when Barringer heard it he apologised for intruding and took his leave.

"I should think that young fellow might kill a man in a row, but he doesn't seem the sort to lay out for one," said Duncarry, and the Saint groaned.

"Don't rack my brains. The crime *is* manifestly impossible, as we all know, and I refuse to burst any blood vessels over it this evening."

"Friste was a shipping agent, wasn't he? What did he ship?"

"Various things. Some of them legitimate, and some of them not. I think I told you he was a nasty man. He had one boat on the South American run. Get me? Some souls travelled to hell on that ship."

Duncarry nodded; and for some moments the Saint smoked with a thoughtful frown. And then, all at once, with one of the electric changes of mood that were so characteristic of the man, the frown vanished, and Simon sprang to his feet, smiling.

"Come on, Dun! I'm tired of this. Let's leave it to Teal and his staff of high-brow stars. That bomb stunt was probably the beginning and the end of the entertainment for tonight, so we'll go out and be riotous. I'll take you down the Wild West End and show you some gay life."

"So long as you don't take me to a place that Teal's likely to raid—"

"I'll try to think of one of which he's a leading member," promised the Saint.

They went out with some circumspection; but the Saint's guess seemed to have been accurate, for there was no disturbance, and the Mews was deserted.

On the Embankment, the Saint stopped his car and got out. With the tin box in his hand he leaned against the parapet, watching the river; and then he gave the box a heave, lighted a cigarette, and went back to Detective Duncarry.

"One of my brilliant inspirations has just struck me, Dun." The American raised inquiring eyebrows.

"Pat and Eileen have been together half the evening, and our recent fake postman probably wasn't the first man to take a look at Upper Berkeley Mews. The great thought is that Jack or Vittorio, or both, who've never set eyes on Pat, though they've probably heard of her, may have got the two girls mixed. Suppose they got the great idea of grabbing Pat in the hope of getting a pull over me—it's nearly as easy to kidnap a girl in this motor-car age as to do a smash-and-grab stunt and get away with it."

"It certainly is, Saint."

"I've got no down on Eileen," said the Saint, "but still, I almost wish that's what's happened. If Jack and Vittorio have butted in and mixed their stuff, I believe I shall be able to view even that Gaydon's Wharf murder without feeling sea-sick."

It was half-past eleven when Patricia Holm arrived with Lady Susan Hannassay and her party at the club that the Saint had selected.

They were greeted with the edifying spectacle of Simon Templar seated on the back of a chair playing the banjo, while Detective Duncarry, in spite of his limp, was dancing to the melody and at the same time balancing a champagne bottle on his head. While the dancer was receiving his meed of applause the Saint spoke to Patricia.

"At what time did Eileen leave you?"

"About ten-past eight, I think—we dropped her at Piccadilly Circus. Why?"

"She missed her boy, somehow. Barringer has been round with his hair on end. He waited for her till nearly nine, and then came along to see if she was still with you."

Patricia looked at him anxiously.

"What do you think has happened?"

"I've got a very good idea," said the Saint rather grimly. "And so have you, lass. But at the moment there's just nothing we can do. We haven't a clue in the wide world. Of course, Barringer may have located her since—"

He shrugged. As a matter of fact, the problem was plaguing him, and only the sober knowledge of his own helplessness kept him in exasperated inaction.

The club band was taking a breather, and the Saint resumed his strumming on the borrowed banjo as if no such joy-shattering nuisances as Gaydon's Wharf murders, infernal machines thrust into letter-boxes, and blood-thirsty gunmen, had any existence in a glad world.

He raised his cheerful voice, and continued with his self-appointed task of entertaining the assembled company.

> "Dearest, the jaunt is over, Ended the jag divine;
> You must go back to your wife, I must go back to mine—"

"Zoom! Boom! Ta-ra-ra!" aided and abetted Detective Duncarry with enthusiasm.

A waiter approached and whispered something in the Saint's ear.

"Spill the rest for yourself, Dun, and get yourself hated," said the Saint, saddling the American with the instrument of torture. "There's an infuriated laundress outside, flourishing a club and my unpaid washing bill."

He went through into the vestibule, and greeted Charles Barringer blithely.

"I came here because I found this address in my pocket, Mr Templar," he said, holding out a scrap of paper.

"Sure. I put it there for you to find". So you haven't found Eileen yet?"

"I haven't."

"Have you mentioned her disappearance to the sleuth from Scotland Yard who's watching over your welfare?"

Charles Barringer shook his head hopelessly. He looked strained and worried beyond his years; and suddenly the Saint gripped him by the shoulders, swung him round, and looked long and searchingly into his troubled brown eyes.

"Son," he said, "don't be too sure that you're desperately wanted for killing Friste, because it isn't true. I can't deny that Teal's alleged brain is running that way, but mine isn't. And I'm also on the job, and I have a very good reason for knowing that you didn't do it."

He smiled encouragingly.

"Keep the stiff upper lip, old chap. If you like to hang around here a few minutes longer, I'll get on the phone to Teal right away and tell him all about it. I'd toddle off with you myself, but I can't abandon Duncarry, who's getting happy and ready and willing to play the superb ass. If you like, I'll fetch in your bloodhound as well, or he'll be getting nervous. I promise you the poor boob isn't the man-eating horror you think he is, and you may get quite sociable over a smoke and a glass of beer. He's only holding down his job."

"It's a dirty job," said the boy bitterly. "Why don't they arrest me again, and get it over?"

The Saint hitched his shoulders.

"Search me. The intricacies of British law are beyond me. Leave it to Teal, and I'll collect the sleuth."

Simon moved on past the doorkeeper and beckoned the plain-clothes man across the road.

"Two friends of mine," he said to the suspicious waiter. "Supply them with beer and cigarettes, and add the debt with Mr Duncarry's to my death warrant."

"Mr Duncarry has just ordered a magnum of champagne, sir."

"He would," said the Saint mournfully. "If I'd had any sense, I'd have made him a member for half a guinea and entitled him to pay for himself."

He went to the telephone and asked for Teal's private number. By this time, Chief Inspector Teal should either have retired to bed, or have been seated at the domestic fireside listening to the radio and putting innumerable threepences into the pockets of Mr Wrigley's shareholders. The latter guess appeared to hit the bull's-eye, for Teal himself answered the call, promptly.

"Oh, you," he said, almost with a moan. "Oh, damn!"

"Glad you're sitting up and taking notice, dear old Antipon. Eileen Wiltham has faded into the great unknown, so you'd better shed those carpet slippers and get busy. I'm at the Jericho with Duncarry, who's full of pep. Gin and pep."

"What the—what's this about the Wiltham girl?" asked Teal sourly.

"I'm only guessing," said the Saint, who was also hoping it with considerable horsepower, "but I've got a hunch that my loving pals Jack

Farnberg and Vittorio Ardossi have mixed her up with Pat. Get on the job, old dear."

Mr Teal breathed so hard that the Saint almost fancied he could smell peppermint, and hung up the receiver. Simon grinned gently. He was practically certain now that his guess had been correct, and, with certain humane reservations, he welcomed the idea. Commonplace crimes like the Gaydon's Wharf murder mystery had a very transient appeal for him, and the idea of inviting Teal's assistance against Farnberg and Ardossi over a strictly personal slab of hatred would have made him laugh; but if Farnberg and Ardossi had been insane enough to entangle themselves in the Gaydon's Wharf affair, the resulting developments might have their entertaining angles.

"You can push on now, Charles," he said, returning to the vestibule. "I've started things moving, so don't be too anxious about your beloved. Goodnight, son."

A couple of hours later the Saint gathered up the wreckage of Detective Duncarry, conveyed it forth into the night, and handed it over to the porter of the American's hotel. He went down the steps again to his car, fresh and smiling; and at that moment another car purred into the quiet square and pulled up within a yard of his own tail light.

The chauffeur jumped down to open the door, and the passenger stepped out. The fur collar of his overcoat rose above his ear-tips, and from under a glossy silk hat a sallow face peered out through gold-rimmed glasses. Even so, Simon recognised him at once.

"I'll telephone when I want you again."

"Thank you, sir. Goodnight, sir."

Simon felt inclined to burst into song. This sort of thing smithereened all Teal's cautious ideas and painstaking methods of forging the chain link by link and ratting after his man from hole to hole. It was pure unadulterated luck, of course, but it was so.

"Welcome, Vittorio mio," cried the Saint with extended arms. "Why did you run so fast when I last saw you? And why didn't you inform the police of your address? You may be a proud American citizen, but you're an alien over here, my pet, and the police may jug you for it. Hadn't I better come in and explain the law?"

Ardossi began to protest, but the Saint shepherded him irresistibly up the steps. "What's Mr Duncarry's number?" he asked the night porter.

"Twenty-eight, sir."

The little hotel in a quiet corner of Elmbury Square suited Detective Duncarry's pocket, but it was not the kind of place for a recently fledged plutocrat like Ardossi to select unless he felt that it might be unhealthy to be too much in the limelight. There was no lift. The Saint followed Ardossi up the stairs, and patted him tenderly about the person for any hard bulge suggestive of a hidden weapon.

Ardossi's room was on the second floor, and the lights went up in his sitting-room as he unlocked the door. The room looked comfortable enough, but slightly dingy.

"Lead on, little one," said the Saint persuasively. "I want to inspect the rest of your dovecote."

The Italian, finding that his protests were ignored, obeyed meekly enough. A small bedroom adjoined the sitting-room, and beyond that was the bathroom. They returned when the Saint was satisfied with his tour of inspection.

"A jolly-looking overcoat, Vittorio," commented the Saint critically, as Ardossi divested himself of that expensive garment and removed his gloves. "These are happy days."

Ardossi sat down without removing his glossy hat. In the centre of his shirt front was a fine pink pearl, and he spread out his hands with an opulent sparkle of diamond rings.

"What do you want?" he asked.

"Not much, Vittorio—only the lady you kidnapped. Funny thing to want, isn't it? But I want it very much, so don't let's have any trouble. Open your mouth and wag your chin, sweetheart, or I'll start at your ears and peel the hide off you in strips."

"I don't know what you're talking about."

Ardossi sighed. The Saint was expecting him to lie and keep on lying, but there were certain methods of overcoming such trifling difficulties. Simon took out his cigarette-case and lighted a cigarette as if he had all the time in the world to spare. Then his unfriendly gaze returned again to the Italian.

"You're not so bat-eyed as all that," he said. "Jack up those glasses and let's have a look at you."

The glasses went, revealing the Italian's eyes, black as sloes and unwinking.

"What's the game over here, Vittorio?"

The Italian gave the ghost of a smile. "The same game, Mr Templar."

"Running in with Jack Farnberg now?"

Ardossi shook his head. "I haven't seen Jack Farnberg for two years. Not since the cops got him."

The Saint's blue eyes seemed to grow even lazier.

"Is—that—so? . . . Vittorio, you'd lie the legs off a full-grown elephant! I think it's time for us to take a little walk, and if I catch you telling any more lies about Jack Farnberg I'll be damned sure you're lying about the lady, and by the time I've finished with you every bone in your body will be softer than five cents' worth of Vaseline in a heat-wave."

Detective Duncarry had certainly revelled; but he had a tough head, and the Saint hoped to find him not absolutely dead to the world. He took the Italian firmly by the scruff of the neck and jerked him out of the chair; and a glint of fear came into the man's beady eyes at last.

"Where are you taking me?"

"You sing when I tell you to sing," instructed the Saint curtly.

He led Ardossi along the dimly lighted corridor and on to the second flight of stairs. Half-way up Ardossi stumbled, and as he fell his right hand closed on a loose brass stair-rod and wrenched it away. The savage sidelong lunge which he made with it would have spiked the Saint from eye-socket to occiput if the Saint had not seen the yellow gleam of the polished rod in the very nick of time and jumped back. But in avoiding the thrust he was compelled to release his prisoner, and like a leaping puma, his mouth open and his white teeth showing, the Italian turned and slashed a second vicious blow at him.

The rod scraped the wall, and that took some of the sting out of it, but it paralysed the Saint's arm, and the automatic he had whipped from his pocket slipped from his fingers. He aimed an upward kick at Ardossi, but it was inches short, for the Italian went over the banisters like a monkey, and the left-handed blow that Simon slatted down at him with the stair-rod he had abandoned only dented the silk hat and forced it down more firmly on the sleek black head.

Simon picked up his automatic again. He could have dropped Ardossi as he ran, but he thought it wiser not to make a sticky mess of the Italian in a peaceful London hotel, for the resulting complications might be tiresome.

Ardossi sprinted for his sitting-room. He had trouble with the door, which had locked itself behind them as they came out, and if the trouble had occupied him another two seconds the Saint's grip would have been on his collar. He kicked the door to behind him, but Simon sliced the stair-rod in between lock and catch and kept it from fastening.

The Saint knew that Ardossi would have no qualms about splashing gun lead around, but he took a chance on that and barged in. The sitting-room was empty, and it offered no hiding-place, but the bedroom door was closed. The Saint put his shoulder to the door and made the flimsy bolt look like a bent pin, but that room also was empty. And although the bed looked innocent he stabbed the stair-rod into it without eliciting a squeal.

The bathroom was also empty, but the window was open, and the Saint peered out into the gloom. A corkscrew staircase, a way of escape from fire for the tenants of the loftier bedrooms, twisted down and slanted away from the bathroom. If Ardossi had jumped the wide gap from sill to staircase, the Saint figured he must have been a world-beater at the jumping game. He looked down and saw a small balcony below him, and a thin stream of light. Lower down still, and too far to drop without inviting the aid of a surgeon to do something with splints and bandages, was a square, paved yard. Then he saw something else, and cursed gently.

A rope dangled from a staple hammered into the brick wall under the sill, and its lower end might have been tied to the fire escape and cast loose when Ardossi had clawed his way across. Or the Italian might have slid down to the balcony and made the drop into the yard from there.

The life had returned to Simon's right arm, and he swung himself over the sill in pursuit with no uncertain enthusiasm. He was a third of the way down the rope when something whipped out of the darkness from the spiral staircase and clattered against the brickwork. The Saint came down with a run and crashed on to the balcony, and a knife with a broken point rebounded from the wall and fell into the yard.

Simon remained just where he had fallen, crouching on hands and knees and glad to feel that Ardossi was without a gun. He reckoned himself anyone's equal at the knife-throwing game, but although the hilt of Belle was between his fingertips, he could see nothing upon which to use her. After a moment he glanced round at the window behind him, and then he could not repress a grin at what he saw between a gap in the curtains.

Obviously the night porter had blundered, and Duncarry's number was not twenty-eight. For there inside Simon saw the American himself, who had apparently gone to sleep in his chair after shedding his overcoat and one shoe.

The hammering of knuckles on the pane shook the drowsiness out of Duncarry's eyes, and he saw the Saint's features through the glass. He shot back the catch and raised the window, and the Saint jumped in.

"Ardossi himself," said the Saint briskly. "He may have shunted up the fire escape and be prancing about on some distant roof by this time, or he may not. Get your gun and watch for me from here, Dun."

"Sure," said Duncarry as unconcernedly as though he had been asked for a match.

The Saint ran down the stairs and through the hall where the night porter was nodding in a chair, and took cover in the shelter of a pillar at the end of the steps. His hunch was that the Italian had not lingered on the fire escape for the mere pleasure of slinging a knife at him, but was waiting for some further incident—possibly the arrival of Jack Farnberg himself.

And the Saint was right, for within thirty seconds he saw Ardossi again, sidling round from the side entrance.

Suddenly the Italian darted into the road. Expecting that he would try to climb the railings and vanish into the obscurity of the gardens, the Saint chanced the wrath of Scotland Yard and all the vials of fury that might be poured hissing hot upon his head, and fired low. Ardossi squealed, rocked on one leg, and tumbled into the gutter, and his silk hat rolled off.

Then headlights flashed, and a car turned into the square. The Saint took one look at the blue-black object that protruded from a window of the car, and dropped flat on the muddy pavement. The next moment a stammer of shots turned the silent square into a clamour of noise. The door behind the Saint opened, someone grunted throatily, and the night porter came rolling down the steps and lay still at the bottom, gazing up glassy-eyed at the dark drizzling sky.

Rising on one knee, the Saint emptied his automatic at the tyres of the retreating car, but it turned the next corner on two wheels, and the only souvenir that remained was a flattened silk hat.

Windows were open and police whistles were shrilling.

The Saint bent over the night porter, saw that he was beyond human help, and ran up the steps to meet Duncarry. The New Yorker was still minus one shoe, and his left trouser-leg, pulled up to the knee, revealed a silk sock anchored by a sock-suspender of dazzling blue embroidered with golden rosebuds.

"I heard the fireworks," he said. "Am I too late?"

"Sorry—you are." The Saint clapped him on the shoulder. "And I really think this is the end of tonight's festival. So you can pull down the shutters on that leg and find your other shoe."

"Did you get him?" asked the American with a yawn.

"I don't know. He squealed and dropped, but that may have been a bluff. Then a car came, and they lifted him in. I couldn't see who was working the machine-gun, but I'll bet ready money it was Jack Farnberg, Vittorio's certainly unlucky with tall hats—this is the second time he's been stung.

In spite of the late hour a crowd was already gathering in the square, and the police were arriving thick and fast. The Saint paused to give the police sergeant the number of the car, and spent some time answering questions before Duncarry was able to secure his release.

They went back to the American's room at last. Duncarry dispensed whisky, and the Saint gazed at his gun moodily.

"I never was the hell of a shot with these things," he said. "Next time I ever get a sight of either of those bright lads, I'll use my knife or my bare hands—and when that day comes, Dun, you're going to see something you can take home and tell the children. And the day is coming soon!"

7

AMAZING BATTLE IN LONDON SQUARE

NIGHT PORTER SHOT DEAD

MACHINE-GUNS AND REVOLVERS

The Saint had no more than glanced at the headlines in the newspaper, for he was not curious to know what the Press had made of the little carnival in Elmbury Square in the early hours of that morning.

After that casual glance he dropped the newspaper into the waste-paper basket and made for the bathroom in his dressing-gown and slippers. He had risen towards noon, as was his pleasant custom, and his breakfast followed at an appropriate hour. He was treating a plateful of bacon and eggs with anything but gentleness when Detective Duncarry drifted in.

The American's lean face and keen eyes did not suggest that on the previous night he had been looking upon much champagne when it was bubbly.

"Was I canned?" he demanded, extending a cool, steady set of fingers. "Did I burble and bleat, Saint?"

"Not a bit. Gay and festive, and developing symptoms of sleeping-sickness towards the close—but those symptoms were only the natural outcome of a long day of toil and tribulation."

"I must have shifted a thankful," grinned the American impenitently. "And coming from an arid and boozeless land, you must admit I'm a good amateur at pulling round. Cigar?"

The Saint shook his head.

"Not yet, old son. Do you know, I've an idea that show last night isn't going to be anything like the end of the fun."

Duncarry nodded.

"I'm not arguing," he said.

The Saint clicked over a switch, and when the coffee was bubbling in the glass bulb of the machine he turned the tap and handed a steaming and fragrant cup to the New Yorker.

"There's a bottle of Biscuit '15 in the corner," he said. "If you've got a heavy feeling, spray your coffee with it and you'll be ready to drop into the deep end of the next course like a penguin off a high springboard." He fetched the bottle over and regarded his guest whimsically. "Damn you, Dun, I'm afraid I'm beginning to like you!"

Duncarry gave one of his curt nods.

"I'll say the same to you. We've fought on different sides, but that's all over now. I'm staying here for another eighteen days, and if there's any trouble around, and you want a willing volunteer, you can count me in. I mayn't be so decorative, but in a wild corner you won't find me squeal or quit."

"Maybe I'll be taking you at your word," said the Saint. "The trouble will be coming sure enough."

They sat and yarned for a while longer, and then the Saint rose and flicked a cigarette-end out of the window.

"Let's get out of here before the phone rings again and we hear some more grousing from Teal," He smiled gently, smoothing his hair, with his eyes on the ceiling. "Know anything about spiders, Dun?"

It was a most disconnected question to have jerked at him without any warning, but Duncarry never blinked.

"Not much," he answered. "I did once read a book about 'em by a guy named Fabre. Lady spiders, it seems, eat their husbands, so I gather their divorce courts have a thin and hungry time."

"I don't know at what time of the year spiders are in season," said the Saint meditatively, "but there's a very fine specimen hanging from the electrolier right now. It looks ominous. Jack Farnberg will have to go for a ride, Dun, but I don't want Teal to get me hanged for it."

"Do it quick, and I'll help you and chance the hanging," said Duncarry recklessly.

The Saint laughed, and then a ring on the front-door bell interrupted his reply. He slipped to the window and peered out cautiously.

"It's Charles Barringer's employer, backer, and prospective pa-in-law," he said, turning to find Duncarry pushing back his chair. "Sir Enoch Wiltham, K.B.E. Don't bother to buzz off."

He went out and admitted the visitor, and a couple of minutes later Sir Enoch Wiltham entered the sitting-room. His legs were short, his body had a prosperous bulge, and his few remnants of hair were divided equally into two parts. His round, red face was founded upon more chins than were strictly necessary.

"Mr Templar?" he asked huskily.

"My name. This is Mr Duncarry, of the New York Detective Bureau."

"I wish to speak to you on a rather delicate matter," said Wiltham, and Simon turned to the New Yorker with a shrug.

"Sorry, Dun. I'll see you at the Piccadilly in about half an hour."

Duncarry nodded and picked up his hat; and Sir Enoch lowered himself into a chair.

"Barringer has spoken of you in terms of great admiration," said Sir Enoch. "He gave me to understand that you were assisting the police in the Gaydon's Wharf case, and I wondered—could you tell me, or would it be exceeding your duty to say—whether he is still under suspicion?"

"I'm afraid he is. Personally, I think it's ridiculous—"

"And I'm certain of it. Why, I myself can account for every moment of his time during the period when the murder is supposed to have been committed! The suggestion is preposterous."

Simon Templar spread out his hands.

"Nobody knows that better than I do," he said. "In fact, I have very good reason for knowing that Charles is indisputably innocent."

Sir Enoch clasped his hands over his prosperous bulge, and went on to explain that he was putting up the money to develop Barringer's new method of producing commercial alcohol. It all seemed absolutely square and above-board; and although the Saint had a constitutional dislike for men with multitudinous chins and husky voices, he made one of his intuitive decisions that Sir Enoch Wiltham did not belong to the ancient and crowded order of grafters.

"Charles is a good boy—I'm immensely fond of him. He'll be a rich man one day, and—"

"And he's going to marry your daughter. Isn't that it?"

"There's no one I'd be happier to see her marry."

Simon nodded, and lighted another cigarette.

"I think we shall find a way of clearing him before very long," he said.

"If you can do that, I shall be deeply in your debt." Sir Enoch gazed at his feet and appeared to hesitate. Presently he added, jerkily, "I had another question to ask—"

"Shoot."

"I wondered if you could give me any information . . . . The fact is . . . well, to tell you the truth I've been invited to embark in the American bootleg business."

Simon's eyebrows lifted faintly.

"I'm afraid I'm not the greatest authority in the world on that game," he said. "Duncarry could tell you more about it than I can. Would you like to meet him again?"

"Is he in the business?"

"On the contrary, his job is to stop it—but he should know pretty well all there is to know about it. The risks are big, but the profits are in proportion. Naturally, you can't insure your cargo, and so you may be badly stung. Come along to the Piccadilly with me and talk it over with Duncarry. The morality of it won't worry him as long as you don't propose to butt into his area."

Wiltham seemed doubtful, but the Saint was curious. He pressed Sir Enoch irresistibly, and won his point. They were at the door when the telephone-bell began ringing, but with the sure and certain knowledge that it was Chief Inspector Teal butting in again, the Saint ignored the call. Sir Enoch's car and chauffeur were in attendance, and they were quickly wafted to the portals of the Piccadilly.

Detective Duncarry cared considerably less than a hoot about bootlegging, provided it was not carried on in the placid and law-abiding district of New York which he controlled, but when the Saint gravely presented Sir Enoch as a gentleman eager to enter the booze racket, even the unemotional American betrayed mild surprise. But when, after lunch, Sir Enoch ordered a bottle of Napoleon brandy and half a dozen cigars listed at a guinea each, Duncarry's heart softened.

Sir Enoch Wiltham, it appeared, had a good many irons in the financial fire. He had purchased a large quantity of second-hand champagne, some vitriolic whisky, and a reservoir of French brandy that would have served admirably as fuel for spirit stoves if the quantity of water it contained had not rendered it completely fireproof.

"And you got the bright idea of shoving this stuff over to the land of the thirsty and free?" said the Saint.

"As a matter of fact, I was only wondering how to make a fair profit out of the stuff when this offer came," answered Sir Enoch, "and I was promised that a ship would be found if I would provide the cargo."

"What did the guy who made this offer know about the game?" inquired Duncarry lazily.

"He said he knew it inside-out and had his own organisation on the other side to distribute the liquor. He was quite frank about it, in a way—he told me he was in touch with one of the big gangs who were ready to handle and pay for any quantity of genuine wines and spirits."

The New Yorker nodded.

"There's a market for the genuine article," he said. "They make the cheap stuff themselves, but they can always find a home for good imports. All the same, my advice to you is to keep out. Sell this guy the stuff in London, and leave the rest to him. Once you let it go over the other side you mayn't find it so easy to cash their cheque."

Having said his piece, which, was unusually long for him, Duncarry relapsed into silence behind his cigar. The eye which came within Sir Enoch's line of vision was dreamy and impassive, but the eye that the Saint could see had a question in it.

"I'm afraid I'm too old and fat to be an outlaw," said Sir Enoch in his throaty voice, "but my mind is sometimes so young and foolish that I had even thought of making the trip myself to enjoy the thrill."

"Depends on what you call enjoyment," said the American, still with that questioning eye on the Saint; and then Simon raised his eyes and saw a vision in the offing that made him cover his brow with a slight groan.

"Good afternoon," said Mr Teal.

The Saint sighed, performed the necessary introductions, and invited the detective to be seated. Sir Enoch offered a cigar.

"Sorry the number of that car didn't help you," said the Saint.

"Faked plates," said Teal sleepily. "I wasn't expecting it would be any use."

He refused brandy, and chewed monotonously. It did not seem to be his radiant morn.

"There's nothing else you can tell me?" he asked.

"Nothing."

"There wouldn't be. I could murder that guy with the machine-gun with my own hands, and smile while I was doing it. Why didn't he hit you?"

"Probably wanted to annoy you, Claud." The Saint blew a perfect smoke-ring and turned to Duncarry. "The way this country is run is weird and wonderful. I pay rates and taxes which go towards maintaining the comic-opera police force of which Claud Eustace is such a distinguished member, but if I put in a claim for a rebate on account of a nice new suit ruined because I was compelled to lie down and soak up the London mud while the police allowed someone to spray the landscape with bullets, I'll bet any money it would be turned down."

"If you'd stood up and got sprayed yourself, I'd have stood you a coffin," said Teal acidly.

He departed soon afterwards, with the air of a Christian martyr going into cold storage.

Again Duncarry glanced at the Saint as if expecting a cue, and this time he received one. The tip of the Saint's cigar traced a word in the air; and Duncarry rose, muttering something about a forgotten telegram, and cruised off in quest of his overcoat and hat. He finished his cigar in the lounge, and there the Saint rejoined him later.

"Dun, I have been had for a mug. I've promised his Knighthood to clear Charles Barringer. I suppose we all have our moments of insanity."

"How come?"

"I saw your inquiring eye fixed on me like a gimlet, and guessed you were on the point of asking the old boy the name of the man who was going to handle his cargo. But I'd sized him up. Knowing who you were, he'd have seen trouble coming for those birds, and the question would have frozen him stiff. I set about it in another way. Enoch really is fond of Barringer, and really does want to get him out of this police mess. That's where I made my break. I promised to clear Barringer as white as if he had just been bleached."

"And what did you get for that?"

"Kellory," answered the Saint briefly.

Duncarry pursed his lips and emitted a low whistle.

"Blinder Kellory? Is that where Jack Farnberg drifted to, then? "

"Seems like it. And it seems that Jack is proposing to work a bit of business into his trip over here."

"And Ardossi, and that yacht of his—"

"Fits in. Vittorio told me he was still in the old game. The rest seems fairly easy—but the promise I gave about Barringer is going to give real trouble."

The lean American meditated for a moment.

"If Jack Farnberg's in this, and you meet, I suppose you'll bump him off?"

"Yeah." The Saint gazed glumly at the table-cloth. "Killing Jack has never been the ambition of my young life, but it's one of the things that are thrust upon one. If I don't kill him, he'll certainly kill me—and that would be too dreadful."

Duncarry frowned.

"If it's all the same to you," he said, "I'd like to know why you're so sure Barringer didn't kill Friste."

The Saint looked at him.

"Because I know who did," he said.

Something in the set of his mouth discouraged further questions, and there was silence for a few moments. And then the Saint laughed, and all the old careless gaiety danced back into his eyes.

"My brain seems to improve every day," he said. "In the last two hours I've had two brilliant inspirations."

"And what are they?"

"At the moment I can only tell you one of them. You remember my mentioning a dragon when we were having a look at Gaydon's Wharf? The idea I've just had about that dragon is probably one of the most brilliant ideas I shall ever have. The first time I said anything about it, I wasn't any too sure how it was going to fit in, but I think it's in its place now. You may get ready to scream at the joke when the time comes, sonny boy."

8

"Taxi, sir?"

The thick-set man who had just emerged from Pattman Buildings nodded. "Farringay Mansions, Chelsea."

The door of the cab closed with a bang. It was a fairly long journey from the heart of the City to Chelsea, but the driver made good time of it, and, without consulting the meter, his passenger pushed a ten-shilling note into his hand.

Ten seconds later, the taxi driver entered the building and approached the hall porter with an envelope in his hand.

"Where does the chap I just drove up live?" he asked. "I found this in the cab. Will you take it?"

"Take it yourself, and he may spring a couple of bob," said the porter. "Number eleven."

"Thanks, mate."

The driver hurried up the carpeted staircase, and near the end of a corridor he saw the number of the flat blinking at him in polished brass figures above a shining knocker. He lifted the knocker and rapped.

The passenger opened the door himself. "You left this on the floor of the cab, sir."

The man frowned.

"It isn't mine," he said.

"Better look at it and make sure, sir. It isn't sealed."

The thick-set man with the drawling nasal accent turned back the flap of the envelope, and drew out a card. Then he saw what was drawn on it, and his heavy jaw dropped.

"Jolly sort of day, isn't it, Jack?"

The taxi driver took off his peaked cap and straggling walrus moustache, and Farnberg stared at him. The silent automatic which Detective Duncarry had admired gleamed blue-black in the Saint's right hand.

Jack Farnberg dropped the card, and his big hands went up slowly.

"Am I on the spot, Saint?" he asked huskily.

"Near enough."

The gunman's tongue flicked over his lips. He was the abysmal brute, but he had no lack of courage. He gave his shoulders a shrug, and grinned crookedly.

"Get on with it, then," he said. "You stacked this deck, Saint, and it's your ante this time."

"Yes, I'm going to kill you, Jack," said Simon Templar softly. "And if Vittorio happens along, he'll be able to split the funeral with you. I'm a forgiving sort of bloke, honey, but the man who says that the Saint framed him is asking for something hot and nasty."

"Shoot—and preach the damned sermon afterwards," snarled Farnberg, and again his tongue slid over his dry lips.

"Not yet, dear one," answered the Saint gently. "Just now I've got a promise to keep, and that lets you out. But I wanted you to know what was coming to you. Now yelp, Jack. There's a hall porter down below. Open your mouth and exercise your lungs!"

Someone came pattering along the corridor, and the Saint took two swift steps backwards and shifted his automatic to his left hand. In the mirror behind Farnberg he saw the handle turn.

Then the door opened, and a woman came in. In the mirror, with one watchful eye fixed on Farnberg and the other looking behind him, the Saint took stock of her swiftly and comprehensively. She wore a brown, fur-trimmed coat, brown close-fitting hat, silk stockings, and high-heeled shoes. Between her carmined lips was a lighted cigarette. Her face was powdered and her cheeks were rouged.

The Saint crooked his arm and straightened it again. His fist smashed against the hat just where the lobe of an ear, with an ear-ring in it, showed below the felt. It was a mule-kick of a punch, and the slim figure sprawled face downwards on the carpet without a sound.

The Saint shifted his gun back into his right hand, closed the door, and put his foot on a smouldering cigarette.

"Not good enough, Jack," he said regretfully. "Vittorio hasn't practised enough with those shoes—it was the way he walked gave him away. Come on, Jack—let's hear you yell."

Farnberg showed his teeth.

"See here," he said, "if you didn't sell me to the cops in Brooklyn, I know you're in with them now, and I guess you've got a squad of them outside. I couldn't shoot straight the other night because the car lurched. So it's your turn now."

"Beautiful," said the Saint, "you may tell me one thing before I go. And you may say it quick. What have you done with Patricia Holm?"

He saw the sudden crinkling of Farnberg's forehead. And all at once he had a blinding, dazzling flash of understanding. Yet the most amazing thing about it was that it made him wonder why he had never thought of it before. It was superb, splendiferous—far too good to be true. But true it must have been. He had no further doubt on that score, and the realisation filled him with a real and wild delight.

"Don't bother to answer," he said quickly. "I guess we'll be hearing from you again pretty soon. Till then, you can hold that for me!"

In one lightning movement the Saint lashed a terrific undercut into the point of the gunman's jaw, garnered him with a sweep of his arm as his body sagged, and let him drop gently forward over his outstretched leg. Smiling happily at the scene of slaughter, he paused to light a cigarette. Then he went out, shutting the door behind him.

"Did he drop?" asked the hall porter, and the taxi driver smiled seraphically under his replaced face-hair.

"Not half," he answered. "And now—where do we go?"

"There's one round the corner," replied the porter.

They went round the corner together.

Simon treated the porter to a pint of beer and a packet of cigarettes, and drove him back to the flats.

"Married?" he asked, as his unrecorded fare stepped out.

"Don't I know it! One kid, eighteen months, and the best yeller in England."

"Put that in its money-box," said the Saint.

He crammed the ten-shilling note that Farnberg had paid him into the porter's hand and drove away.

Two hours later, resplendent in perfectly fitting evening clothes, the Saint was filling a slim, gold cigarette-case in preparation for what he reckoned was a well-earned reward for his afternoon's work.

Simon had repaired his previous omission and made Duncarry a member of the Jericho Club, and there he knew he would find the American.

The Club was down by the river, within a furlong of Farringay Mansions. On his way the Saint passed the door, and saw his friend the porter standing there looking up at the moon.

"Have you got a match?"

"Certainly, sir."

The porter fished out his matchbox and was rewarded with a cigarette. Not for a moment did he suspect that the slim and supremely elegant young man was none other than the princely taxi driver who had given him the ten-shilling note which even then was warming his pocket.

As he passed on, Simon Templar glanced up at the windows of the flats which fronted the river. In one of them—unless they had already taken fright and wing—there were two people with sore and sorry heads.

He chuckled and passed on. At the Jericho Club there was no crowd at that hour, for most of the members were late birds. In a quiet corner of the supper-room he discovered Duncarry entertaining a select company with some bewildering card tricks. Seeing the Saint, Duncarry put the cards aside and drifted over to the bar. His quick eyes noticed the slight abrasions on the Saint's knuckles at once.

"More trouble?" he inquired laconically.

"Nothing much."

The New Yorker pulled thoughtfully at his cigar.

"Both of them?" he asked lazily.

The Saint told his story briefly, and Duncarry listened in silence. At the end he grunted.

"I'll bet you don't tell Teal that story," he said. "Gee, he'd murder you."

"He'd want to."

Duncarry gave him a puzzled look.

"I still don't know why you left 'em."

"I explained that long ago," said the Saint. "Furthermore, Wiltham came through on the phone this morning to say he had fixed up the sale of his cargo to Kellory, and that Kellory's representative would come to his office at five o'clock to pay for it. I guessed that representative would be Jack Farnberg, and so I was waiting outside."

"Sure. But when you'd got the skunks down and out—"

"Why didn't I collect and deliver them to Scotland Yard? Well, for one thing I wanted Jack Farnberg for myself; and for another, I've got to let Jack run around until his cheque's cleared—according to my terms to Ali Baba of the forty chins."

"Beats me," said Duncarry helplessly. "That precious pair will never stop running now— and they've still got that girl."

"That's why I'm letting them run," said the Saint. "Nothing will happen to Eileen—you can take that from me."

"But does Wiltham know that the man who shot you up the other night is the same man that's got his daughter?"

"He doesn't—naturally. But he'd be a fool if he hadn't noticed that there was something in the wind and that you were some of it. If I'd told him what we know, he mightn't have been so keen to make me promise that you'd do nothing to ball up his sale."

"You're playing with fire," said Duncarry grimly. "Not that I expect that's news to you, but you'd better take my tip and watch your step. If I was interested in that Wiltham girl, I wouldn't be too sure she's safe."

"And yet I know she is—for a day or two."

Duncarry shrugged.

"It's your affair," he said briefly. "Are we free for the rest of the evening?"

"So far as I know," said the Saint, and Duncarry expressed his unqualified approval.

The band struck up, and Duncarry produced and placed upon his head a most outrageous paper hat. From another pocket he brought a contraption which he elongated into a diabolical instrument of noise and discord. Blowing shrill blasts, he proceeded to give a gratuitous example of what he considered a one-man cabaret should be.

It was later when the Saint was presented with the banjo and requested to give one of his blasphemous recitals. But in these days he seemed destined to leave everything of that sort unfinished.

"Roes in the bud,
Sweet ova of the sturgeon—"

Again a waiter approached, and the Saint abandoned his attempt and went out to find Barringer in the vestibule.

"I had a letter tonight—"

"I know," said the Saint, and the young man stared.

"How do you know?"

Simon smiled.

"My spies are everywhere," he said calmly. "The letter said that you will disclose the secret of your alcohol invention in an arranged manner, or something unpleasant will happen to Eileen."

Barringer gaped at him wide-eyed.

"How the devil did you know that?"

"There's precious little I don't know, son," replied the Saint airily. "But I produced that brainwave by concentration alone, combined with many hours of fasting and prayer."

"But what are we going to do?"

"Nothing—tonight."

The Saint's hand fell on Barringer's shoulder, and the Saintly smile was quiet and reassuring.

"Don't think twice about answering that letter or obeying it. The occasion will not arise. Tomorrow night you shall see Eileen again—I give you my word for that."

A few minutes later the Saint was continuing his song as if nothing had happened.

The Saint had not brought his car, but that night he had no wreckage to deliver to the hotel in Elmbury Square, for at the close of play Detective Duncarry was showing no signs of unsteadiness or sleeping sickness.

"We'll take a stroll and get some fresh air, Dun, and then pick up a taxi."

The night was crisp and dry, and they walked slowly along the Embankment enjoying the peace of the evening. As they came near the Farringay Mansions, Simon pointed upwards.

"That's where Jack and I had our little heart-to-heart talk."

Detective Duncarry looked. Except for a light in the entrance hall, the flats were in darkness, and the face of the building was broken only by arrays of drawn blinds.

"It must have been a great moment when they both woke up," grinned the New Yorker.

"They're awake now," said the Saint. "See that?"

A pale light suddenly gleamed through three of the lowered blinds. Then one of the windows went dark again, and the other two followed suit.

"It beats me why they haven't made their getaway hours ago," said Duncarry.

The Saint glanced round.

"There's an empty taxi with its flag down—I guess they're making that getaway this minute. Fade into the sheltering shadows, Dun. I shouldn't think Jack's temper is any too good just now, and if he sees two suspicious characters hovering around he might do something sticky with a gun. I've promised to go and help Pat buy a new hat tomorrow and I couldn't cope with the problem on a stretcher."

The taxicab stopped before the front entrance, and the driver jumped down and swung his arms, for there was a frosty nip in the air. He had to wait several minutes for his fares, but they emerged in due course—a man and a woman. Duncarry, sheltering behind the iron cage round an almost leafless tree, almost wept as the cab moved away.

"This country of yours is a damned sight too civilised," he said bitterly. "I suppose over here you've got to have a written permission from the Prime Minister and the Archbishop of Canterbury to kill a mosquito. I've a gun in my pocket, and I could have settled the whole thing in two pops."

The Saint laughed.

"Keep off the grass," he said. "That couple of hoodlums is my preserve. But I'll tell you something, Dun."

Another taxi came prowling up beside them, and the Saint waved his hand and opened the door.

"What have you got to tell me?" asked Duncarry as they settled back and the cab moved forward.

"Only that I made one little tiny mistake a day or two ago," said the Saint. "And that was when I thought Eileen Wiltham had been taken in mistake for Pat. Didn't you say those lads made the cheap stuff on their own premises?"

"I did."

"Then everything is going to be quite all right," said the Saint comfortably, and lighted another cigarette.

9

From Sir Enoch Wiltham the Saint had gathered a few facts. The cargo that he had sold to the Kellory gang was to be picked up at sea by a ship lying three miles off Brest—the *Missolonghi*. The ship might have taken on the cargo more conveniently in a French port, and there was no law against it, but there was always the danger that a local American consul with a suspicious eye and an inquisitive nose might have queried the deal. It might have soaked into his head that the *Missolonghi*, registered at Sourabaya and flying Dutch colours, might not be travelling straight back to Java with so much throat oil on board. He might even, in his nastiness, have cabled across the Atlantic and advised the U.S. revenue cutters to sit up and take notice—and that would not have fitted in with Kellory's plans at all.

Simon Templar spent an idle day, and he was yawning over a book when two telegrams were delivered by the same messenger. The first was from Patricia Holm, who had been spending a couple of days with friends in Sussex, announcing that she would return about six that evening. The second telegram was more cryptic, but it only took him a second or two to absorb its meaning.

L. S. D. O. K. K. B. K.

The Saint gathered that Sir Enoch Wiltham's L.S.D. was O.K., and that was the information that he had been waiting for all day.

He rose thankfully, lighted a cigarette, and for a few moments paced the room in thought. Patricia would be driving her own car, and since she was a careful driver and the car was a good one she would probably arrive about the time she had promised. Simon wrote a note and propped it up conspicuously on the mantelpiece. Then he went to his bedroom, and remained there for some time.

In the gathering dusk, he slipped like a shadow into the street and hurried away.

The man who guarded the gate leading to Deepsands Wharf looked out of his box.

> *"In Plymouth town there lived a maid, (Bless you, young*
> *woman!)*
> *In Plymouth town there lived a maid,*
> *(O mind what I do say!)*
> *In Plymouth town there lived a maid,*
> *And she was mistress of her trade;*
> *I'll go no more a-roving with you, fair maid—"*

The man who trolled out the old sea shanty had a good voice, though at this time it was slightly disturbed by occasional diaphragmatic spasms. He was tall, unshaven, unwashed, and not too steady on his feet.

"Who are you, and where do ye think you're going?" demanded the gate-keeper.

"Me? Wotcher mean?" The dirty stranger took a couple of inches of black clay pipe out of his mouth. "I'm a dustman, a bleedin' stoker on the Miss—something. Never can remember the name. Something Irish."

"The *Missolonghi*?"

"That's right. *Miss O'Longhi*. Where is she?" The gate-keeper pointed.

"Down along there." "Thanks, mate."

The Saint continued his erratic passage. He crossed a single line of railway and saw his objective. The *Missolonghi* was made fast to the wharf bollards, and a crane with a noisy spluttering engine was swinging wooden cases into her—apparently Jack Farnberg and Vittorio had been making some other purchases besides the one in which the Saint had a deputy interest.

"For if that hooker isn't Vittorio's," figured the Saint, "my name is also Bobblibobblio."

She was a craft of about 1,600 tons, and had recently been painted a dirty drab tint over her original white. She was on the narrow side for carrying cargo, but the Saint knew that it did not require a *Bremen* to carry a large consignment of wines and spirits in cases that pack handily away.

The Saint refilled his cutty with black shag. He was not sure that Jack Farnberg and Vittorio Ardossi were within a hundred miles of the yacht—they might have eluded Teal's net and got away to France by boat or aeroplane to board the *Missolonghi* by the vessel that was to meet her at sea with Sir Enoch Wiltham's contribution—but somehow the Saint was prepared to bet that his first deduction was right. And there was a very good reason why it should be right, for although Farnberg and Ardossi might have made a slick getaway on their own, they would have found it quite a different proposition to make that getaway with Eileen Wiltham for an unwilling third. Besides which, there was the other little spot of business in which Eileen Wiltham was concerned still to be settled. Farnberg's note to Barringer had instructed him to meet a car that would be waiting for him at a certain point on the road north of St. Albans at six o'clock. There would be no one there to meet that car—the Saint had arranged for that—and he expected that Farnberg and Ardossi would remain on the north side of the Channel at least until after the time limit they had issued had expired.

None of the men at work on the wharf took the least notice of him as he sat on a bollard smoking his pipe. He could see the tallyman checking the cases as they swung over on the wire and slid down out of view. In the glare of the electric lights an occasional Lascar moved across the deck, a familiar figure enough in the vicinity of Deepsands Wharf and still more familiar farther down the River where great docks open their water gates to the shipping of the world.

Still the Saint sat and smoked. The only white man he saw was the checker with his book and pencil. But even if the crew consisted entirely of Lascars, the yacht would be officered by Europeans, for all the navigation Farnberg and Ardossi had learnt would not have steered a paper boat across a puddle.

There was a shimmer of heat above the funnel, and an upward trail of thin, grey smoke; but suddenly the banked furnaces were stoked and the funnel vomited a black sooty cloud. The craneman's mate was adjusting the chains to the last of the cases.

"'Arf a mo," cried the Saint. "I might as well ride as walk. Right away!"

He stepped on the cases, and the wire cable slid over the pulley.

"Don't forget to put me down in the book," he said as he sank past the tallyman. "Shove me down as dynamite."

The tallyman closed his book and went ashore, and the Saint walked forward along the alley-way. A Goanese boy, who was carrying a pail of steaming rice from the cuddy, looked up at him with a swift, slant-eyed glance. They were busy below, and the Saint could feel the growing heat of the stokehold.

He went on, humming a tune. The stevedores had been paid off, and the wharf was deserted. A heavy goods train rumbled through from the dockhead with a continuous warning whistle. Farther on, he found that the carpets had vanished from the saloon companion, and the saloon itself was strewn with packing cases.

The Saint put a match to his pipe, went on deck again, and ran into a stiff little man with a pointed beard and a braided pea-jacket with many buttons.

"Vot in Himmel you vant here?" he snapped. "You voss not on this ship belong."

The Saint's teeth gleamed in a smile through the grime on his face.

"I want all sorts of things, dear lad," he said. "I'm a dustman. I've got a ship somewhere, but I've lost it."

"Then get oud of this, or I kick you oud!"

"I'm on my way," said the Saint affably. "It may console you to know that the fact that I don't like your face has very little to do with it. Also, I wouldn't sail on your ship for fifty quid a week. And if I have any lip from you, dear heart, I'll knock those nice whiskers of yours through the back of your neck, and you can use them to fasten your collar."

He pushed the flat of his hand into the man's face and sent him staggering, and wandered over the gangway before the officer had regained his balance.

This meeting with the bearded man was unfortunate, for Simon Templar's brief but effective tour had led him to the conclusion that neither Farnberg nor Ardossi was at present on board the *Missolonghi*. The question of whether Eileen Wiltham was on board he had not had time to deal with—besides, he wanted to get all his eggs into one basket before the market opened. Somehow or other he would have to board the yacht again, and do his stuff on the high seas.

And then suddenly Simon Templar met his man under the light of a spluttering arc lamp, and heedless of what it might bring from the ship the Saint raised his voice in a crescendo of joy.

"Jack Farnberg—my little pet!"

Like a panther the Saint crouched and leapt, and his hurricane rush swept Farnberg from his feet and brought him crashing down. Though by profession a bootlegger, Farnberg never touched strong drink, and he was as strong as a bull. The Saint's hands were at his throat. Farnberg managed to get his other hand under him, but Simon Templar's left hand got there first and whipped the gun from his pocket. The Saint sent it flying through the air with a wide swing of his arm; it clattered on the side of the yacht and splashed down into the water.

With an upward jab of his fist at the Saint's face, and a violent writhe, the gunman managed to free his throat. And then they locked and rolled together, heaving and straining in the coal dust and litter under the arc lamp, with the railway lines gleaming behind them.

Over the rails of the *Missolonghi* a little knot of Lascars watched the fight with stolid faces.

The two men were well matched. The Saint tried half a dozen tricks that had rarely failed him, but though the Saint remained uppermost he failed to smash the grip of the gunman's thick, steel-muscled arms. Farnberg's face was smeared with coal-dust and slimy with sweat, and the plaster was peeling from the cut on his chin which the Saint's uppercut had inflicted at their last meeting; the Saint could see red murder glaring up at him in Farnberg's eyes, and he laughed softly.

They lurched over again, and something glinted white over the edge of the Saint's left sleeve—the ivory hilt of the knife strapped in its sheath to his forearm. He got his teeth to it, bit down until he had a firm grip of the hilt, and drew the knife with a sidelong jerk of his head.

Farnberg, squinting down, saw it pointed towards his throat, thin and razor sharp, and the dark eyes of the Lascars on the yacht's deck glinted expectantly. Farnberg's collar had been torn away, showing his naked throat and bulging windpipe. The knife dipped closer, and Farnberg saw death an inch away, and the horror of it made his mouth sag and froze the glare in his eyes.

The point of the knife came nearer still. It pricked the skin, drawing a drop of blood, and the watchers on the deck shuffled their feet. And then Simon Templar lifted his head and spun the knife away.

"I won't dirty a good knife on you," he said. "I'll have you with my hands!"

The big arc lamp suddenly spluttered more noisily, flamed in unusual brilliance, and then the carbons faded into dull red and the light went out.

With the menace of the knife gone, Farnberg gathered every ounce of his strength. In the gloom he tightened his grip, dug his heels into the slag and coal-dust, and heaved. Again they rolled over, and the Saint felt a momentary chill on his hand, the touch of polished metal. Then they rested again, gripped fast together, panting.

Then out of the darkness came a clash of opening gates, and the warning whistle of an approaching train, and the Saint knew the meaning of that chill touch on his hand.

They were lying on the rails.

Out of the tail of his eye, Simon saw a red globe of light sweeping forward out of the shadows. Startled by the unaccustomed darkness of the wharf, the engine driver opened the throttle of his whistle with a gush of steam that filled the air with shrieks.

"The train!" yelled Simon Templar. "We're in the fairway!"

Iron grips relaxed and they rolled clear—forced into a moment's truce by the threat of simultaneous annihilation.

They staggered up and stood panting. And then, when the train was less than three yards away, Farnberg leapt again. The Saint ducked in the nick of time, stepped back, and sent his fist smashing into

Farnberg's face. The gunman went reeling back. His heel caught against the line, and as he fell he screamed once . . .

The Saint searched for a cigarette mechanically. The train was coming to a stop with a grate and scream of overworked brakes, but the engine had already passed him—and passed Farnberg also . . .

Then the arc lamp spat, reddened, and glowed again into hissing light, and in the light the Saint saw Ardossi only a yard away with a gun in his hand. He dropped on one knee and shot himself forward almost in the same movement, and as he did so he heard two shots, one on top of the other.

The Saint was not hit, but Ardossi, tackled low and brought crashing to the ground, lay curiously still. Simon pulled himself to his feet and saw a familiar face.

"Your prophecies were certainly right," said the voice of Detective Duncarry. "It's lucky I came along. You ducked quick enough, but he had his bead on you, just the same."

He looked thoughtfully at the silent form of the Italian. "And I guess that was the last bead he'll ever draw, or my shooting isn't what it was."

The Saint nodded.

"Jack Farnberg's another—he had a nasty accident."

A moment later Chief Inspector Teal loomed up in his somnambulistic way.

"Miss Holm bust a valve spring, and came in a couple of hours late," he explained. "She found your note and phoned me, and we came right along. Why didn't you tell me you'd located this ship of Ardossi's?"

"I had a promise to keep," said the Saint. "Did you see me keep part of it? It was a really beautiful bit of accidental death, Claud."

"It would be," said Teal sleepily.

He was not alone. Charles Barringer came up in the company of a detective-sergeant and joined the group. The youngster's face was white and strained.

"What's happened?" he asked, and the Saint looked at him and grinned.

"Just a few brief moments of law and disorder," he said cheerfully. "I guess you'll find Eileen on that tub all right, if you look long enough. Push on and do the rest of the rescue yourself, son—and make it romantic!"

10

Chief Inspector Teal unlocked the door of the offices at Gaydon's Wharf, and a stale and musty smell emerged to greet him, slightly disinfected by the aroma of Duncarry's cigar.

"And now you've dragged us here, what have you got to say?" he inquired, without noticeable optimism.

"Blowed if I know," said the Saint. "Struggle with it, old dear. I've promised Wiltham to clear up the mystery, and I'm relying on you. I'm not a detective."

He sat down on the desk.

"Stuffy," he said. "An open window would improve matters. Will you oblige, heart's delight?"

"Look here, Saint," said Teal patiently, "I know you're not altogether the fool you look and sometimes pretend to be. You've brought us down here—"

"And I promised to pay for lunch afterwards, didn't I?" murmured the Saint sweetly. "Do you want the whole earth for nothing? Didn't I offer you the best lunch that London could provide?"

"You certainly did," said Detective Duncarry. The Saint raised his hat.

"Got a fag to spare, Teal?"

Teal threw the cigarette at him, and the Saint caught it adroitly in his mouth.

"Got a match, beloved?"

The matchbox came flying through the air with a rattle.

"Your taste in cigarettes is septic," said the Saint as he lighted one, and the American grinned.

The Saint clasped his hands over his knee and leaned back.

"Have you solved the great dragon mystery that I mentioned last time I was here?" he asked.

"Friste certainly had a kind of brass dragon ornament," Teal said. "I've verified that. What about it?"

"Granted that our mysterious murderer slipped in and out through a keyhole, as he apparently did," said the Saint, "he'd find the trick a bit difficult if he was taking that dragon with him, wouldn't he?"

Teal's eyes opened a little wider.

"Go on," he said.

"Do you really give it up?"

"Go ahead."

"Then I'll show you a little trick," said the Saint.

From his pocket he took a length of string. A brief inspection of the books in a rack beside the desk produced a bulky *Who's Who*, and this the Saint tied firmly to one end of the string. He carried the book over to the window and balanced it precariously on the outside edge of the sill.

"Can you lend me a gun?" he said, turning to Duncarry.

The American produced a weapon, and Simon, after cautiously unloading it, tied the other end of the string to the trigger.

Then he picked up the window pole and backed some distance away from the window without taking up more than half the slack of the string. He rested one end of the pole on the sill, almost touching the book that was balanced there; the other end of the pole he rested against his body. He gripped the automatic firmly between the open palms of his two hands, aiming it at the centre of his forehead, and the watching eyes of the two detectives suddenly gleamed with a wild surmise.

"So simple, really," said the Saint, and took one step forward.

The pole pushed the balanced *Who's Who* off the sill, and the book vanished into space. The string tightened with a jerk, and the empty automatic clicked as the jar fired the trigger. Simon dropped his hands, and the gun, towed by the sinking weight of the book, slithered up to the window sill and stuck there.

As the Saint stepped away, the window pole dropped to the floor inside the room.

"With a weight like that dragon at the other end of the string, the gun wouldn't have stuck—it would have gone right out," he said.

Chief Inspector Teal drew a deep breath and stared at him, blinking, and the Saint pitched his half-smoked cigarette into the fireplace.

"Friste seems to have been some hater," he said. "He'd lost the girl that he wanted more than anything else in the world, and it was Charles Barringer who had beaten him to it. He must have known that even if he killed Barringer he'd still have no chance himself, and perhaps he had a feeling that life wasn't worth living without that one thing that he wanted and couldn't have. But even then, for a fellow to hate hard enough to blow out his own brains in the loving hope and belief that someone would swing for it, and thereby solve two problems at once, is something new and strange and wonderful."

Chief Inspector Teal tilted back the bowler hat that he had not troubled to remove, and scratched his head. He gazed at the Saint with a kind of reluctant admiration in his eyes.

"Did you say you weren't a detective?" he asked.

"I did," said the Saint.

"I'm not sure that I couldn't run you in for perjury," said Mr Teal, and the Saint laughed.

He lighted one of his own cigarettes, and adjusted his wide-brimmed hat at its jauntiest angle.

"Do we move on to this lunch?" he suggested insinuatingly.

But it was never noted in the official records of the case that, as they sat at lunch, the Saint saw a look in Duncarry's keen eyes which suggested that a curious medley of thoughts and emotions were seething within the American. And to say that Simon Templar was surprised when Duncarry called round at Upper Berkeley Mews alone at six o'clock would be a blatant lie.

"I've always heard you were some thinker, Saint," said Duncarry. "And now I know it."

"Why?" asked the Saint innocently.

Duncarry reverently deposited an inch of ash from one of the Saint's cigars in an ashtray.

"Did you kill Friste?" he asked.

For a moment Simon Templar looked at him thoughtfully, and then the Saintly smile twitched at the corners of his mouth.

"I'm afraid I'd never heard anything about your brain, Dun," he said. "But you can have a testimonial from me any time you want it."

"You did kill him, then?"

"Of course I did," said the Saint. "Didn't I tell you he was a nasty man? I tapped on the door just after the last of the staff had gone, and he let me in himself. He was closing the windows and preparing to lock up, and he dropped the pole where it was found when he saw my gun. I rigged myself up to look like him at a casual glance and went past the doorkeeper next morning just to make it more mysterious; on the first landing I changed back into my usual beautiful self and went out again."

Duncarry nodded.

"And I suppose it's occurred to you that Teal may have the river under those windows dragged to prove your theory?"

"Naturally it has," said the Saint calmly. "I made a special trip out there last night to plant the whole outfit for him to find."

Duncarry trickled some smoke through his nostrils and frowned.

"That dragon's still worrying me," he confessed. "It's the one thing I haven't been able to figure out."

"Oh, that!" said the Saint. "That's easy. After the shooting I was drifting through a selection of Friste's private papers for some time, and that dragon got on my nerves. The sight of it offended me. So I simply heaved it through the window. But the time I spent figuring out a spare way of fitting all the facts together is neither here nor there." The Saint sighed, the sigh of a mind wearied after much righteous labour. "And now, what do you say we go and beat up the Jericho?"

THE NATIONAL DEBT

1

On a certain day in November, three men sat over the remains of dinner in the Italian Roof Garden of the Elysion Restaurant.

Outside, a thin drizzle of sleet and rain was falling. It lay like glistening oil on the streets, and made the hurrying throngs of pedestrians turn up the collars of their coats against the cold, and huddle numbed hands deep into their pockets. But in the Roof Garden all was warmth and light and colour. In the high, dim glass roof overhead, softly-tinted lights gleamed like artificial stars, and an artificial moon shone in the centre of the dome. Vine-decked loggias surrounded the room, and the whole of one wall was covered with a beautifully executed fresco of a Mediterranean panorama, bathed in sunshine. The Elysion had a reputation for luxury, and its Italian Roof Garden was the most elaborately comfortable of all its restaurants.

The three men sat at dinner in an alcove. The curtains of the window beside them were drawn, and they could look out on to Piccadilly Circus, a striking contrast to the sybaritic warmth of the room in which they were, with gaily coloured electric sky-signs flashing and scintillating through the wet.

The meal was over, and in front of each man was a cup of coffee, and a glass of the 1875 brandy of which the Elysion is justly proud, served in the huge-bowled bottle-necked glasses which such a brandy merits. They smoked long, thin, expensive cigars.

The man at the head of the table spoke.

"By this time," he said, "you are justly curious to discover how many of my promises I have fulfilled. It gives me great satisfaction to be able to tell you that I have fulfilled them all. Every inquiry has been made, and every necessary item of information is docketed here." He tapped his forehead with a thin forefinger. "My plans are complete; and now that you have tasted the brandy, which I trust you find to your liking, and your cigars are going satisfactorily, I should like your attention while I outline the details of my project."

He was tall and spare, with a slight stoop—you would have taken him at first glance for a retired diplomat, or a University professor, with his thin, finely cut face and mane of grey hair. He looked to be about fifty-five years of age, but the very pale blue eyes under the shaggy white eyebrows were the eyes of a much younger man.

"I'm waiting to hear the story, Professor," said the man on his left.

He was squat, bull-necked, and blue of chin, and his ready-made evening clothes seemed to cause him considerable discomfort.

The third man signified his readiness to listen by a silent expressive gesture with the hand that held his cigar. This third man was small and perky, his hair muddily grey and in the state tactfully described by barbers as "a little thin on top." A long, scraggy neck protruded from a dress collar three sizes too large.

"It is quite simple," said the man who had been addressed as "Professor," and leaned forward.

The other two instinctively drew closer.

He spoke for three-quarters of an hour, and the other two listened in an intent silence which was broken only by an occasional staccato query, a request for a repetition, or a demand for more lucid explanation of a point which arose in the recital. The Professor dealt smoothly with each question, speaking in a low, well-modulated voice, and at the end of the forty-five minutes he knew that the alert brains of the other two had grasped the essential points of his plan and adjudged it for what it was—the scheme of a genius.

"That is the method I propose to adopt," he concluded simply. "If either of you has any criticism to make you may speak quite freely."

And he leaned back with a slight smile, as though he was convinced that there could not possibly be any valid criticism.

"There's one thing you haven't told us," said the man on his right. "That is—where are we going to get hold of the stuff?"

"It cannot be bought," answered the Professor. "Therefore we shall make it."

The man appeared to continue in doubt.

"That's easy to say," he remarked. "Now consider it practically. Neither Crantor nor I know anything about chemistry. And you're clever in many ways, I know, but I don't believe you can do that."

"That is quite true," said the Professor. "I can't."

"A chemist must be bought," said Crantor.

The Professor shook his head.

"No chemist will be bought," he said. "We cannot afford to buy anybody. Bought men are dangerous. The man who can be bought by one party can be bought by another party if the price is big enough, and I never take risks of that sort. We will compel a chemist to do what we require, and it will be so arranged that we shall be insured against betrayal. I have already selected the agent. Her name is Betty Tregarth. She is very young, but she has taken a degree with honours, and she is a fully qualified analytical chemist. At present she is on the staff at Coulter's, the artificial silk people. I have made all the necessary inquiries, and I know that she has all the qualifications for the task."

The man with the long neck turned, and took his cigar out of his mouth.

"Do you mind telling us how you are going to make her do it, Professor?" he asked.

"Not at all, my dear Marring," answered the Professor, and proceeded to do so.

This plan also they were unable to criticise, but Gregory Marring remained dissentient on one point.

"It oughtn't to have been a woman," he declared with conviction. "You never know where you are with women."

The Professor smiled.

"That remark only demonstrates the crudity of your intelligence," he said. "My contention is that with a woman one can always be fairly certain where one is, but men are liable to be obstinate and difficult."

The point was not argued further.

"I may take it, then," suggested the Professor, "that we are prepared to start at once?"

"There's nothing to stop us," said Marring.

"Thasso," said Crantor.

The Professor turned and gazed thoughtfully out of the window. It looked very cold and bleak outside, but what he saw seemed to please him, for he smiled.

Three nights later, at about nine o'clock, Betty Tregarth was roused from the book she was reading by the ringing of the telephone.

"Is that Miss Betty Tregarth?"

"Yes. Who is that?"

"I am speaking for your brother, Miss Tregarth. My name is Raxel—Professor Bernhard Raxel. Your brother was knocked down by a taxi outside my house a little while ago, and he was carried in here to await the arrival of an ambulance. The doctors, however, have decided against moving him."

The girl's heart stopped beating for a moment.

"Is he—is he in danger?"

"I am afraid your brother is very seriously injured, Miss Tregarth, but he is quite conscious. Will you please come at once?"

"Yes, yes!" She was frantic now. "What address?"

"Number seven, Cornwallis Road. It is only a few hundred yards from your front door."

"I know. I'll be round in five minutes. Good-bye."

She hung up the receiver and dashed for a hat and coat.

Only an hour ago her brother had left the flat which they shared, having declared his intention of visiting a West End cinema. He would have passed down Cornwallis Road on his way to the tube station. She dared not think how bad his injuries might be. She knew the significance of these quietly ominous summonses, for her father had been fatally injured in a street accident only three years before.

In a few minutes she was ringing the bell of number seven, Cornwallis Road, and almost immediately the door was opened by a butler.

"Miss Tregarth?" he guessed at once, for there was no mistaking her distress. "Professor Raxel told me to expect you."

"Where's my brother?"

The man threw open a door.

"If you will wait here, Miss Tregarth, I will tell the Professor that you have arrived."

She went in. The room was furnished as a waiting-room, and she wondered what the Professor's profession was. There were a couple of armchairs, a book-case in one corner, and a table in the centre littered with magazines. She sat down, and strove to possess herself in patience, but she had not long to wait.

In a few moments the door opened, and a tall, thin, elderly man entered. She sprang up.

"Are you Professor Raxel?"

"I am. And you, of course, are Miss Tregarth." He took her hand. "I am afraid you will not be able to see your brother for a few minutes, as the doctor is still with him. Please sit down again."

She sat down, struggling to preserve her composure.

"Tell me—what's happened to him?"

Before answering, the Professor produced a gold cigarette-case and offered it. She would have refused, but he insisted.

"It doesn't take a Professor to see that you are in a bad state of nerves," he said kindly. "A cigarette will help you."

She allowed him to light a cigarette for her, and then repeated her demand for

information.

"It is difficult to tell you," said Raxel slowly, and suddenly she was terrified.

"Do you mean—"

He placed the tips of his fingers together.

"Not exactly," he said. "In fact, I have no doubt that your brother is in perfect health. I must confess, my dear Miss Tregarth, that I lured you here under false pretences. I have not seen your brother this evening, but I have been told that he went out a little over an hour ago. There is no more reason to suppose that he has met with an accident tonight, than there would be for assuming that he had met with one on any other night that he chose to go out alone."

She stared.

"But you told me—"

"I apologise for having alarmed you, but it was the only excuse I could think of which would bring you here immediately."

At first he had been geniality itself, but now, swiftly and yet subtly, a sinister element had crept into his blandness. She felt herself go cold, but managed somehow to keep her voice at its normal level.

"Then I fail to see, Professor Raxel, why you should have brought me here," she remarked icily.

"You will understand in a moment," he said.

He took a small automatic pistol from his pocket, and laid it on the table in front of her. She stared at it in amazement mingled with fear.

"Please take it," he smiled. "I particularly want you to feel safe, because I am going to say something that might otherwise frighten you considerably."

She looked blankly at the gleaming weapon, but did not touch it.

"Take it!" insisted the Professor sharply. "You are here in my power, in a strange house, and I am offering you a weapon. Don't be a fool. I will explain."

Hesitantly she reached out and took the automatic in her hand. Since he had offered it she might as well accept it—there could be no harm in that; and, as he had remarked, it was certainly a weapon of which she might be glad in the circumstances. Yet she could not understand why, in those circumstances, he should offer it to her. Certainly he could not imagine that she would make use of it.

"Of course, it isn't loaded," she said lightly.

"It is loaded," replied the Professor. "If you don't believe me, I invite you to press the trigger."

"That might be awkward for you. A policeman might be within hearing, and he would certainly want to know who was firing pistols in this house."

The Professor smiled.

"You could shoot me, and no one would hear," he said. "I ask you to observe that there are no windows in this room. The walls are thick, and so is the door—the room is practically soundproof. Certainly the report of that automatic would not be audible in the street. I can be quite positive about that because I have verified the statement by experiment."

"Then—"

"You may understand me better," said the Professor quietly, "if I tell you first of all that I intend to keep you here for a few hours."

"Really?"

She was becoming convinced that the man was mad, and somehow, the thought made him for a moment seem less alarming. But there was nothing particularly insane about his precise, level voice, and his manner was completely restrained. She settled back in her chair, and endeavoured to appear completely unperturbed. Then she thought she saw a gleam of satisfaction light up in his eyes as she took another puff at the cigarette he had given her, and her fingers opened and dropped it suddenly as though it had been red hot.

"And I suppose the cigarette was doped?" she said shakily.

"Perhaps," said the Professor.

He rose and went quickly to a bell-push set in the wall beside the mantelpiece, and pressed it.

Betty Tregarth got to her feet feeling strangely weak.

"I make no move to stop your going," said Raxel quickly. "But I suggest that you should hear what I have to say first."

"And you'll talk just long enough to give the dope in that cigarette time to work," returned the girl. "No—I don't think I'll stay, thanks."

"Very well," said Raxel. "But if you won't listen to me, perhaps you will look at something I have to show you."

He clapped his hands twice, and the door opened. Three men came in. One was the butler who had admitted her, the other was a dark, heavy-jowled, rough-looking man in tweeds.

The third man they almost carried into the room between them. He was tall and broad-shouldered, and he was so roped from his shoulders to his knees that he could only move in steps of an inch at a time unaided. His face was divided into two parts by a black wooden ruler, which had been forced into his mouth as a gag, and which was held in position by cords attached to the ends, which passed round the back of his head.

"Does that induce you to stay?" asked Raxel.

"I think it means that I am induced to go out at once, and find a policeman," said the girl, and took two steps towards the door.

"Wait!"

Raxel's voice brought her to a stop. The command in it was so impelling, that for a moment it was able to overcome the panicky desire for light which was rapidly getting her in its grip.

"Well?" she asked, as evenly as she could.

"You are a chemist, Miss Tregarth," said Raxel, "and therefore you will be familiar with the properties of the drug known as Bhang. The cigarette you half-smoked was impregnated with a highly-concentrated and deodorised preparation of Bhang. According to my calculations, the drug will take effect about now. You still have the automatic I gave you in your hand, and there, in front of you, is a man gagged and bound. Stand away, you two!"

The Professor's voice suddenly cracked out the order with a startling intenseness, and the two men who had stood on either side of the prisoner hurried into the opposite corner of the room and left him standing alone.

Betty Tregarth stared stupidly at the gleaming weapon in her hand, and looked from it to the bound man who stood stiffly erect by the door.

Then something seemed to snap in her brain, and everything went black; but through the whirling, humming kaleidoscope of spangled darkness that swallowed up consciousness, she heard, a thousand miles away, the report of an automatic that echoed and re-echoed deliriously through an eternity of empty blackness.

She woke up in bed, with a splitting headache.

Opening her eyes sleepily, she grasped the general geography of the room in a dazed sort of way. The blinds were drawn, and the only light came from a softly shaded reading lamp by the side of the bed. There was a dressing-table in front of the window, and a wash-stand in one corner. Everything was unfamiliar. She couldn't make it out at first—it didn't seem like her room.

Then she turned her head and saw the man who sat regarding her steadily, with a book on his knee, in the arm-chair beside the bed, and the memory of what had happened, before the drug she had inhaled overcame her, returned in its full horror. She sat up, throwing off the bedclothes, and found that she was still wearing the dress in which she had left the flat. Only her shoes had been removed.

The effort to rise made the room swim dizzily before her eyes, and her head felt as if it would burst.

"If you lie still for a moment," said Raxel suavely, "the headache will pass in about ten minutes."

She put her hand to her forehead and tried to steady herself. All her strength seemed to have left her, and even the terror she felt could not give her back the necessary energy to leap out of bed and dash out of the door and out of the house.

"You'll be sorry about this," she said faintly. "You can't keep me here forever, and when I get out and tell the police—"

"You will not tell the police," said Raxel soothingly, as one might point out the fallacies in the argument of a child. "In fact, I should think you will do your best to avoid them. You may not remember doing it, but you have killed a man. What is more, he was a detective."

She looked at him aghast.

"That man who was tied up?"

"He was a detective," said Raxel. "This is his house. I may as well put my cards on the table. I am a criminal, and I had need of your services. The detective you killed was on my trail, and it was necessary to remove him. I killed two birds with one stone. We captured him in the north, and brought him back here to his own house in London, a prisoner. His housekeeper's absence had already been assured by a fake telegram summoning her to the death-bed of her mother in Manchester. I then brought you here, drugged you with Bhang, and gave you an automatic pistol."

She was aghast at a sudden recollection.

"I heard a shot—just as everything went black . . ."

"You fired it," said Raxel smoothly, "but you are unlikely to remember that part."

Betty Tregarth caught her breath.

"It's impossible!" she cried hysterically. "I couldn't—"

Raxel sighed

"You will disappoint me if you fail to behave rationally," he said. "The ordinary girl might be pardoned for such an outburst; but you, with your scientific training, should not need me, a layman, to explain to you the curious effects that Bhang has upon those who take it. A blind madness seizes them. They kill, not knowing who they kill, or why. This is what you did. Your first shot was successful. Naturally, you fired first at the unfortunate Inspector Henley, because I had so arranged the scene that he was the first man you saw at the instant when the drug took effect! I might mention that we had some difficulty in overpowering you afterwards, and taking the pistol away from you. Henley died an hour later."

It was true—what Raxel had said was an absolute scientific fact. Granted that she had been drugged as he said, she would easily have been capable of doing what he said she had done.

"The terrifying circumstances," Raxel went on unemotionally, "probably hastened your intoxication. Your immediate impulse was to escape from the room at all costs, and Henley was the one man who stood between you and the door. You shot your way out—or tried to. It is all quite understandable."

"Oh, God!" said Betty Tregarth softly.

Raxel allowed her a full five minutes of silence in which to grasp the exact significance of her position, and at the end of that time the pain in her head had abated a little.

"I don't care," she said dazedly. "I'll see it through—I'll tell them I was drugged."

"That is no excuse for murder," said Raxel, "and taking drugs is, in itself, an offence."

"But I can tell them everything about it—how you brought me here. There's proof. You telephoned. The Exchange can prove that."

"The Exchange can prove nothing," said Raxel. "I did not telephone—I should be a very poor tactician to have overlooked such an obvious error. Your line was tapped, and the Exchange has no record of the call. I must ask you to realise the circumstances. You will be taken away from here, and the house will be left exactly as we found it. The only fingerprints will be yours on the automatic you used. Nothing has been moved, and Inspector Henley will be found lying dead here when the police are summoned by his housekeeper on her return. We have treated him very gently during his captivity; and before we leave, the ropes that bound him will be removed, so that from an examination of his body it will be impossible to prove that he was not completely at liberty, in his own house—as any man, even a detective, has every right to be. The scene will be staged in such a way that the detectives, unless they are absolute imbeciles, will deduce that Henley was entertaining a woman here, and that for some reason or other she shot him. The woman, of course, will be you. But your fingerprints are not known to the police, and there will be nothing to incriminate you unless I should write and tell them, in an anonymous letter, where they can find the owner of the fingerprints on the gun. I don't want to have to do that."

"Then what do you want?"

"Your loyal support," said Raxel. "Tomorrow you will go to Coulter's and tell them that your doctor has advised you to take a rest cure, as you are in danger of a nervous breakdown. You will tell your brother the same story. Then you will go down with me to an inn in South Wales, which I have recently purchased, and in which I have installed an expensive laboratory. There you will work for me— and it will only be for three weeks. At the end of that time, if you have done your work satisfactorily, you will be free to go home and return to your job, and I will pay you a thousand pounds for your services. Incidentally, I can assure you that you will not be asked to do anything criminal. I required a qualified chemist on whose silence I could rely—that is all. Therefore I took steps to secure you. I do not think any jury would be likely to hang you, but you would certainly go to prison for a long time—if you were not sentenced to be detained at Broadmoor during His Majesty's pleasure—and fifteen years spent in prison would rob you of the best part of your life. As an alternative to such a punishment, I think you should find my suggestion singularly acceptable."

"And what am I supposed to do in this laboratory?"

He answered her question in three brief sentences, and she gasped.

"Why do you want that?" she answered.

"That is no concern of yours," answered Raxel. "You will not be asked to associate yourself with my use of it, and so you need have no fear that you will be incriminating yourself. I promise you that when you have made a sufficient quantity for my ends, I shall ask nothing more of you. Nothing shall be done to stop your return home, and no one need ever know what you have been doing. You can, if you like, adopt me as your physician, and tell any inquirers that you are taking a cure under my personal supervision. We can arrange that. Also, I give you my word of honour that no harm shall come to you while you are in my employ."

He looked at his watch.

"It is half-past ten," he said. "You have hardly been unconscious an hour, though I expect you have been wondering how many days it has been. There is plenty of time for you to give me your answer and be back at the flat by the time your brother returns. And there is only one answer that you can possibly give."

2

Besides the huge flying Hirondel that was the apple of his eye, Simon Templar possessed another and much less conspicuous car which ran excellently downhill, and therefore he was able to descend upon Llancoed at a clear twenty miles an hour.

The car (he called it Hildebrand, for no reason that the chronicler, nor anyone else in this story, could ever discover) was of the model known to the expert as "Touring," which is to say that in hot weather you had the choice of baking with the hood down, or broiling with the hood up. In wet weather you had the choice of getting soaked with the hood down, or driving to the peril of the whole world and yourself while completely encased in a compartment as impervious to vision as it was intended to be impervious to rain. It dated from one of the vintage years of Henry Ford, and the Saint had long ago had his money's worth out of it.

On this occasion the hood was up, and the side-screens also, for it was a filthy night. The wind that whistled round the car and blew frosty draughts through every gap in the so-called "all-weather" defences, seemed to have whipped straight out of the bleakest fastnesses of the

North Pole. With it came a thin drizzle of rain that seemed colder than snow, which hissed glacially through a clammy sea-mist. The Saint huddled the collar of his leather motoring-coat up round his ears, and wondered if he would ever be warm again.

He drove through the little village, and came, a minute later, to his destination—a house on the outskirts, within sight of the sea. It was a long, low, rambling building of two storeys, and a dripping sign outside proclaimed it to be the Beacon Inn. It was half-past nine, and yet there seemed to be no convivial gathering of villagers in any of the bars, for only one of the downstairs windows showed a light. In three windows on the first floor, however, lights gleamed from behind yellow blinds. The house did not look particularly inviting, but the night was particularly loathsome, and Simon Templar would have had no difficulty in choosing between the two even if he had not decided to stop at the Beacon Inn nearly twelve hours before.

He climbed out and went to the door. Here he met his first surprise, for it was locked. He thundered on it impatiently, and after some time there was the sound of footsteps approaching from within. The door opened six inches, and a man looked out.

"What do you want?" he demanded surlily.

"Lodging for a night—or even two nights," said the Saint cheerfully.

"We've got no rooms," said the man.

He would have slammed the door in the Saint's face, but Simon was not unused to people wanting to slam doors in his face, and he had taken the precaution of wedging his foot in the jamb.

"Pardon me," he said pleasantly, "but you have got a room. There are eight bedrooms in this plurry pub, and I happen to know that only six of them are occupied."

"Well, you can't come in," said the man gruffly. "We don't want you."

"I'm sorry about that," said the Saint, still affably. "But I'm afraid you have no option. Your boss, being a licensed innkeeper, is compelled to give shelter to any traveller who demands it and has the money to pay for it. If you don't let me in, I can go to the magistrate tomorrow and tell him the story, and if you can't show a good reason for having refused me you'll be slung out. You might be able to fake up a plausible excuse by that time, but the notoriety I'd give you and the police attention I'd pull down on you, wouldn't give you any fun at all. You go and tell your boss what I said, and see if he won't change his mind."

At the same time, Simon Templar suddenly applied his weight to the door. The man inside was not ready for this, and he was thrown off his balance. Simon calmly walked in, shaking the rain off his hat.

"Go on—tell your boss what I said," said the Saint encouragingly. "I want a room here tonight, and I'm going to get one."

The man departed, grumbling, and Simon walked over to the fire and warmed his hands at the blaze. The man came back in ten minutes, and it appeared at once that the Saint's warning had had some effect.

"The Guv'nor says you can have a room."

"I thought he would," said the Saint comfortably, and peeled off his coat. There were seventy-four inches of him, and he looked very lean and tough in his plus-fours.

"There's a car outside," he said. "Shove it in your garage, will you, Basher?"

The man stared at him.

"Who are you speaking to?" he demanded.

"Speaking to you, Basher Tope," said the Saint pleasantly. "Put my car in the garage."

The man came nearer and scowled into Simon's face. The Saint saw alarm dawning in his eyes.

"Who are you?" asked Tope hoarsely. "Are you a split?"

"I am," admitted the Saint mendaciously. "We wondered where you'd got to, Basher. You've no idea how we miss your familiar face in the dock, and all the warders at Wormwood Scrubs have been feeling they've lost an old friend."

Basher's mouth twisted.

"We don't want none of you damned flatties here," he said. "The Guv'nor better hear of this."

"You can tell the Guv'nor anything you like after you've attended to me," said the Saint languidly. "My bag's in the car. Fetch it in. Then bring me the register, and push the old bus round to the garage while I sign. Then, when you come back, bring me a pint of beer. After that, you can run away and do anything you like."

It is interesting to record that Simon Templar got his own way. Basher Tope obeyed his injunctions to the letter before moving off with the obvious intention of informing his boss of the disreputable policeman whom he was being compelled to entertain. Of course, Basher Tope was prejudiced about policemen, and it must be admitted that the Saint used menaces to enforce obedience. There was the little matter of a robbery with violence, for which Basher Tope had been wanted for the past month, as the Saint happened to know, and that gave him what many would consider to be an unfair advantage in the argument.

Left alone with a tankard of beer at his elbow, the register on his knee, a cigarette between his lips, and his fountain-pen poised, Simon read the previous entries with interest before making his own. The last few names were those which particularly occupied his attention.

A.E. Crantor	*Bristol*	*British*
Gregory Marring	*London*	*British*

| *E. Tregarth* | *London* | *British* |
| *Professor Bernhard Raxel* | *Vienna* | *Austrian* |

All these entries were dated about three weeks before, and none had been made since. Simon Templar smiled, and signed directly under the last entry.

| *Professor Rameses Smith-Smyth-Smythe* | *Timbuctoo* | *Patagonian* |

"And still," thought the Saint, as he carefully blotted the page, "the question remains—who is E. Tregarth?"

3

The Saint went to bed early that night, and he had not seen any of the men he hoped to find. That fact failed to trouble him, for he reckoned that the following day would give him all the time he needed for making the acquaintance of Messrs. Raxel, Marring, and Crantor.

He got up early the next morning, and went out to have a look round. The mist had cleared, and although it was still bitterly cold the sky was clear and the sun shone. Standing just outside the door of the inn, in the road, he could see on his left the clustered houses of the village of Llancoed, of which the nearest was about a hundred yards away. On the other side of the road was a tract of untended ground which ran down to the sea, two hundred yards away. A cable's length from the shore, a rusty and disreputable-looking tramp steamer, hardly larger in size than a sea-going tug, rode at anchor. A thin trickle of black smoke wreathed up into the still air from her single funnel, but apart from that she showed no signs of life.

Simon returned to the inn, and discovered the dining-room.

It contained only three tables, and only one of these was laid. In the summer, presumably, it catered for the handful of holiday-makers who were attracted by the quietness of the spot, for there were green-painted chairs and tables stacked up under a tarpaulin outside; but in December the place was deserted except for the villagers, and those would be likely to eat at home. The table was laid for four. The Saint chose the most comfortable of the selection of uninviting chairs that offered themselves, and thumped on the table with the handle of a knife to attract attention. It was Tope who answered.

"Breakfast," said the Saint laconically. "Two boiled eggs, toast, marmalade, and a pint of coffee."

Tope informed him that the table he occupied was engaged, and Simon mildly replied that he was not interested.

"It's the only table that looks ready for use," he pointed out, "and I want my breakfast. You can be laying a table for the other guys while I eat. Jump to it, Basher, jump to it!"

Basher Tope muttered another uncomplimentary remark about interfering busies what thought they owned the earth, and went out again. The Saint waited patiently for fifteen minutes, and at the end of that time Tope re-entered, bearing a tray, and banged eggs, toast-rack, and coffee-pot down on the table in front of him.

"Thank you," said the Saint. "But you don't want to be so violent, Basher. One day you'll break some of the crockery, and then your boss will be very angry. He might even call you a naughty boy, Basher, and then you would go away into a quiet corner and weep, and that would be very distressing for all concerned."

Basher Tope was moved to further criticisms of the police force and their manners, but Simon took no further notice of him, and after glaring sullenly at the detective for some moments Tope turned on his heel and shuffled out again.

The Saint was skinning the top of his second egg when the door opened and a girl came in. She was wearing a plain tweed costume, and

Simon thought at once that she must be the loveliest thing that had ever walked into that sombre room. He rose at once.

"Good morning," he said politely. "I'm afraid I've pinched part of your table, but the cup-smasher who attends to these things couldn't be bothered to lay another place for me."

She came up hesitantly, staring at him in bewilderment. She saw a tall, broad-shouldered young man, with twinkling blue eyes, smooth dark hair, and the most engaging smile she had ever seen in her life. Simon, modestly realising that her amazement at seeing him was pardonable, bore her scrutiny without embarrassment.

"Who are you?" she asked at length.

The Saint waved her to a chair, and she sat down opposite him. Then he resumed his own seat and the assault on the second egg.

"Me? . . . Professor Smith, at your service. If you want to call me by my first name it's Rameses. The well-known Egyptian Pharaoh of the same label was named after me."

"I'm sorry," she said, at once. "I must have seemed awfully rude. But we—I mean, I wasn't expecting to see a stranger here."

"Naturally," agreed the Saint conversationally. "One's never expecting to see strangers, is one? Especially of the name of Smith. But I'm the original Smith. Look for the trade-mark on every genuine article, and refuse all imitations."

He finished his egg, and was drawing the marmalade towards him when he noticed that she was still looking at him puzzledly.

"Now you'll be thinking I'm rude," said Simon easily. "I ought to have noticed that you weren't being attended to. The service is very bad here, don't you think?"

He banged the table with his knife, and presently Tope came to answer.

"The lady wants her breakfast," said the Saint. "Jump to it again, Basher, and keep on jumping until further notice."

The door closed behind the man, and Simon began to clothe a slice of toast with a thick layer of butter.

"And may one ask," he murmured, "what brings you to this benighted spot at such a benighted time of year?"

His words seemed to bring her back to earth with a jerk. She started, and flushed, and there was a perceptible pause before she found her voice.

"Couldn't one ask the same thing about you?" she countered.

"One could," admitted the Saint genially. "If you must know I shall be strenuously occupied for the next few days with the business of being Professor Rameses Smith."

"The famous charlatan, humbug, and imitation humorist?" she suggested.

Simon regarded her delightedly.

"None other," he said. "How ever did you guess?"

She frowned.

"You were so obviously that sort."

"True," said the Saint, unabashed. "But in my spare time I am also a detective."

He was watching her closely, and he saw her go pale. Her hands suddenly stopped playing with the fork which she had picked up and with which she had been toying nervously. She sat bolt upright in her chair, absolutely motionless, and for the space of several seconds she seemed even to have stopped breathing.

"A—detective?"

"Yes." Simon was unconcernedly providing his buttered toast with an overcoat of marmalade. "Of course, I was sitting down when you came in, so you wouldn't have noticed the size of my feet."

She said nothing. Tope came in with a tray and began unloading it, and Simon Templar went on talking in his quiet, flippant way without seeming to notice either the girl's agitation or the other man's presence.

"Being a detective in England," he complained, "has its disadvantages. In America you can always prove your identity by clapping one hand to your hip and using the other to turn back the left lapel of your coat, thereby revealing your badge. It's a trick that always seems to go down very well—that is, if you can judge by the movies."

The colour was slowly ebbing back into the girl's face, but her hands were trembling on the table. She seemed to become conscious of the way they were betraying her, and began twisting her fingers together in a fever. In the silence that followed, Tope shambled out of the room, but this time he did not quite close the door. The Saint had no doubt that the man was listening outside, but he could see no reason why Basher Tope should be deprived of the benefits of a strictly limited broadcasting service. As for the girl, it was plain that the Saint's manner had started to convince her that he was pulling her leg, but he couldn't help that.

"Is there any reason," he said, "why I shouldn't be a detective? The police force is open to receive any man who is sufficiently sound of mind and body. I grant you I have a superficial resemblance to a gentleman, but that's the fault of the way I was brought up."

She had no time to frame a reply before there came the sound of voices approaching outside, and a moment later the door swung open and three men came in.

Simon Templar looked up with innocent interest at their entry, but he also spared a glance for the girl. Obviously she was one of their party, but she did not strike Simon as being the sort of girl he would have expected to find in association with the men he was after, and he had some hopes of getting a clue to her status with them by observing the way in which she greeted their arrival. And he was not unpleasantly surprised to find that she looked up furtively—almost, he would have said, in terror.

The three men, as the Saint might have foreseen, showed no surprise at finding him at their table. They came straight over and ranged themselves before him, and Simon rose with his most charming smile.

"Good morning," he said.

The tallest of the three bowed.

"Our table, I think, Professor Smith?"

"Absolutely," agreed the Saint. "I've just finished, and you can step right in."

"You are very kind."

Simon screwed up his napkin, dropped it on the table, and took out his cigarette-case. His eyes focused thoughtfully on the man who stood on the left of the tall man who appeared to be the leader.

"Mr Gregory Marring, I believe?"

"Correct."

"Six months ago," said the Saint, "a special messenger left Hatton Garden for Paris, with a parcel of diamonds valued at twenty thousand pounds. He travelled to Dover by the eleven o'clock boat-train from Victoria. He was seen to board the cross-Channel packet at Dover, but when the ship arrived at Calais he was found lying dead in his cabin with his head beaten in, and the diamonds he carried have not been heard of since. I don't want you to think I am making any rash accusations, Marring, but I just thought you might be interested to hear that I happen to know you travelled on that boat."

His leisurely gaze shifted to the man on the extreme right.

"Mr Albert Edward Crantor?"

"Thasso."

"The Court of Inquiry could only find you guilty of culpable negligence," said the Saint, "but the Special Branch haven't forgotten the size of the insurance, and they're still hoping that it won't be long before they can prove you lost your ship deliberately. The case isn't ready yet, but it's tentatively booked for the next Sessions. I'm just warning you."

The man in the centre smiled.

"Surely, Professor Smith," he remarked, "you aren't going to leave me out of your series of brief biographical sketches?"

"For the moment I prefer to," answered the Saint steadily. "At any moment, however, I may change my mind. When I do, you'll hear from me soon enough. Good morning, my lovely ones."

He turned his back on them, and walked quietly to the door, but he opened the door with an unexpectedly sudden jerk, and the movement was so quick that Basher Tope had no time to recover his balance and fell sprawling into the room. Simon caught him by the collar and yanked him to his feet.

"This reminds me," said the Saint, turning. "There was another man skulking around when I came down this morning. I know him, too."

The other three were plainly surprised.

"Everyone here of importance is present in this room," said Raxel. "You must be suffering from a delusion."

"The man I saw was no delusion," Smith replied. "His name is Duncarry. He's a much-wanted American gun artist who's come to England for his health. We still don't know how he slipped into the country, but he's one of the men I'm taking back to London with me when I go. There's a seat reserved for him in the hot chair at Sing Sing, and if you see him loafing around here again you can tell him I said so!"

With that parting shot he left them, and as he closed the door softly behind him he began to whistle.

"Now I guess I've rubbed the menagerie right on the raw!" Simon Templar thought cheerfully. "If my after-breakfast speech doesn't make those gay birds hop, I wonder what will?"

4

Simon spent the morning reading and drinking beer. The three men and the girl sat late over breakfast, and he guessed that his arrival had been the occasion for a council of war. When they came out of the dining-room, however, they walked straight past him without speaking, and ignored his existence. They went upstairs, and none of them even looked back.

They did not appear again for the rest of the morning, but at about twelve o'clock Detective Duncarry was ushered upstairs by Basher Tope. He was there twenty minutes, and when he came down again he was peeling off his coat and generally conveying the impression of being there to stay. Simon shrewdly surmised that the congregation of the ungodly was now increased by one, but Basher Tope took no notice of the Saint, and led Duncarry round in the direction of the public bar without speaking a word. It must be recorded that Simon Templar took a notably philosophic view of this sudden passion for ignoring his existence.

He lunched early, and Basher Tope returned exclusively monosyllabic replies to the cheerfully aimless conversation with which

Simon rewarded his ministrations. After about the fourth unprofitable attempt to secure the observation of the conversational amenities, the Saint sighed resignedly and gave it up as a bad job.

After lunch he put on his hat and went out for a brisk walk, for he had decided that there was nothing he could do in broad daylight as long as the whole gang were in the house. With characteristic optimism, he refused to consider what particular form of unpleasantness they might be preparing for his entertainment that night, and devoted himself whole-heartedly to the enjoyment of his exercise. He covered ten miles at a brisk pace, and ended up with a ravenous appetite at the only other inn which the village boasted.

They were clearly surprised by his demand for a meal, but after first being met with the information that they were not prepared to cater for visiting diners, he successfully contrived to blarney the proprietor and his wife into accommodating him. The Saint thought that that was only a sensible precaution to take, for by that time no one could tell what curious things might be happening to the food at the Beacon.

He ate simply and well, stood the obliging publican a couple of drinks, and went home about ten o'clock.

As he approached the Beacon he took particular note of the lighting in the upstairs windows. Lights showed in only two of them, and these were two of the three that had been lighted up on the night he arrived. There were few lights downstairs—since the change of management, the Beacon had become very unpopular. The Saint had gathered the essential reasons for this from his conversation with the villagers in the rival tavern. The new proprietor of the Beacon was clearly running the house not to make money, but to amuse himself and entertain his friends, for visitors from outside had met with such an uncivil welcome that a very few days had been sufficient to bring about a unanimous boycott, to the delight and enrichment of the proprietor of the George on the other side of the village.

The door was locked, as before, but the Saint hammered on it in his noisy way, and in a few moments it was opened.

"Evening, Basher," said the Saint affably, walking through into the parlour. "I'm too late for dinner, I suppose, but you can bring me a pint of beer before I go to bed."

Tope shuffled off, and returned in a few moments with a tankard.

"Your health, Basher," said the Saint, and raised the tankard.

Then he sniffed at it, and set it carefully down again.

"Butyl chloride," he remarked, "has an unmistakable odour, with which all cautious detectives make a point of familiarising themselves very early in their careers. To vulgar people like yourself, Basher, it is known as the knock-out drop, and one of the most important objections that I have to it is that it completely neutralises the beneficial properties of good beer."

"There's nothing wrong with that beer," growled Basher.

"Then you may have it," said the Saint generously. "Bring me a bottle of whisky. A new one—and I'll draw the cork myself."

Basher Tope was away five minutes, and at the end of that time he came back and banged an unopened bottle of whisky and a corkscrew down on the table.

"Bring me two glasses," said the Saint.

Basher Tope was back in time to witness the extraction of the cork, and Simon poured a measure of whisky into each glass and splashed water into it.

"Drink with me, Basher," invited the Saint cordially, taking up one of the glasses.

Tope shook his head.

"I don't drink."

"You're a liar, Basher," said the Saint calmly. "You drink like a particularly thirsty fish. Look at your nose!"

"My nose is my business," said Tope truculently.

"I'm sorry about that," said Simon. "It must be rotten for you. But I want to see you have a drink with me. Take that glass!"

"I don't want it," Tope retorted stubbornly.

Simon put his glass down again.

"I thought the lead cap looked as if it had been taken off very carefully, and put back again," he said. "I just wanted to verify my suspicions. You can go. Oh, and take this stuff with you and pour it down the sink."

He left Basher Tope standing there, and went straight upstairs. The fire ready laid in his bedroom tempted him almost irresistibly, for he was a man who particularly valued the creature comforts, but he felt it would be wiser to deny himself that luxury. Anything might happen in that place at night, and Simon decided that the light of a dying fire might not be solely to his own advantage.

He undressed, shivering, and jumped into bed. He had locked his door, but he considered that precaution of far less value than the tiny little super-sensitive silver bell which he had fixed into the woodwork of the door by means of a metal prong.

He had blown out the lamp, and he was just dozing when the first alarm came, for he heard the door rattle as someone tried the handle. There followed three soft taps which he had to strain to hear.

With a groan, Simon flung off the bedclothes, lighted the lamp, and pulled on his dressing-gown. Then he opened the door.

The girl he had met that morning stood outside, and she pushed past him at once and closed the door behind her. The Saint seemed shocked.

"Don't you know this is most irregular?" he demanded reprovingly.

"I haven't come here to be funny," she flashed back in a low voice. "Listen to me—were you talking nothing but nonsense this morning?"

"Not altogether," replied Simon cautiously. "Although I don't mind admitting—"

"You're a detective?"

"Er—occasionally," said Simon modestly.

The girl bit her lip.

"Who are you after?" she asked.

Simon's eyebrows went up.

"I'm after one or two people," he said. "Marring and Crantor, for instance, I hope to include in the bag. But the man I'm really sniping for is Bunnywugs."

"You mean Professor Raxel?"

"That's what he calls himself now, is it? I've heard him spoken of by a dozen different names, but he's best known as the Professor. He has a certain reputation."

The girl nodded.

"Well," she said, "you gave the gang some pretty straight warnings at breakfast. Now I'm warning you. If the Professor's got a reputation, you can take it from me he's earned it. You've bitten off a lot more than you can chew, Smith, and if you go on playing the fool like this it'll choke you!"

"Rameses is rather a mouthful, I grant you, so my friends usually call me Simon," said the Saint wistfully.

The girl stamped her foot.

"You can be funny at breakfast tomorrow, if you live to eat it," she shot back. "For God's sake—can't you see what danger you're in?"

"Now I come to think of it," murmured the Saint, "you must have a name, too."

"Tregarth's my name," she told him impatiently.

"It must have been your father's," said the Saint with conviction. "Tell me—what else do the family call you to distinguish you from him?"

"Betty Tregarth."

Simon held out his hand.

"Thanks, Betty," he said seriously. "You're rather a decent kid. I'm sorry you're mixed up in this bunch of bums."

"I'm not!" she began hotly, and then suddenly fell silent with her face going white, for she realised how impossible it would be to tell him the true circumstances.

And the realisation cut her like a knife, for Simon Templar was smiling at her in a particularly nice way; and she knew at once that if there was one man in the whole world whom she might have trusted with such a story as hers, it was the smiling young man with the hell-for-leather blue eyes who stood before her arrayed in green pyjamas and a staggering silk dressing-gown that would have made Joseph's coat look like a suit of deep mourning. And by the cussedness of Fate it had had to so happen that he was also one of the few men in the world in whom she could not possibly confide. She felt hot tears stinging her eyelids—tears that she longed to shed, and could not.

"Shake, Betty," said the Saint gently, and she took his hand.

He looked down at her, still smiling in that particularly nice way.

"Thanks for coming," he said. "But it's no use, though—I'm staying here as long as the job takes. If you'll adopt me as a sort of honorary uncle and take my advice, you'll get out of this as quick as you can. Pack your bag tonight, and hike for the station first thing tomorrow morning. That's a straight tip. And if you do decide to get out, and the other tumours cut up queer, just blow me the wink, and I'll see you through. That's a promise."

He opened the door for her, and he had to let go her hand to do it.

"Goodnight," said the Saint.

"Goodnight," she said with quivering lips and an ache in her throat.

He closed the door on her, and she heard the key turn in the lock.

5

He rolled back into bed again, blew out the lamp, snuggled down, and he was asleep in a few minutes. The prospect of being the object of the attentions of other nocturnal visitors not so kindly disposed towards him failed to disturb his slumbers, for he knew exactly how far he could trust his powers of sleeping as lightly as he wished to.

His confidence was justified; for when, three hours later, the door began to swing open under the impulse of a steady hand, the almost inaudible *ting!* of the little bell he had attached to it was sufficient to rouse him, and in an instant he was wide awake.

He pushed back the blankets and slid soundlessly out of bed, taking with him the electric torch and automatic pistol which were under his pillow.

The room was in pitchy darkness. The Saint waited a moment until he judged that the intruder was right inside the room, and then switched on his torch. It picked up the figure of Basher Tope, advancing cat-footed towards the bed, and in Basher Tope's right hand was the instrument which had won him his nickname—a wicked-looking blackjack.

"Hullo, Basher!" said the Saint brightly. "Come to hear a bedtime story from Uncle Rameses?"

For answer Tope leapt, swinging his bludgeon, but the blinding beam of light that concentrated in his eyes was extinguished suddenly, and he struck empty air. He felt his way round cautiously, and found the bed empty. Then he heard a mocking laugh behind him, and spun round. The torch was switched on again, and focused him from the other side of the room.

"Blind Man's Buff," said the Saint's cheery voice, out of the darkness. "Isn't it fun?"

Then Simon heard a sound from the door on his left, and whirled the beam round. The door had opened and closed again, and now Professor Bernhard Raxel stood with his back to it, and in his hand was an automatic pistol with a silencer screwed to the muzzle.

Raxel fired six times all round the light, and it was quite certain that in whatever contorted position Simon Templar had been holding that torch one of the bullets would have found its mark. But Simon Templar was not holding the torch at all; and when Raxel's automatic was empty Simon struck a match and revealed himself in the opposite corner of the room—revealed, also, was the electric torch lying on its side on the table where he had put it down.

"That's a new one on you, I'll bet!" said the Saint.

He lighted the lamp, put on his dressing-gown, and ostentatiously dropped his gun into a pocket. Tope looked inquiringly at the Professor, and Raxel shook his head.

"You can go, Basher."

"You can go also, Raxel," said the Saint. "It's two o'clock in the morning, and I want to get some sleep. Run away, and save up your little speech for breakfast."

Raxel inclined his head.

"Tonight was intended to be a warning to you," he said. "It was purely on the spur of the moment that I resolved to turn the warning into a permanent prohibition. It was clever of you to think of leaving your torch on the table. It is even flattering to remember that you did me the honour of crediting me with having heard before of the time-honoured device of holding the torch at arm's-length away from you. But next time I may be a little cleverer than you."

"There won't be a next time," said the Saint. "You ought to know that it was a fool thing to do, to come to my room and try to put me out tonight, but it was no more than I expected. Now be sensible about it, sonny boy. I've got a little more to learn about you yet, and so you can carry on until I've learnt it. But you can't kill me, and you needn't think I'm afraid of being killed. You made a bad break when you overlooked the railway ticket to Llancoed in Henley's wallet. That makes you hop!"

"You're talking in riddles," said Raxel coldly.

"You know the answer to 'em," said Simon. "I could run you in now for attempted murder, but I'm not going to because I want you for something much bigger. I'm going to give you just enough rope to hang yourself. Meanwhile, you will leave me alone. Everyone at Scotland Yard knows that I'm here and you're here, and if I happen to die suddenly, or do a mysterious disappearance, they'd have you in about two shakes of a sardine's trailing edge. Now get out—and stay out."

Raxel went to the door.

"And finally," Simon called after him, as a parting shot, "tell Basher not to put any more butyl in my beer. It kind of takes the edge off my thirst!"

The Saint breakfasted alone the next morning, but he waited about the inn for some time afterwards in the hope of seeing the girl. Crantor and Marring came down, and the cheerful "good morning" with which he greeted each of them was replied to in a surly mutter. Raxel followed, and remarked that it was a nice day. The Saint politely agreed. But the girl did not come down, and half an hour later he saw Basher bearing a tray upstairs, and gave it up and went out. His walk did not seem so satisfying to him that morning as it had the previous afternoon, for he was honestly worried about his first visitor of the night before. He made a point of being late for luncheon but although the three men were sitting at their usual table (the Saint found that a separate table had been prepared for himself) the girl was not with them. He took his time over the meal, having for the moment no fear that his food might have been tampered with, and sat on for an hour after the other three had left, but Betty Tregarth failed to make an appearance.

When he had at last been compelled to conclude that she was lunching as well as

breakfasting in her room, he went upstairs to his own room to think things out. There, as soon as he opened the door, a scene of turmoil met his eye. The suitcase he had brought was open on the floor, empty, and all its contents were strewn about the place in disorder. The search had been very comprehensive—he noticed that even the lining of the bag had been ripped out.

"Life is certainly very strenuous these days," sighed the Saint mildly, and began to clear up the mess.

When he had finished, he lighted the fire and sat down in a chair beside it to smoke a cigarette and review the situation.

He ended up exactly where he started, for everything there was to say had been said at two o'clock that morning. His entry had been staged with a deliberate eye to its effect—it would have been practically impossible to pretend to be an entirely innocent tourist for long, in any case, even if the first man he met had not put into his head the old trick of posing as a detective. And if he had to introduce himself flatly as a detective, the obvious course was to do it with a splash, and the Saint was inclined to congratulate himself on having made a fairly useful splash, as splashes go. But there it ended. Having made his splash he could only sit tight and wait.

Simon Templar was prepared to back himself against all comers in a patient-waiting competition. That decided, he raked some magazines out of his bag and sat down to read.

At half-past seven he washed, brushed his hair carefully, and went down to dinner full of hope. But once again he was unrewarded by a glimpse of the mysterious Betty Tregarth.

He sat out the other three, but they rose and left the table at last, and the girl had not joined them. The Saint stopped Raxel as he passed on his way to the door.

"I hope you have not suffered a bereavement," he said solicitously.

Raxel seemed puzzled.

"Miss Tregarth," explained the Saint.

"You mean my secretary?" said Raxel. "No, she has not been with us today."

A flicker of hope fired up deep down inside Simon Templar.

"Unfortunately," volunteered Raxel smoothly, "she has been indisposed. Nothing serious—a severe cold, with a slight temperature—but in this weather I thought it advisable to keep her in bed."

Simon watched the three men go with mixed feelings. The Professor had been just a little too aggressively plausible. His manner had indicated quite clearly that whether Simon Templar chose to believe that Betty Tregarth was indisposed or not, his interest in her was not appreciated and would be discouraged.

Not that that worried the Saint.

When he went up to bed that night he made a careful search of the more obvious hiding-places in his room, and found what he had expected to find, tucked into the pocket of his pyjama-coat. It was a rough plan of the upper part of the house, and each room was marked with initials to indicate the occupant. One room was marked with a cross, and against this was a scrawled note.

Kept locked. R., M., and C. go in occasionally.
T. is there nearly all day.

The Saint studied the plan until all its details were indelibly photographed on his brain, and then dropped it on the fire and watched it burn. Then he went to bed.

He woke at four o'clock, got up, and dressed. He slipped his automatic into his hip pocket, took his torch in his hand, opened the door silently, and stole out into the corridor.

6

His first objective was the room which had been marked "T" on the plan. Trying the handle with elaborate precautions against noise, he found, as he expected, that the door was locked. But the locks on the doors were old-fashioned and clumsy, as he had discovered by some preliminary experiments in his own room, and it only took him a moment to open that lock with a little instrument which he carried. He passed in, and closed the door softly behind him. The ray of his torch found the bed, and he stole across and roused the girl by shining the light close to her eyes. She stared, and the Saint switched out the light and clapped a hand swiftly over her mouth.

"Don't scream!" he whispered urgently in her ear. "It's only me—Smith."

She lay still, and Simon took his hand from her lips and switched on the torch again.

"Talk in a whisper," he breathed, and she nodded understandingly. "Listen—have you really been ill?"

She shook her head.

"No. They're keeping me here—I was caught coming back from your room last night. How did you get in?"

Simon gave her a glimpse of the skeleton key which he had spent part of the afternoon twisting out of a length of stout wire.

"Have you thought of getting away?" he asked, "I'll smuggle you out now, if you care to try it."

"It's no good," she said.

Simon frowned.

"You're being kept here a prisoner, and you don't want to escape?" he demanded incredulously.

"I'm not a prisoner," she replied. "It's just that they found out I'd got enough humanity in me to risk something to save you. If you went away I'd be free again at once."

"And you'd rather stay here?"

"Where could I go?" she asked dully.

Instantly he was moved to pity. She seemed absurdly young, like a child, lying there.

"Haven't you any—people?"

"None that I can go back to," she said pitifully, desperately. "You don't know how it is . . ."

"I guess I do," said the Saint gently, even if he was wrong. "But maybe I could find you some friends who'd help you."

She smiled a little.

"It wouldn't help," she said. "It's nice of you, but I can't tell you why it's impossible. Go on with what you've got to do, if you're too reckless to get out while there's time. Don't think anything more about me, Mr Smith."

"Simon."

"Simon."

"I never knew how revolting 'Mr. Smith' sounded until you said it just now," he remarked lightly, but he was not thinking of trivialities.

Presently he said, "There's another room I was meaning to visit tonight, but maybe you can save me the trouble. I'm told it's kept locked, but you spend best part of the day there. What's inside?"

Her eyes opened wide, and she shrank away from him.

"You can't go in there!"

"I hope to be able to," said the Saint. "The little gadget that let me in here—"

"You can't! You mustn't! If Raxel knew that you knew what's in there he'd take the risk— he'd kill you!"

"Raxel need not know," said the Saint. "I shall try not to advertise the fact that I'm going in there, and I shan't talk to him about it afterwards—unless what I find in there is good enough to finish up this little excursion. Anyhow," he added, watching her closely, "what can there be in that room that you can spend every day with, and yet it would be fatal for me to see it?"

"I can't tell you . . . but you mustn't go!"

Simon looked straight at her.

"Betty," he said, "as I've told you before, you're heading for trouble. I've heard of real tough women who looked like angels, but I've never really believed in them. If you're that sort, I'll eat the helmet off every policeman in London. I don't know why you're in this, but even if you are as free as you say, you don't seem to be enjoying it. I'm giving you a chance. Tell me everything you know, help me all you can, and when the crash comes I'll guarantee to see you through it. You can take that as official."

She moved her head wearily.

"It's useless . . ."

"You mean Raxel's got some sort of hold over you?"

"If you like."

"What is it?"

"I can't tell you," she said hopelessly.

The Saint's mouth tightened.

"Very well," he said. "On your own head be it. But remember my offer—it stays open till the very last moment."

He rose, and found her hand clutching his wrist.

"Where are you going?" she asked frightenedly.

"To unlock that door, and find out what's in this mysterious room," said the Saint, a trifle grimly. "I think I told you that before."

"You can't. These locks are easy, but there's a special lock on that door."

"And right next door is an empty room, and there's nobody else but myself on that side of the house. Also, there's plenty of ivy, and it looks pretty strong to me. I don't think the window will keep me waiting outside for long."

He disengaged her hand, and stepped away a little so that she could not grab him again.

"I'll lock your door when I go out," he said.

He went out, and she had not tried to call him back. It was the work of a few moments only to re-lock the door from the outside, and then he stole across the corridor to the door of the room which he had marked down because of its window, which was separated by no more than a couple of yards from the window of the locked room.

The ivy, as he had guessed, was strong; and as he had said, there was no one but himself sleeping on that side of the house, so that the noise he made was of no consequence. Better still, the Professor, when fitting the special lock to the door of the mystery room, had clearly overlooked the possibilities that the ivy-covered walls presented to an active young man, and the catch of the window was not even secured.

Simon slid up the sash cautiously, and slithered over the sill. Then he switched on his torch, and his jaw dropped.

The centre of the room was occupied by a rough wooden bench, and on this was set up a complicated arrangement of retorts, condensers, aspirators, and burners. They seemed to form a connected chain, as if they were intended for the distillation of some subtle chemical substance which was submitted to various processes of blending and refinement during the course of its passage through the length of the apparatus. The chain terminated in a heavy cylinder such as oxygen is supplied in.

Simon studied the arrangement attentively; but he was no chemist, and he could make nothing of it. In his cautious way, he decided not to touch any of the components, for he appreciated that any chemical process which had to be surrounded with so much secrecy might possibly be pregnant with considerable danger for the ignorant meddler, and the association of Bernhard Raxel with the mystery would not have encouraged anyone to imagine that all those elaborate precautions had been taken to protect the secret of the manufacture of some new kind of parlour fireworks to amuse the children. But the Saint did take the liberty of peering closely at the apparatus, and the result was somewhat startling—so startling that it was some time before he was in a condition to pass on to the examination of the rest of the room.

On another bench, against one wall, was a row of glass bottles, unlabelled, containing an assortment of crystals, powders, and liquids, none of which had an appearance with which the Saint was familiar.

This, then, was the secret. A comprehensive tour revealed nothing more, and Simon, his object accomplished, prepared to go. He lighted a cigarette and hesitated over his departure for a few moments, but he could think of nothing that a longer stay might achieve, and presently he accepted the inevitable with a shrug. Yet that delay had certain consequences— he was so absorbed with his problem that he did not visualise those consequences that night.

He returned to his own room as stealthily as he had left it, but the house remained shrouded in unbroken silence. The Saint's careful and expert examination had revealed a neat and inconspicuous burglar alarm attached to the door of the locked room. This, he had divined immediately, worked a buzzer under Raxel's own pillow, and therefore Raxel would have no fear that the Saint would be able to make an attempt to discover his secret without automatically calling the attention of the whole house to his nocturnal prowling. In which comfortable belief Professor Bernhard Raxel was beautifully and completely wrong.

Simon climbed into bed, and for the first time in his life failed to fall asleep immediately. He wanted to know what sinister secret lay behind the mysterious laboratory in that house, and most of all he wanted to know why Betty Tregarth should spend most of her time there. Betty Tregarth wasn't likely to be a willing associate of a man like the Professor—he was ready to swear to that. Was it possible that she had some special knowledge of chemistry, and had been blackmailed or coerced into assisting the Professor? . . . And then Simon Templar suddenly remembered the curious feeling that had come over him when he was peering at the apparatus in the locked room, and gasped aloud in a blinding blaze of understanding.

7

He was up early next morning, and the first thing he did was to go down, to the village post office. He got a call through to London, to a friend who could help to answer some of the questions that were bubbling through his brain. And what he heard fascinated him.

It was on his way back to the Beacon that he suddenly recalled a detail of his delay the previous night, and therefore the immediate development failed to surprise him.

He had just finished breakfast when Raxel, Marring, and Crantor entered the dining-room, and Simon saw at once from their bearing that they had already made an interesting discovery. Raxel came straight over to his table, and the other two followed.

"Good morning," said the Saint, in his cheerful way.

"Good morning, Mr Smith," said the Professor. "I am sorry to hear that you walk in your sleep."

Simon looked blank.

"So am I," he said. "Do I?"

"I think so," said the Professor, and an automatic pistol showed in his hand. "Please put your hands up, Mr Smith—I have just seen your cigarette-ash on the floor of the laboratory."

Simon rose, yawning, with his arms raised.

"Anything to oblige," he murmured. "Have you put it under the microscope and discovered the brand of tobacco?"

"That is not what is puzzling me just now," said the Professor blandly. "Search him, Marring. We have already ransacked your room, Mr Smith, and the letter which I was expecting to find was not there, so that if you have written it, it is likely to be on your person."

Simon submitted to the search without protest, and smiled at the look of savagely restrained consternation that broke momentarily through Raxel's mask of suavity when the search proved fruitless. "Rather jumping to conclusions, weren't you?" he suggested mildly.

Basher Tope stood in the doorway.

"I saw him go out before breakfast," said Tope clamorously. "He went down to the village. He must have used the telephone."

For a moment Simon thought Raxel would shoot, and keyed himself up for a desperate grab at the gun the Professor carried. But with a tremendous effort the man controlled himself, and the Saint smiled again.

"That's where you're stung, isn't it, dear one?" he drawled. "And now, let me tell you the tragic story of the mutilated onion, which never fails to melt the iciest eye. Or are tears a tender subject with you?"

The Professor shrugged, and bowed gracefully, but his eyes were flaming with fury.

"It is certainly your point, Mr Smith," he said in an icily level voice.

Without another word he turned, and went on to his own table, the other two following, and then Simon knew that the hours in which he would be able to bet on remaining at the Beacon in safety were numbered.

Immediately the three men were seated, a buzz of low-voiced guttural argument broke out. Both Crantor and Marring seemed to be advancing suggestions. They spoke in a language which was included in the Saint's extensive repertoire, and he could follow the whole of their discussion. From the glances of baffled hate that were flung in his direction from time to time he reckoned that he had been more popular in his day than he was at that moment.

Raxel listened to the incoherent babbling of the other two men for some time with ill-concealed impatience, and then he silenced them with a wave of his hand.

"*Hören Sie zu*," he said, with a note of incontestable command in his voice, and spoke a few rapid, decisive sentences.

Out of these sentences Simon caught one word. The word was *töten*, and it did not require a German scholar to grasp the general idea. "*Wir müssen ihn töten*," Raxel had said, or words to that effect.

"So at last they've decided to kill me," thought the Saint, eating toast and marmalade. "Presumably my demise will be arranged at the earliest possible opportunity. Well, that means I've got them on the hop at last!"

However, the thought failed to disturb him visibly, and in a few moments he rose and left the room. Betty Tregarth had not put in an appearance, but he had not expected that, and so he was not disappointed. The venomous eyes of the other three men followed him out.

In the parlour he found a tall, lean-limbed man wielding a broom.

"Morning, Dun," said the Saint.

The man turned a leathery face towards him, and grinned.

"Morning, Saint."

"How are things?"

Duncarry grinned.

"O.K. so far. I haven't heard or seen anything to speak of—I don't think they're sure of me yet. You told me to lie low, so I haven't been nosing around at all."

"That's right," said the Saint. "Keep on being quiet. I've done all the nosing that need be done. But keep your eyes skinned. There's going to be trouble coming to me soon, I gather, and it's coming good and fast. So long!"

He drifted away.

There seemed to be no point in hanging about the inn that morning, and he decided to walk down to the George and have a drink. In the bar he remembered the ship which was anchored opposite the Beacon, and mentioned it to the proprietor.

"I think it belongs to one of the gentlemen up the road," that mine of local gossip informed him. "Gentleman of the name of Crantor. It came in here about a fortnight ago, and the crew all drove away in a car. I don't think there's anybody on board now."

"There's smoke comes up from her funnel," Simon pointed out. "You can't keep a fire going without somebody to look after it."

"Maybe there's a man or two just looking after the ship. Anyway, half a dozen men drove away with Crantor the day the ship came in, and he came back alone. One of the boys did ask what the ship was for—we don't get ships like that in here so often that people don't talk about it. That was in the days when some of the boys used to go up to the Beacon for their drinks, before the new boss there got so rude to them that nobody could stand it any longer. I think it was Bill Jones who asked what the ship was doing. Mr Raxel said they were working on a new invention—a new sort of torpedo or something—and they were going to use the ship for trying it out at sea. That might easily be true, because about a month ago a lorry came in and delivered a lot of stuff at the Beacon, and the drivers had a drink here on their way out of the village. Chemistry apparatus it was, they said, and Raxel ordered it."

The Saint nodded vaguely, and then suddenly he stiffened. The proprietor also listened. That sort of thing is infectious.

Simon went over and looked out of the window. His ears had not misled him—a rickety Ford truck was crashing down the street. It stopped outside the door of the George, and two men came in and walked up to the counter.

"Couple o' quick halves, mate," ordered one of them.

They were served. The drinks were swallowed quickly. They seemed to be in a hurry.

"Got a rush order," one of them explained. "A couple of boxes to get to Southampton to catch a boat that's sailing tomorrow morning, and all luggage has got to be on board tonight. Can you tell us where the Beacon is?"

"Drive on to the end of the road, and turn to your right," said the Saint. "You'll find it on your right, about three hundred yards up. What ship are these boxes going to?"

"Couldn't tell you, mate. All I know is that we've got to get them to Southampton by nine o'clock tonight. Cheerio!"

They went out, and after that the publican felt that he had lost his audience, for the Saint was noticeably preoccupied.

Half an hour later, the lorry clattered past the window again, and Simon followed its departure with a thoughtful eye.

He went back to the Beacon at about half-past twelve, and he was having a drink in the parlour preparatory to attacking luncheon, when he saw a fast-looking touring car driven round from the garage at the rear by Basher Tope. A moment later Raxel, Marring, and Crantor came out. Crantor was wearing a heavy leather coat, and appeared to be receiving instructions. Raxel spoke, and Crantor nodded and replied. Then he climbed into the car, and took the wheel. The others stepped back, and with a wave of his hand Crantor let in the clutch and went roaring out of sight eastwards along the coast road.

Raxel and Marring came in again, followed by Basher Tope, and Simon heard Raxel and Marring go through into the dining-room. He banged hopefully on the bell, and felt that luck was with him when Duncarry answered the summon.

"Another half-pint, Dun," said Simon, and tendered a pound note.

Duncarry was back in a moment with the replenished tankard and the change. There was some silver, and a ten-shilling note. When Duncarry had gone, Simon pocketed the silver, and unfolded the note. Inside the note was a slip of paper, and on it was written one word.

"Megantic."

The *Megantic*, Simon knew, was on the quick run from Southampton to New York, and he guessed that Duncarry must have been called in to help carry the trunks downstairs, and had noticed the inscription on the labels. But that wasn't particularly helpful, and Simon went in to his lunch a very worried and puzzled man. Theoretically, of course, there was no reason why Raxel should not take a consignment of xylyl bromide to New York if he had to take it somewhere, but on the other hand there was also no earthly reason that the Saint could see why he should.

8

"And, now, my dear Marring," said Raxel, "there is very little more to delay us."

Marring moved a couple of Bunsen burners to one side, and sat on the edge of the table.

"There is Smith," he said.

"I will attend to Smith," said Raxel. "Fortunately for us, he arrived on the scene a little too late. The boxes have already been despatched, and once Crantor has returned with his crew, we can embark on his ship and disappear. The police will not hurry—I know their methods. They will see no reason to make any special effort, and I shall not expect anything to happen before this evening. By that time we shall be on the high seas, and Smith will be—disposed of. Now that this place's period of usefulness is over, there is no reason for us to move cautiously in fear of a police raid."

"That's all very well," said Marring. "But what about the girl? Do you think she's as safe as you make out?"

Raxel frowned.

"Once, I was certain," he said. "Unfortunately, the arrival of Smith has rather shaken that certainty. I do not profess to be a psychologist, but I consider my intuition is fairly keen. The girl is now debating in her mind whether she can trust Smith with her secret. It may seem ridiculous to you that a girl could confess to a detective that she had committed a murder, and hope that he would help her. But she is fascinated by him, and that will have altered her outlook."

"Then what are you going to do?"

"That also has been arranged—I think, very neatly. We will deal with it at once."

He led the way out of the laboratory and across the corridor. After unlocking Betty Tregarth's door he knocked, and they went in.

Betty Tregarth was sitting in the chair by the fire, reading, but she looked up listlessly at their entrance.

"Oh, it's you," she said dully.

Raxel came over, and stood in front of the fire.

"I have come to tell you that you have now served your purpose, Miss Tregarth," he said, "and there is nothing to stop your departure as soon as you choose to go. I promised you one thousand pounds for your services, and I'll write you a cheque for that amount now."

He did so, sitting down at the table. She took the cheque, and looked at it without interest.

"Now," he said, replacing the cap on his fountain-pen, "I wonder what your plans are?"

"I haven't made any," said the girl, in a tired voice. "I don't know what I'm going to do."

"I understand," said the Professor sympathetically. "That was a difficulty in your path which occurred to me shortly after you'd started work, and I have given it a good deal of thought. In fact, I have prepared a solution which I should like to offer you. You may accept or reject it, as you please, but I beg you to give it your consideration."

She shrugged.

"You can tell me what it is."

"I suggest that you should leave the country, and start life afresh," said Raxel. "The thousand pounds which I have given you will provide you with enough capital to last you for several months, and that should give you plenty of time to find fresh employment. With your qualifications that should be fairly easy."

"But where am I to go?"

"I suggest that you go to America. In fact, I have taken the liberty of booking a first-class passage for you on the *Megantic*, which sails from Southampton early tomorrow morning. You may, of course, decline to go, but I think you would be wise to take it."

The girl spread out her hands in a weary gesture.

"America's as good as any other place," she said. "But I haven't got my passport down here, and there isn't time to go back to London for it. Besides, I haven't a visa."

"That also I have taken the liberty of arranging," said Raxel.

He produced a newspaper of the day before, and pointed to a paragraph. She read:

> "Burglars last night forced an entry into the first-floor
> flat at 202 Cambridge Square, Bayswater, occupied
> by Mr Ralph Tregarth and his sister . . . sister away in
> the country . . . bureau broken open . . . Mr Tregarth
> said . . . nothing of value taken . . ."

"The report was quite correct—nothing of value was taken, except this," said Raxel.

He took a little book from his pocket, and handed it over to her. It was her own passport.

"I caused one of my agents in London to obtain it," explained Raxel. "The following morning he took it to the United States Consulate and obtained a visa. There should now be nothing to stop you leaving for Southampton this afternoon. If you are agreeable, Mr Marring will drive you to Southampton tonight. You can board the Megantic at once, and go to sleep; by the time you wake up, England and all your fears will have been left behind."

Betty Tregarth passed a hand across her eyes.

"I've no choice, have I?" she said, "Yes, I'll go. Will you let me write a couple of letters?"

"Certainly," said Raxel obligingly. "In fact, if you would like to write them now, I will post them myself on my walk through the village this afternoon."

"And read them first, I suppose," said the girl cynically, "to see that there's nothing in them to incriminate you. Well, there won't be— you're quite safe. They'll be just ordinary good-bye letters."

Raxel waited patiently while she wrote two short notes—one to her brother, and one to Rameses Smith. She addressed the envelopes, and pointedly left the flaps open. Raxel smiled to himself, and stuck them down in her presence.

"I don't need to read them," he said. "The fact that you were prepared to allow me to do so proves at once that the precaution is not necessary."

"Will you let me say good-bye to Mr Smith?" she asked.

Raxel shook his head regretfully.

"I am afraid that is impossible, Miss Tregarth," he said. "It is the only privilege that I am forced to deny you."

She nodded.

"It doesn't matter, really," she said flatly. "I didn't think you'd let me."

"Circumstances forbid me," said Raxel, and put the letters in his pocket. "The car will be ready for you directly after dinner, if not before. You will remain in your room until then. In any case you would be busy with your packing. Good afternoon."

He left the room, Marring following him, and locked the door again on the outside.

9

At half-past five that afternoon Crantor returned. The Saint heard the car draw up outside the hotel, and opened his window. It was quite dark, but he could hear voices below, and several men seemed to be moving about in the road. Then the car was turned so that the headlights shone seawards, and they began to flicker. Simon read the Morse message: "Send boat." The men did not go into the hotel, but walked about outside, stamping their feet, and conversing in undertones. Presently a lamp winked up from the shore, and Crantor's voice could be heard gathering the men together. They set out to cross the patch of waste land that lay between the road and the sea—

Simon saw the torch which Crantor carried to light the way bobbing and dipping towards the edge of the water. He waited patiently, and saw lights spring out on the ship.

After some time the light came flickering over the foreshore like a will-o'-the-wisp, but it was Crantor alone who crossed the road and entered the hotel.

The Saint was about to close his window when the door of the hotel opened again, and three people came out. They could be seen in the shaft of light that was flung out into the road by the lamp in the hall. One was Raxel, the other Marring, in hat and coat, the third was a muffled figure in furs. Simon realised who it must be, and his lips hardened.

A moment later, Tope came out, carrying a couple of heavy suitcases. These he packed into the back of the car. Then the girl walked to the car alone, and got into the front seat. Raxel and Marring stood for a few moments on the doorstep. Their voices drifted clearly up to the listener above their heads. Only four sentences were spoken.

"You have not forgotten to pack your revolver, my dear Marring?"

"Is it likely?"

"Then, *au revoir*—and a pleasant voyage."

Marring chuckled.

"I shall breakfast with you on Thursday," he said. "*Au revoir*, Professor."

He went round to the driver's seat, and clambered in.

Simon Templar watched the car drive away. Raxel, standing on the step, watched it out of sight also, and then turned and went indoors. The door closed.

"Hell!" said the Saint.

The balloon was now fairly launched, and he'd been compelled to stand by and watch the performance. And the Saint hated standing by. Yet he'd had to let the girl go, and never make a move to stop her, or even try to get a word with her before she went, because he realised quite clearly that there was nothing he could have done. She must have known that he was in the hotel—even if she didn't, and she had been taken away against her will, she could have cried for help and hoped that he would hear. But she seemed to have left quite willingly. She had walked to the car of her own accord, and although she had not joined in the conversation of Raxel and Marring, there did not seem to have been any coercion. And he realised, of course, that he had nothing to go on, anyway—to all intents and purposes she had been one of the gang. The rest was merely theory—a theory which he would cling to till the bitter end, he admitted, but at the same time a theory which the girl herself had done precious little to encourage. If she'd wanted to see him before she left, she'd have tried to. She wouldn't have gone as quietly as that.

At that moment he heard the voices of Raxel and Crantor coming down the corridor outside. Simon slid noiselessly across the room, and stood motionless at the side of the door, in such a position that if it were opened he would be hidden.

His intuition had served him well, for he had hardly taken up his position when the handle rattled under somebody's hand, and there was a knock.

The Saint kept silence. The knock was repeated, and then the door opened. Simon held his breath, but Raxel only took one step into the room.

"He's not here," said the Professor's voice. "We might have expected that he was out. If I have correctly diagnosed the relationship between our Mr Smith and our Miss Tregarth, one might safely say that he would not have let her leave without trying to get at least a few minutes' conversation with her."

"Thasso," said Crantor. "He seems to spend most of his time out of doors, walking. I guess he's out on a tramp now."

"We shall be ready for him when he returns," said Raxel, and the door closed.

Simon breathed again. The ancient ruse of hiding behind an opening door had worked for the thousandth time in history. He waited a moment, and then opened the door a cautious two inches. He was in time to hear another door close farther up the passage, and crept out.

He padded down the corridor on tiptoe, listening at each door as he passed, and located the two men in the laboratory.

He paused, listening. Their voices came to him quite distinctly. Raxel was speaking.

"The *Megantic* makes a steady twenty-five knots. My inquiries have been very complete. Here is the route—I have marked it out in red ink for you. They sail punctually at six o'clock tomorrow morning. By six o'clock on Thursday morning they should therefore be—here."

"That's right," said Crantor. "Here, pass me those compasses. I'll just check that, and work out the position now."

There was a silence, and then Crantor spoke again.

"I've jotted down the position against your mark," he said, and mentioned some figures. "So that's that. We've only got to wait till Smith comes back, and then we can be off."

"I've told Tope to watch for him, and report as soon as he arrives," said Raxel.

"What are you doing about Duncarry?" asked Crantor.

"For a time," answered Raxel, "I thought of enlisting him. He seemed to me to have distinct possibilities. But I have since revised that opinion. It is just an idea of mine—I feel that Duncarry might be dangerous. We will leave him behind."

"Right," said Crantor. "My bag's packed. If yours is ready we might send them down to the boat now. Then we can beat it as soon as we've got rid of Smith."

Simon Templar turned the handle, and kicked the door open. He stepped into the room. Crantor jumped up with an exclamation, but the Professor was unperturbed.

"We have been expecting you, Mr Smith," he remarked.

"Then you've got what you wanted, old dear," said the Saint cheerfully. "Stick your hands up, both of you."

He showed his gun, and Crantor obeyed, but Raxel's hand went to his pocket, and Simon pressed the trigger.

Nothing happened.

"It is now your turn to put up your hands, Mr Smith," said Raxel, and his silenced automatic gleamed in his hand. "It was careless of you to leave your gun in your bedroom when you went to your bath this morning, but it gave me an invaluable opportunity of unloading it."

Simon's hands went up slowly.

"I congratulate you," he said.

"You flatter me," said the Professor. "It was really quite easy. On the other hand, I am able to thank you for saving us the trouble of waiting for you any longer."

The Saint smiled.

"If the bit of conversation I heard before I came in hadn't been so helpful, you might have had to wait a lot longer," he murmured. "However—since we're all happy, may I smoke?"

Raxel produced his own case.

"So," he remarked, "you are no longer mystified?"

"Well—no," admitted the Saint. "Not exactly. I never imagined you and Marring and Crantor went into partnership to discuss new ways of accelerating the growth of sweet-peas. On the other hand, I definitely didn't know what was going on, though I've been watching you ever since you teamed up. Then when I took a peek at your workshop—"

"You were enlightened?"

"To the extent of four or five candle-power," said the Saint carefully. "I won't say that I jumped to the meaning of the bottled onions right away, and the diphenylcyanoarsine was way beyond my scientific powers, but I got some expert advice that cleared a lot of air. And now you've answered the other questions, so that lets me out. It was only Betty Tregarth that I hadn't one good clue about."

"Ah—you were interested?"

Simon lounged against the wall. He had no idea what turn the situation would take next, so, characteristically, he declined to overheat his brain with the problem.

"I was curious," he said. "But even that riddle is rapidly untangling itself with the help of other information recently acquired. I seem to remember that when you murdered Inspector Henley, who was also interested in you, there was a woman in the house. At least, the police found traces of her presence, though they had nothing to help them to identify her. And it appears that Betty Tregarth is your tame chemist." The Saint's eyes rested thoughtfully on Bernhard Raxel. "Now suppose—just suppose—a trio of tough babies had figured out a dandy scheme of up-to-date piracy, using poison gas and all that sort of dope. They'd want someone to make the stuff for them, wouldn't they? Anyone out of the street can't walk into a shop and ask for half a dozen cylinders of assorted smells to be sent round right away in a plain van. And the number of crooked chemists isn't so colossal that people would be queuing up in front of your house to get the billet. But suppose you had located a very good woman for the job, full of qualifications and knowledge, but still feminine enough to be frightened—and then suppose you framed her for a murder that you were going to commit anyway, framed her well enough to convince her even if the police never noticed it—and then demanded her services as the price of your protection? It might work—women have been blamed fools before now—and a scheme like that would just suit your kind of brain—"

He read the accumulating confirmation in Raxel's eyes even while he was elaborating his theory, and laughed.

"That's about it, isn't it, Uncle?" he drawled.

Raxel nodded calmly.

"Your logic is admirable, Mr Smith. If you had not been so foolish as to take up this case, your powers might have won you a high position in your profession. As it is—" he shrugged. "I fear our time is short. Will you kindly precede us to the cellar?"

"With all the pleasure in life," answered the Saint politely.

They went down the corridor, and down the stairs in procession. On the ground floor, Crantor opened a door under the staircase, and went through, switching on a torch as he did so. The Saint saw a flight of stone stairs leading down into darkness.

"What's going to happen when I get down there?" he asked.

"We shall leave you," answered Raxel, "I do not think you will live very long."

He gave the Saint a glimpse of the small glass bulb that he had carried down with him from the laboratory—and Simon could recognise the contents of that on sight. And the Saint had led too full a life to doubt that Raxel's intentions were perfectly deliberate and cold-blooded. He knew that Raxel intended to kill him. For an instrument there was the twinkling glass bowl of concentrated death in the Professor's hand. And the quiet, unemotional ruthlessness of Raxel's voice was very real. But for that, the whole situation might have seemed like the last fragment of a grotesque nightmare; but the Professor's gentleness was more convincing than any vindictive outburst could have been.

"Nice of you," said the Saint thoughtfully.

"I'm sorry," said Raxel, although his deep-set, faded blue eyes showed neither sorrow nor any other trace of humanity. "I bear you no malice. It is simply that my interest in my own safety demands it."

Simon smiled.

"Of course, that's an important consideration," he murmured. "But I think you ought to do the thing in style while you're about it. There's a tradition in these matters, you know.

I've never been executed before, and I'd like this to be something I can remember. It's too late for breakfast, and I suppose it'd delay you too much to ask you to let me eat a final dinner, but at least you can give me a couple of bottles of beer."

Crantor came up the stairs again, and was visibly relieved when he saw that the Saint was still holding up his hands.

"Why don't you send him along down, Professor?" he demanded. "We haven't got a lot of time to waste."

"The conventions must be observed," said Raxel. "Mr Smith has asked the privilege of being allowed to consume two bottles of beer, and I shall let him do so. Tope!"

Basher Tope came shambling out of the bar, and the Professor gave the order. The beer was brought. Simon poured it out himself, and drank the two glasses with relish. Then he picked up the bottles.

"I'll take these with me," he said, "as mementoes. Right away, Professor!"

Crantor led the way down the stairs, and the Saint followed. Raxel brought up the rear.

At the foot of the stairs was a short flagged passage ending in a door. Crantor opened the door, and motioned to the Saint to enter. Raxel came up, and the two men stood in the doorway, Crantor lighting up the cellar with his torch.

It was fairly large, and at one end was a row of barrels. The floor was covered with stone paving, and the roof was supported by wooden buttresses. But the house was an old one, and Simon had banked everything on the walls not being bricked up, and his hopes went up a couple of miles when he saw that there was nothing but bare earth on three sides of the room.

He turned with a smile.

"Good-bye, Professor," he said.

"Good-bye," said Raxel.

His left hand swung up with the glass globe, and the green liquid it contained caught the light of the torch, and it shone like a monstrous jewel.

The next instant the bowl had smashed on the floor, and before the light of the torch was taken away Simon saw the green vapour boiling up from the stone.

Then the door slammed, and the key turned in the lock. The footsteps of Raxel and Crantor could be heard hurrying down the echoing passage and stumbling up the stairs; and Simon Templar, holding his breath, was knocking the bottoms off the bottles he carried, and packing them with earth torn from the walls of the cellar with desperate speed.

10

With the first bottle packed with earth, the Saint put the neck in his mouth, and used it to breathe through, closing his nostrils with his fingers. It had been a forlorn hope, but it had been the only thing he had been able to think of; and he remembered having read in a book that such a device formed one of the most efficient possible respirators. It was something to do with molecular velocity—the Saint was no profound scientist, and he did not profess to understand the principle. The main point was whether it would work effectively. He waited, breathing cautiously, while the luminous dial on his wrist-watch indicated the passing of ten minutes. At the end of that time he felt no distress other than that caused by the difficulty of squeezing air through the packed earth, and decided that his improvised gas-mask was functioning satisfactorily.

He turned his attention to the door. Hampered as he was by having to take care not to draw a single breath of air which did not pass through his packed bottle, he was not able to fling his whole weight against it, but the efforts he was able to make seemed to produce no impression. He felt all round the door, but the wall in which it was set was the only one which was bricked up. Then he went down on his hands and knees, and tested the stone flags. Two of them, right beside the door, were loose. Handicapped though he was by having only one free hand, he succeeded in getting his fingers under each slab in turn, and dislodging it, and dragging it away. The earth underneath was moist and soft.

Simon Templar began to dig.

It took him three hours by his watch to burrow under the door, but at last he achieved an aperture large enough to worm his way through. He leaned against the wall on the other side for a few moments, to rest himself, and then felt his way down the corridor and up the stairs.

Mercifully, the door at the top of the stairs was unlocked, and it opened at once. Manifestly, Raxel had had no doubt that the Saint would not live long enough to find any way out of the cellar. Simon burst through, and rushed for the nearest window. He had not even time to open it—he smashed it with his respirator-bottle, and filled his aching lungs with great gasping breaths of frosty fresh air.

After a short time he was able to breathe more easily, and then he made a round of the ground floor, opening every window and door to give free passage to the sea breeze, which was soon blowing strongly enough through the house to sweep away any of the gas which filtered up from the cellar.

It was in the kitchen that he found Detective Duncarry securely trussed up and gagged in a chair. Simon cut him loose and heard the story.

"I don't know how it happened. One minute I was cleaning up a saucepan, and then I got a sickening welt on the back of the head that knocked me right out. Next thing I knew, I was tied up like a Christmas turkey."

"And I suppose if I'd died, as I was meant to, you'd have sat here till you starved to death," said the Saint. "It's a great life if you don't weaken."

He lighted a cigarette, and paced the room feverishly, refusing to talk. Raxel, Crantor, and Basher Tope had gone—he did not have to search the inn to know that. And the ship had gone. Looking out of the window, he could see nothing but blackness. Nowhere on the sea was visible anything like a ship's lights. But then they'd had a long start while he was sapping under that cellar door.

And now he knew exactly what the Professor's scheme was, and the magnitude of it took his breath away.

He wasted only a few minutes in coming to a decision; and then, with Duncarry to help him, he went round to the garage and examined the dilapidated Hildebrand. It had not been touched—but, of course, Raxel could not have foreseen that the Saint would be in a position to use it. Anyway, it didn't look up to much, as cars went, and Simon eyed it disparagingly.

"Now, why did I ever think it might be a comic stunt to arrive here in this ruin?" he wanted to know.

But certainly that car was the only vehicle which would take him out of Llancoed that night, for there would be no trains running from a one-horse village like that, at that hour.

"Where are you making for?" asked Duncarry, as Simon let in the clutch and the car moved off with a deafening rattle.

"Gloucester," said the Saint briefly. "And Hildebrand is going to touch the ground in spots, like he's never skipped before. Now get down on your knees in front of the dashboard, Dun, and pray that nothing busts!"

Duncarry pulled his nose.

"This show will be all over before I even know what it's about," he said. "I've followed you right from the beginning without asking a single question, and I've never beefed about it. I've waltzed around looking villainous—I've swept floors and washed dishes—I've been tied up and left to starve—and you haven't heard me complain. But now . . ."

"Know anything about the *Megantic*, son?" asked the Saint, and Duncarry, who was an earnest student of the newspapers, nodded.

"Sure—she's carrying another instalment of your War Debt over to the States. Just a few million pounds' worth of gold," he said, and the Saint's eyebrows moved slowly northwards.

It was the one item of information that he lacked, and the revelation made his hair curl. "Up-to-date piracy" he had diagnosed without revving his brain up to any point where it would have been liable to seize, but that the subject of the piracy should be such a colossal sum, in the shape of such an easily negotiable metal, was a factor of which he had never dreamed.

And then he laughed.

"There's nothing much for you to know, old dear," he drawled. "It's only that the Professor has arranged to lift that little flock of ingots on the way."

Duncarry revolved his long-nosed face towards the Saint, and inhaled sibilantly.

"What's that?" he demanded.

"Exactly what I told you," murmured Simon, and passed on what he had seen and what he had overheard.

Now that he had all the threads in his hands, this did not take him long.

Mysteries are long and complicated, but facts are always plain and to the point.

"The Professor has a few million cubic feet of compressed poison gas in his heavy luggage for the benefit of the strong-room guards. I'll bet any money he also has a cabin in a good strategic position for conferring the same benefit. There is also a quantity of tear-gas to deal with minor disturbances. That's what they were manufacturing when I butted in—I got a whiff of it, and the mystery literally made me burst into tears. Crantor will come up in the ship we saw to take off the boodle. I can guess that, though I can't tell you how it's going to be arranged."

"And what do we do about it?" asked Duncarry, and the Saint grimaced.

"That depends upon the efficacy of your prayers," he said.

If anything can be deduced from subsequent events, Duncarry was no mean intercessor. Or perhaps the Saint's magnificent luck was working overtime. At least it is a simple fact that they covered the eighty-five miles to Gloucester without a mishap, though it took them nearly five hours.

It was three o'clock on the Wednesday morning when the Saint entered the police station in Gloucester, and by some means best known to himself succeeded in so startling the sleepy night shift that they allowed him to use the official telephone for a call to Chief Inspector Teal's private address.

And the means by which he convinced Chief Inspector Teal that he was not trying to be funny may also never be known. But he passed on Teal's parting words to Duncarry verbatim.

"Leave this end to me," Teal had said, and for once in his life his voice was not at all drowsy. "I'll get through to the police at Portsmouth and tell them to be looking out for you; and after that I'll get on to the Admiralty, and make sure that they'll have everything ready for you when you arrive. You'll see the thing through yourself—it's hopelessly illegal, but I'm afraid you've earned the job."

"Does that mean that we're temporary policemen?" inquired Duncarry, when the speech had been reported and Simon Templar nodded.

"I guess it does."

A constable had already been sent round to knock up the biggest garage and commandeer the fastest car in stock, and at that moment a huge Bentley roared up and stopped outside the station. Simon took the wheel, and Duncarry settled in beside him.

They were well on their way before the American voiced his opinion of the whole affair.

"This is a great day for a couple of outlaws," he remarked, and the Saint, remembering the almost grovelling farewell of the Gloucester police-station personnel, could not find it in him to disagree.

11

Passengers on the *Megantic* who were up early for breakfast that morning were interested to see the low, lean shape of a destroyer speeding towards them. As the destroyer came nearer, a string of flags broke out from the mast, and then the passengers were amazed and fluttered, for the Megantic suddenly began to slow up.

The destroyer also hove to, and a boat put out from its side and rowed towards the

Megantic.

Betty Tregarth was one of the early risers who crowded to the side to watch the two men from the destroyer's boat climbing up the rope ladder which had been lowered for them. She saw the first man who clambered over the rail quite clearly, and the colour left her face suddenly, for it was the man whom she knew as Rameses Smith.

The *Megantic* had got under way again, and the destroyer was rapidly dropping astern, when she received the expected summons to the captain's cabin.

Besides the captain, Rameses Smith was there, and another man with an official bearing whose face seemed vaguely familiar. Marring was also there, an unsavoury and dishevelled sight in his dressing-gown, and she saw that there were handcuffs on his wrists.

"This is the other one," said the Saint. "Miss Tregarth, I don't think I need to put you in irons, but I must ask you to consider yourself under arrest."

She nodded dumbly.

Simon Templar turned to his companion.

"Dun, you can take Marring below. Don't let him out of your sight. I'll arrange for you to be relieved later." Then he turned to the captain. "Captain Davis, may I ask you to allow me a few words alone with Miss Tregarth?"

"Certainly, Mr Templar."

The captain followed Duncarry and Marring out of the room, and Simon Templar closed the door behind them, and faced the girl.

"Sit down," he said, and she obeyed. She had never imagined that he could look so stern.

Simon took a chair on the other side of the table.

"Betty," he said, "I'm giving you your last chance. Spill all the beans you know, and you mayn't do so badly. Stay in with the rest of 'em, and you're booked for a certain ten years. Which is it going to be?"

"I'll tell you everything I know," she said. "It doesn't matter much now, anyway."

She told him the story from the beginning, and he listened with rapt attention. She expected incredulity, but he showed none. At the end of the recital he was actually smiling.

"That's fine!" said the Saint, almost with a sigh. "That's the best thing I've heard for a long time!"

"What do you mean?" she asked dazedly.

"Only this," answered the Saint. "I guessed you were framed, but the police never knew anything about it. Raxel never bothered to try and deceive them. He just wanted to make sure of you. I don't know every single idea that waddles through the so-called brains of the police, but if you're wanted for murdering Inspector Henley you may call me Tiglath-Pileser for short."

She stared.

"But you're a detective yourself. Your name isn't Smith of course, but—"

Simon smiled cherubically.

"The captain called me by my right name," he said. "I am Simon Templar."

She stared.

"Not—the Saint?"

"None other," said Simon; and it is the chronicler's painful duty to record that he said it as if he was very pleased about it. Which he was.

"Then—is all this—"

Simon shook his head.

"I'm afraid it isn't," he said, almost lugubriously. "This enterprise is catastrophically respectable. You may take it that the full power and majesty of the Law is concentrated in these lily-white hands. Is there anyone else you'd like arrested?"

"Do you mean that I'm free?" she asked, with a wild hope springing up in her voice.

"Well, that's a matter for Claud Eustace Teal. You're too deeply involved to be set free without a considerable flourishing of red tape, but within a week or so, say . . . Here, have a handkerchief."

The Saint pushed a gaudy square yard or two of silk into her hands, and went in search of Duncarry.

"Betty Tregarth is drenching the skipper's carpet," he said. "Would you like to go and lend a shoulder?"

The destroyer returned some hours later from the task of rounding up and capturing the co-operating vessel that was Crantor's charge;

and it was Duncarry who escorted the girl on board and supervised the transhipment of Gregory Marring and the two expert safe-smashers who were discovered among the passengers. The Saint himself seemed to have lost interest, and his interview with Professor Raxel was very brief.

"I have just learnt your real name, Mr—er—Smith," Raxel said. "If I had known it earlier, I should not have made the mistake of underestimating your dangerousness. You should have been killed the first night you arrived at the inn."

"You should have been strangled at birth," said the Saint unpleasantly.

It was evening when Duncarry found him hanging over the rail and gazing at the approaching coast of England with the same moody countenance.

"What's wrong?" asked the American, and Simon turned and chucked his cigarette-end over the side.

"We've crashed, Dun," said the Saint, as if he were announcing the end of the world.

Duncarry frowned.

"What are you getting at, Saint?"

"Isn't it obvious? Here we've spent weeks of sleuthing and spadework, and seen our share of the rough stuff as well, and we're never going to see a cent out of it. Have you forgotten that I'm a business organisation?"

Duncarry shrugged.

"If the authorities see it the way I do, they'll say we paid an instalment of your National Debt all by ourselves. Isn't that enough for you?"

Simon Templar lighted another cigarette, and resumed his disparaging inspection of the horizon.

"I cannot live by paying National Debts," he said. "We shall have to find some other bunch of tough babies, and soak 'em good and proper to make up for this. I was trying to think of some sheep who are ripe for the slaughter. There's a couple of muttons in Vienna I was thinking of shearing one time——"

"Maybe I'll be taking a holiday," said Duncarry.

He had taken a place at the rail beside the Saint, and Simon looked at him suddenly.

"Why?" demanded the Saint. "Wouldn't you like a trip to Vienna?"

"I'd love one—for my honeymoon," answered the American dreamily, and the Saint groaned.

PUBLICATION
HISTORY

Whilst the three stories in this book, like many previous Saint stories, have their origins in the work Leslie Charteris did for *The Thriller*, two thirds of this trio differ slightly for they originate from a time when Charteris was still experimenting with heroes.

"The Story of a Dead Man" was his first story for the magazine and was published in issue no. 4, published on 2 March, 1929. The hero was Jimmy Traill, who perhaps unsurprisingly is the Saint in all but name. Not long after this story appeared a reader wrote in to the magazine suggesting that a serial by Leslie Charteris be run so that this popular writer could be read every week. The Editor prudently replied that "too much of a good thing was not good for anyone" so such a serial never materialized, but Charteris went on to have a long and successful career in the magazine.

"The Impossible Crime" appeared under the title of "Bumped Off" in issue no. 109, published on 7 March 1931, so was a relatively young story when collected into this book, by which time Charteris was focused on the adventures of the Saint.

"The National Debt" appeared under the title "The Secret of Beacon Inn" in issue no. 9, published on 6 April 1929. It was the second story Charteris sold to the magazine and the hero was Rameses Smith who was also very similar to the Saint.

The book itself was first published in April 1931 by Hodder & Stoughton with an American edition, of sorts, appearing in November that year. This was a book entitled *Wanted for Murder* (later republished as *The Saint: Wanted for Murder* in March 1943). It collected the stories from *Featuring the Saint* and *Alias the Saint* in one publication.

By June 1951 Hodder & Stoughton were on their twentieth impression of the hardback, suggesting the title to have been a good, reliable seller.

Two out of the three stories have been adapted for television; "The Impossible Crime" was adapted by Terry Nation (creator of Dr Who's most ardent foe, the Daleks) and retitled "The Contract." It was first broadcast on Thursday 7 January 1965 as part of the third season of *The Saint* with Roger Moore. "The National Debt" was retitled "The Crime of the Century" and was also adapted by Terry Nation. It first aired on Thursday 4 March 1965.

Foreign editions were relatively quick off the mark with a German translation, *S. T. rechnet ab*, appearing in 1934 and a Czech edition in 1938, published by Volesky, under the mouthful of *Nemožný zločin: nová dobrodružství svatého*. The French titled the book *Le Saint et les mauvais garcons* ("The Saint and the Bad Boys") and opted for a straightforward translation which was published by Charteris's regular French publishers, Fayard & Co. in 1939. An Italian edition, translated by Mario Lamberti, was published by Garzanti in 1971 under the simple title of *Alias il Santo*. Whilst the Spanish, unsurprisingly, opted for *Alias el Santo* which was published in 1965. An English language audiobook edition appeared in 1991, read by David Case and published by Books on Tape in America.

The most recent edition was a paperback published in May 1994 by Carroll & Graf.

ABOUT THE AUTHOR

I'm mad enough to believe in romance. And I'm sick and tired of this age—tired of the miserable little mildewed things that people racked their brains about, and wrote books about, and called life. I wanted something more elementary and honest—battle, murder, sudden death, with plenty of good beer and damsels in distress, and a complete callousness about blipping the ungodly over the beezer. It mayn't be life as we know it, but it ought to be.

—Leslie Charteris in a 1935 BBC radio interview

Leslie Charteris was born Leslie Charles Bowyer-Yin in Singapore on 12 May 1907.

He was the son of a Chinese doctor and his English wife, who'd met in London a few years earlier. Young Leslie found friends hard to come by in colonial Singapore. The English children had been told not to play with Eurasians, and the Chinese children had been told not to play with Europeans. Leslie was caught in between and took refuge in reading.

"I read a great many good books and enjoyed them because nobody had told me that they were classics. I also read a great many bad books which nobody told me not to read . . . I read a great many popular scientific articles and acquired from them an astonishing amount of general knowledge before I discovered that this acquisition was supposed to be a chore."[1]

One of his favourite things to read was a magazine called *Chums*. "The Best and Brightest Paper for Boys" (if you believe the adverts) was a monthly paper full of swashbuckling adventure stories aimed at boys, encouraging them to be honourable and moral and perhaps even "upright citizens with furled umbrellas."[2] Undoubtedly these types of stories would influence his later work.

When his parents split up shortly after the end of World War I, Charteris accompanied his mother and brother back to England, where he was sent to Rossall School in Fleetwood, Lancashire. Rossall was then a very stereotypical English public school, and it struggled to cope with this multilingual mixed-race boy just into his teens who'd already seen more of the world than many of his peers would see in their lifetimes. He was an outsider.

He left Rossall in 1924. Keen to pursue a creative career, he decided to study art in Paris—after all, that was where the great artists went—but soon found that the life of a literally starving artist didn't appeal. He continued writing, firing off speculative stories to magazines, and it was the sale of a short story to *Windsor Magazine* that saved him from penury.

He returned to London in 1925, as his parents—particularly his father—wanted him to become a lawyer, and he was sent to study law at Cambridge University. In the mid-1920s, Cambridge was full of Bright Young Things—aristocrats and bohemians somewhat typified in the Evelyn Waugh novel *Vile Bodies*—and again the mixed-race Bowyer-Yin found that he didn't fit in. He was an outsider who preferred to make his own way in the world and wasn't one of the privileged upper class. It didn't help that he found his studies boring and decided it was more fun contemplating ways to circumvent the law. This inspired him to write a novel, and when publishers Ward Lock & Co. offered him a three-book deal on the strength of it, he abandoned his studies to pursue a writing career.

When his father learnt of this, he was not impressed, as he considered writers to be "rogues and vagabonds." Charteris would later recall that "I wanted to be a writer, he wanted me to become a lawyer. I was stubborn, he said I would end up in the gutter. So I left home. Later on, when I had a little success, we were reconciled by letter, but I never saw him again."[3]

X Esquire, his first novel, appeared in April 1927. The lead character, X Esquire, is a mysterious hero, hunting down and killing the businessmen trying to wipe out Britain by distributing quantities of free poisoned cigarettes. His second novel, *The White Rider*, was published the following spring, and in one memorable scene shows the hero chasing after his damsel in distress, only for him to overtake the villains, leap into their car . . . and promptly faint.

These two plot highlights may go some way to explaining Charteris's comment on *Meet—the Tiger!*, published in September 1928, that "it was only the third book I'd written, and the best, I would say, for it was that the first two were even worse."[4]

Twenty-one-year-old authors are naturally self-critical. Despite reasonably good reviews, the Saint didn't set the world on fire, and Charteris moved on to a new hero for his next book. This was *The Bandit*, an adventure story featuring Ramon Francisco De Castilla y Espronceda Manrique, published in the summer of 1929 after its serialisation in the *Empire News*, a now long-forgotten Sunday newspaper. But sales of *The Bandit* were less than impressive, and Charteris began to question his choice of career. It was all very well writing—but if nobody wants to read what you write, what's the point?

"I had to succeed, because before me loomed the only alternative, the dreadful penalty of failure . . . the routine office hours, the five-day week . . . the lethal assimilation into the ranks of honest, hard-working, conformist, God-fearing pillars of the community."[5]

However his fortunes—and the Saint's—were about to change. In late 1928, Leslie had met Monty Haydon, a London-based editor who was looking for writers to pen stories for his new paper, *The Thriller*— "The Paper with a Thousand Thrills." Charteris later recalled that "he said he was starting a new magazine, had read one of my books and would like some stories from me. I couldn't have been more grateful, both from the point of view of vanity and finance!"[6]

The paper launched in early 1929, and Leslie's first work, "The Story of a Dead Man," featuring Jimmy Traill, appeared in issue 4 (published on 2 March 1929). That was followed just over a month later with "The Secret of Beacon Inn," starring Rameses "Pip" Smith. At the same time, Leslie finished writing another non-Saint novel, *Daredevil*, which would be published in late 1929. Storm Arden was the hero; more notably, the book saw the first introduction of a Scotland Yard inspector by the name of Claud Eustace Teal.

The Saint returned in the thirteenth issue of *The Thriller*. The byline proclaimed that the tale was "A Thrilling Complete Story of the Underworld"; the title was "The Five Kings," and it actually featured Four Kings and a Joker. Simon Templar, of course, was the Joker.

Charteris spent the rest of 1929 telling the adventures of the Five Kings in five subsequent *The Thriller* stories. "It was very hard work, for the pay was lousy, but Monty Haydon was a brilliant and stimulating editor, full of ideas. While he didn't actually help shape the Saint as a character, he did suggest story lines. He would take me out to lunch and say, 'What are you going to write about next?' I'd often say I was damned if I knew. And Monty would say, 'Well, I was reading something the other day . . .' He had a fund of ideas and we would talk them over, and then I would go away and write a story. He was a great creative editor."[7]

Charteris would have one more attempt at writing about a hero other than Simon Templar, in three novelettes published in *The Thriller* in early 1930, but he swiftly returned to the Saint. This was partly due to his self-confessed laziness—he wanted to write more stories for *The Thriller* and other magazines, and creating a new hero for every story was hard work—but mainly due to feedback from Monty Haydon. It seemed people wanted to read more adventures of the Saint . . .

Charteris would contribute over forty stories to *The Thriller* throughout the 1930s. Shortly after their debut, he persuaded publisher Hodder & Stoughton that if he collected some of these stories and rewrote them a little, they could publish them as a Saint book. *Enter the Saint* was first published in August 1930, and the reaction was good enough for the publishers to bring out another collection. And another . . .

Of the twenty Saint books published in the 1930s, almost all have their origins in those magazine stories.

Why was the Saint so popular throughout the decade? Aside from the charm and ability of Charteris's storytelling, the stories, particularly those published in the first half of the '30s, are full of energy and joie de vivre. With economic depression rampant throughout the period, the public at large seemed to want some escapism.

And Simon Templar's appeal was wide-ranging: he wasn't an upper-class hero like so many of the period. With no obvious background and no attachment to the Old School Tie, no friends in high places who could provide a get-out-of-jail-free card, the Saint was uniquely classless. Not unlike his creator.

Throughout Leslie's formative years, his heritage had been an issue. In his early days in Singapore, during his time at school, at Cambridge University or even just in everyday life, he couldn't avoid the fact that for many people his mixed parentage was a problem. He would later tell a story of how he was chased up the road by a stick-waving typical

English gent who took offence to his daughter being escorted around town by a foreigner.

Like the Saint, he was an outsider. And although he had spent a significant portion of his formative years in England, he couldn't settle.

As a young boy he had read of an America "peopled largely by Indians, and characters in fringed buckskin jackets who fought nobly against them. I spent a great deal of time day-dreaming about a visit to this prodigious and exciting country."[8]

It was time to realise this wish. Charteris and his first wife, Pauline, whom he'd met in London when they were both teenagers and married in 1931, set sail for the States in late 1932; the Saint had already made his debut in America courtesy of the publisher Doubleday. Charteris and his wife found a New York still experiencing the tail end of Prohibition, and times were tough at first. Despite sales to *The American Magazine* and others, it wasn't until a chance meeting with writer turned Hollywood executive Bartlett McCormack in their favourite speakeasy that Charteris's career stepped up a gear.

Soon Charteris was in Hollywood, working on what would become the 1933 movie *Midnight Club*. However, Hollywood's treatment of writers wasn't to Charteris's taste, and he began to yearn for home. Within a few months, he returned to the UK and began writing more Saint stories for Monty Haydon and Bill McElroy.

He also rewrote a story he'd sketched out whilst in the States, a version of which had been published in *The American Magazine* in September 1934. This new novel, *The Saint in New York*, published in 1935, was a significant advance for the Saint and Leslie Charteris. Gone were the high jinks and the badinage. The youthful exuberance evident in the Saint's early adventures had evolved into something a little darker, a little more hard-boiled. It was the next stage in development for the author and his creation, and readers loved it. It became a bestseller on both sides of the Atlantic.

Having spent his formative years in places as far apart as Singapore and England, with substantial travel in between, it should be no surprise that Leslie had a serious case of wanderlust. With a bestseller under his belt, he now had the means to see more of the world.

Nineteen thirty-six found him in Tenerife, researching another Saint adventure alongside translating the biography of Juan Belmonte, a well-known Spanish matador. Estranged for several months, Leslie and Pauline divorced in 1937. The following year, Leslie married an American, Barbara Meyer, who'd accompanied him to Tenerife. In early 1938, Charteris and his new bride set off in a trailer of his own design and spent eighteen months travelling round America and Canada.

The Saint in New York had reminded Hollywood of Charteris's talents, and film rights to the novel were sold prior to publication in 1935. Although the proposed 1935 film production was rejected by the Hays Office for its violent content, RKO's eventual 1938 production persuaded Charteris to try his luck once more in Hollywood.

New opportunities had opened up, and throughout the 1940s the Saint appeared not only in books and movies but in a newspaper strip, a comic-book series, and on radio.

Anyone wishing to adapt the character in any medium found a stern taskmaster in Charteris. He was never completely satisfied, nor was he shy of showing his displeasure. He did, however, ensure that copyright in any Saint adventure belonged to him, even if scripted by another writer—a contractual obligation that he was to insist on throughout his career.

Charteris was soon spread thin, overseeing movies, comics, newspapers, and radio versions of his creation, and this, along with his self-proclaimed laziness, meant that Saint books were becoming fewer and further between. However, he still enjoyed his creation: in 1941 he indulged himself in a spot of fun by playing the Saint—complete with monocle and moustache—in a photo story in *Life* magazine.

In July 1944, he started collaborating under a pseudonym on Sherlock Holmes radio scripts, subsequently writing more adventures for Holmes than Conan Doyle. Not all his ventures were successful—a screenplay he was hired to write for Deanna Durbin, "Lady on a Train," took him a year and ultimately bore little resemblance to the finished film. In the mid-1940s, Charteris successfully sued RKO Pictures for unfair competition after they launched a new series of films starring George Sanders as a debonair crime fighter known as the Falcon. But he kept faith with his original character, and the Saint novels continued to adapt to the times. The transatlantic Saint evolved into something of a private operator, working for the mysterious Hamilton and becoming, not unlike his creator, a world traveller, finding that adventure would seek him out.

"I have never been able to see why a fictional character should not grow up, mature, and develop, the same as anyone else. The same, if you like, as his biographer. The only adequate reason is that—so far as I know—no other fictional character in modern times has survived a sufficient number of years for these changes to be clearly observable. I must confess that a lot of my own selfish pleasure in the Saint has been in watching him grow up."[9]

Charteris maintained his love of travel and was soon to be found sailing round the West Indies with his good friend Gregory Peck. His forays abroad gave him even more material, and he began to write true-crime articles, as well as an occasional column in *Gourmet* magazine.

By the early '50s, Charteris himself was feeling strained. He'd divorced his second wife in 1943 and got together with a New York radio and nightclub singer called Betty Bryant Borst, whom he married in late 1943. That relationship had fallen apart acrimoniously towards the end of the decade, and he roamed the globe restlessly, rarely in one place for longer than a couple of months. He continued to maintain a firm grip on the exploitation of the Saint in various media but was writing little himself. The Saint had become an industry, and Charteris couldn't keep up. He began thinking seriously about an early retirement.

Then in 1951 he met a young actress called Audrey Long when they became next-door neighbours in Hollywood. Within a year they had married, a union that was to last the rest of Leslie's life.

He attacked life with a new vitality. They travelled—Nassau was a favoured escape spot—and he wrote. He struck an agreement with *The New York Herald Tribune* for a Saint comic strip, which would appear daily and be written by Charteris himself. The strip ran for thirteen years, with Charteris sending in his handwritten story lines from wherever he happened to be, relying on mail services around the world to continue the Saint's adventures. New Saint books began to appear, and Charteris reached a height of productivity not seen since his days as a struggling author trying to establish himself. As Leslie and Audrey travelled, so did the Saint, visiting locations just after his creator had been there.

By 1953 the Saint had already enjoyed twenty-five years of success, and *The Saint Detective Magazine* was launched. Charteris had become adept at exploiting his creation to the full, mixing new stories with repackaged older stories, sometimes rewritten, sometimes mixed up in "new" anthologies, sometimes adapted from radio scripts previously written by other writers.

Charteris had been approached several times over the years for television rights in the Saint and had expended much time and effort during the 1950s trying to get the Saint on TV, even going so far as to write sample scripts himself, but it wasn't to be. He finally agreed a deal in autumn 1961 with English film producers Robert S. Baker and Monty Berman. The first episode of *The Saint* television series, starring Roger Moore, went into production in June 1962. The series was an immediate success, though Charteris himself had his reservations. It reached second place in the ratings, but he commented that "in that distinction it was topped by wrestling, which only suggested to me that the competition may not have been so hot; but producers are generally cast in a less modest mould." He resented the implication that the TV series had finally made a success of the Saint after twenty-five years of literary obscurity.

As long as the series lasted, Charteris was not shy about voicing his criticisms both in public and in a constant stream of memos to the producers. "Regular followers of the Saint saga . . . must have noticed that I am almost incapable of simply writing a story and shutting up."[10] Nor was he shy about exploiting this new market by agreeing to a series of tie-in novelisations ghosted by other writers, which he would then rewrite before publication.

Charteris mellowed as the series developed and found elements to praise too. He developed a close friendship with producer Robert S. Baker, which would last until Charteris's death.

In the early '60s, on one of their frequent trips to England, Leslie and Audrey bought a house in Surrey, which became their permanent base. He explored the possibility of a Saint musical and began writing some of it himself.

Charteris no longer needed to work. Now in his sixties, he supervised the Saint from a distance whilst continuing to travel and indulge himself. He and Audrey made seasonal excursions to Ireland and the south of France, where they had residences. He began to write poetry and devised a new universal sign language, Paleneo, based on notes and symbols he used in his diaries. Once Paleneo was released, he decided enough was enough and announced, again, his retirement. This time he meant it.

The Saint continued regardless—there was a long-running Swedish comic strip, and new novels with other writers doing the bulk of the work were complemented in the 1970s with Bob Baker's revival of the TV series, *Return of the Saint*.

Ill-health began to take its toll. By the early 1980s, although he continued a healthy correspondence with the outside world, Charteris felt unable to keep up with the collaborative Saint books and pulled the plug on them.

To entertain himself, Leslie took to "trying to beat the bookies in predicting the relative speed of horses," a hobby which resulted in several of his local betting shops refusing to take "predictions" from him, as he was too successful for their liking.

He still received requests to publish his work abroad but had become completely cynical about further attempts to revive the Saint. A new Saint magazine only lasted three issues, and two TV productions—*The Saint in Manhattan*, with Tom Selleck look-alike Andrew Clarke, and *The Saint*, with Simon Dutton—left him bitterly disappointed. "I fully expect this series to lay eggs everywhere . . . the only satisfaction I have is in looking at my bank balance."[11]

In the early 1990s, Hollywood producers Robert Evans and William J. Macdonald approached him and made a deal for the Saint to return to cinema screens. Charteris still took great care of the Saint's reputation and wrote an outline entitled *The Return of the Saint* in which an older Saint would meet the son he didn't know he had.

Much of his time in his last few years was taken up with the movie. Several scripts were submitted to him—each moving further and further away from his original concept—but the screenwriter from 1940s Hollywood was thoroughly disheartened by the Hollywood of the '90s: "There is still no plot, no real story, no characterisations, no personal interaction, nothing but endless frantic violence . . ." Besides, with producer Bill Macdonald hitting the headlines for the most un-Saintly reasons, he was to add, "How can Bill Macdonald concentrate on my Saint movie when he has Sharon Stone in his bed?"

The Crime Writers' Association of Great Britain presented Leslie with a Lifetime Achievement award in 1992 in a special ceremony at the

House of Lords. Never one for associations and awards, and although visibly unwell, Leslie accepted the award with grace and humour ("I am now only waiting to be carbon-dated," he joked). He suffered a slight stroke in his final weeks, which did not prevent him from dining out locally with family and friends, before he finally passed away at the age of 85 on 15 April 1993.

His death severed one of the final links with the classic thriller genre of the 1930s and 1940s, but he left behind a legacy of nearly one hundred books, countless short stories, and TV, film, radio, and comic-strip adaptations of his work which will endure for generations to come.

> *I was always sure that there was a solid place in escape literature for a rambunctious adventurer such as I dreamed up in my youth, who really believed in the old-fashioned romantic ideals and was prepared to lay everything on the line to bring them to life. A joyous exuberance that could not find its fulfilment in pinball machines and pot. I had what may now seem a mad desire to spread the belief that there were worse, and wickeder, nut cases than Don Quixote.*
>
> *Even now, half a century later, when I should be old enough to know better, I still cling to that belief. That there will always be a public for the old-style hero, who had a clear idea of justice, and a more than technical approach to love, and the ability to have some fun with his crusades.*[12]

---

1 *A Letter from the Saint*, 30 August 1946
2 "The Last Word," *The First Saint Omnibus*, Doubleday Crime Club, 1939

3 *The Straits Times*, 29 June 1958, page 9

4 Introduction by Charteris to the September 1980 paperback reprint of *Meet—the Tiger!* (Charter), the last ever print edition.

5 *The Saint: A Complete History*, by Burl Barer (McFarland, 1993)

6 PR material from the 1970s series *Return of the Saint*

7 From "Return of the Saint: Comprehensive Information" issued to help publicise the 1970s TV show

8 *A Letter from the Saint*, 26 July 1946

9 Introduction to "The Million Pound Day," in *The First Saint Omnibus*

10 *A Letter from the Saint*, 12 April 1946

11 Letter from LC to sometime Saint collaborator Peter Bloxsom, 2 August 1989

12 Introduction by Charteris to the September 1980 paperback reprint of *Meet—the Tiger!* (Charter).

WATCH FOR THE SIGN
OF THE SAINT!

THE SAINT CLUB

*And so, my friends, dear bookworms, most noble fellow
drinkers, frustrated burglars, affronted policemen, upright
citizens with furled umbrellas and secret buccaneering
dreams that seems to be very nearly all for now. It has been
nice having you with us, and we hope you will come again,
not once, but many times.*

*Only because of our great love for you, we would like
to take this parting opportunity of mentioning one small
matter which we have very much at heart . . .*

—Leslie Charteris, The First Saint Omnibus *(1939)*

Leslie Charteris founded The Saint Club in 1936 with the aim of
providing a constructive fanbase for Saint devotees. Before the War, it
donated profits to a London hospital where, for several years, a Saint
ward was maintained. With the nationalisation of hospitals, profits
were, for many years, donated to the Arbour Youth Centre in Stepney,
London.

In the twenty-first century, we've carried on this tradition but have
also donated to the Red Cross and a number of different children's
charities.

The club acts as a focal point for anyone interested in the adventures of Leslie Charteris and the work of Simon Templar, and offers merchandise that includes DVDs of the old TV series and various Saint-related publications, through to its own exclusive range of notepaper, pin badges, and polo shirts. All profits are donated to charity. The club also maintains two popular websites and supports many more Saint-related sites.

After Leslie Charteris's death, the club recruited three new vice-presidents—Roger Moore, Ian Ogilvy, and Simon Dutton have all pledged their support, whilst Audrey and Patricia Charteris have been retained as Saints-in-Chief. But some things do not change, for the back of the membership card still mischievously proclaims that . . .

> *The bearer of this card is probably a person of hideous*
> *antecedents and low moral character, and upon*
> *apprehension for any cause should be immediately released*
> *in order to save other prisoners from contamination.*

To join . . .

Membership costs £3.50 (or US$7) per year, or £30 (US$60) for life. Find us online at www.lesliecharteris.com for full details.

Made in the USA
Columbia, SC
10 July 2022